The Children's Home Mystery Series

The Flutist and the Dancer

This is a story of a six-year-old girl who is left at the Children's Home by her grandmother. She arrives with a rag doll and an unusual nursery-rhyme book. Her grandmother gives the administration a false name and never returns. The trauma of being taken from her loving Nanny and her twin brother results in a memory block against which she struggles all the way through adolescence.

The Pianist and the Locksmith

This novel steps back to World War II and is about the lengths SaraBeth, a young mother, will go to when it comes to protecting her children and the inner battle she has with her abusive father. This is about faith, trust, and forgiveness between SaraBeth, her high-school sweetheart who spent years in a military hospital and their families.

Broken Arrows, Broken Promises

A bachelor minister's prayers battle with the revelation of his secret past. His first love, Tessa, has a daughter, and she too is searching for information. She hires private detective Will Fox, who is torn between helping her and finding his mother's Native American "story arrows."

Trails End Isle & Wings

Jonothan loves to fly, but he can't fly from his father's deathbed request. If only a 1931 Ford Pickup Truck could talk. In the search he also meets his dad's two other children, Jace and Samantha, and sparks fly.

Brandi also seems bent on learning her lessons in life the hard way. After working with the Shadow Angels and her Children's Home sister, Shannon, she becomes a Deputy Sheriff. And she has to learn how to trust from an unlikely teacher: a German Shepherd pup named Pepper.

Published by Workplay Publishing
Bluffton, Ohio 45817
workplaypublishing.com

Copyright © 2014 Marilyn R. Stark
All rights reserved.

ISBN 0-9842122-8-0
Cover design by Alison King
Cover photograph by Marilyn R. Stark
Interior layout by André Swartley

Characters, locations and events in this novel are products of the author's imagination or are used fictitiously. Resemblance to actual historical events or people, living or dead, is purely coincidental.

PRINTED IN THE UNITED STATES OF AMERICA

Safe Passage in Masquerade

*To: Linda
Enjoy
Marilyn R. Stark
June 19, 2021*

Safe Passage in
Masquerade

A New Children's Home Mystery

by

Marilyn R. Stark

For the numerous writers' groups who continue to write, not only for the love of writing, but the joy of publishing, humbly respecting most genres.

Prologue: Granny & Bea
Turtle Crossing, 1962

Granny Oates, widowed owner of a third generation estate just thirty minutes from Turtle Crossing, kept a tight schedule to allow time for a relaxing morning drive on the way to an appointment. Driving alone meant she had time to think. She wasn't one to put much faith in rumors, but when neighbors on either side of her had had their property surveyed within the past two weeks, it was imperative she find out why.

Anything out of the ordinary always brought back memories of the last time she had ignored a foreboding stillness in the air, when two of Henry Carpenter's friends, in their rush to kidnap her, had shot her favorite milk cow. And although Henry and friends were still in jail, she refused to leave anything to chance.

With the windows cranked partially down, the fragrance of springtime in Ohio was comparable to a mid-morning vacation. She had replaced her pre-dawn jeans and boots with a business suit and heels and had the energy and appearance that belied her sixty years of age.

Granny cruised into Turtle Crossing at just the right speed and caught every one of the six street lights on green for a change. The further south she drove, the more the clouds looked like they would dump a shower or two at any moment. Juggling her combination purse/briefcase, layered desert carrier, and umbrella, she exited her car and scurried towards the office of Bea Longacre of Longacre Graham Real Estate to discuss a piece of property they had discussed on the phone.

Because she had parked half a block away, she was forced to dodge around business owners cranking-out their colorful Main Street awnings. The bank on the corner was chiming eight bells as she acknowledged a few quick nods and good-mornings before she finally arrived at Bea's address.

Granny proceeded up the street entrance staircase towards Bea's office. When the staircase door opened and closed behind her with a bang, Granny half-turned at the landing to greet the new arrival, but the entryway was empty, unusually quiet—almost eerie. Her instincts went on alert, reminiscent of the previous week when a fox prowled a bit too close to her hen house. She had learned at a very young age to listen to what you can't see as well as what you can, but as there was nothing to see or hear in this case, she shrugged her shoulders and continued on up the stairs.

The scent of lemon oil hung in the air, which meant the cleaning crew had worked late into the evening. The door at the top of the stairs, which had a tendency to stick, depending on the weather, was propped open with a black cat doorstop.

She turned left only to hesitate because two ceiling lights were out; glanced immediately to her right, towards the sound of diminishing footsteps echoing down the empty, well-lit end of the hall.

She shook off the feeling that something wasn't quite right as her eyes adjusted to the filtered light that shone through the etched glass in the top half of Bea's door. When Granny stepped up to the door, the toe of her gray pump pinged against crystal. Then something as soft as velvet brushed against her leg. A snow-white rose, tipped in strawberry pink, filled the fluted stemware beside the entrance to Bea's office. She shifted everything she was already carrying so she could pick up the vase too. Was this a budding romance Bea had failed to mention?

When Granny opened the door, vase in hand, she was surprised to find Bea standing in the office foyer; rather than diligently working at her file laden desk. Bea's welcoming smile disappeared. "Not another rose! That's the second one today!"

Seeing Bea in such a state, her face flushed and her eyes sparkling with frustration instead of appreciation, Granny realized her indecision about a piece of property she was considering buying couldn't hold a candle to seeing her dear friend trembling and near tears. "Bea, you love flowers. Has something happened to change that?"

When Granny turned to close the door, Bea flipped the *Open* sign to *Closed*. The sound of the lock clicking into place only added to Granny's concern.

Granny set the etched crystal vase alongside several others, and noted the recently installed Will Fox Security mark on the marble window sills. Security had never been a priority, and she hoped Bea would tell her the reason for it. Wasn't that what friends were for?

The floral scent of roses lingered. The petals silky and cool. However, Bea was treating them like poison ivy.

Taking a deep breath, she joined Bea at her desk. Without hesitation, Bea opened Granny's file and began, "That piece of property we discussed earlier, just doubled in price overnight."

Evidently Bea did not want to talk about the flowers just yet.

"What are the odds the two could be connected?" Granny asked. "Yesterday surveyors were all over the property on the East and West sides of my family's pioneer estate. "

"So far," Bea added, "It's just a rumor—or the best-kept-secret known to man, that someone has purchased or is purchasing property as a business investment along the Turtle Crossing River, which happens to meander through your property."

Granny laid her hand on Bea's and said softly, "Well, that answers part of *my* concerns. Now, what has *you* in such turmoil?"

"Someone has been harassing me!" she replied, enunciating each word with great care and pointedly stabbing her desk blotter with each word. The pencil snapped in half. The pieces flew across her desk. Both were so astonished, they gasped, took a deep breath, and then burst out laughing.

"With flowers?" Granny finally replied, disbelief in her tone.

"Don't say it like that," Bea replied as she neatly stacked and re-stacked a dozen folders three times before adding, "There's more."

"I see," Granny replied as she stilled Bea's hands with her own. "Then talk to me. What or who has you so spooked?"

Bea shoved her chair back from her desk and began to pace from one side of her office to the other, her heels clicking on the oak hardwood floor, thumping across the carpet, then clicking to the front windows, to the drinking fountain, and back.

Not looking up, she replied, "I know my personal life is affecting the quality time my clients deserve. You're going to think I'm being foolish, but it isn't my imagination. My secretary is so spooked by all this that her husband took her out of town for a three-day weekend. He wants her to get another job!"

"Have you considered hiring a bodyguard?"

"Yes, I've considered it," Bea replied as she ran her hands across the back of her leather chair. "I've picked up the phone a dozen times, but then I remember my father telling me, 'When you're in business, you take care of your own problems.'"

"And how do you think he would have handled this 'problem,' as you call it?"

"I really don't know," Bea murmured. "I wish he were here—although I doubt anyone ever left *him* roses."

"What about blueberry coffeecake?"

"That's what smells so good. It was his favorite! I haven't had any of your famous blueberry coffeecake since last spring." Her stomach growled in response. Bea smiled and added, "Sorry. I was in a rush this morning and missed breakfast. Would you like a cup of coffee?"

"I would love a cup. Hot and strong!"

Granny released the lid on the carrier while Bea collected silverware, napkins and delicate iris-patterned dessert chinaware from the depths of her supply closet.

Bea said, "Only good thoughts while we eat, okay?"

"Good thoughts," Granny mused. "I haven't heard you mention your little redhead for awhile." Granny waited. She knew her dear friend would not have a moment's peace until she had some answers about what had happened to a little girl she had tried to adopt nearly ten years ago.

"No," Bea said finally. "But that doesn't mean I don't think about her."

"That's not hard to believe. I remember how happy you were with her."

"I quit volunteering at Children's Services when my adoption request was denied, and she was either fostered-out or adopted by another family but I never gave up. My prayer is that she'll remember me, should our paths ever cross again."

"That's understandable. Although it will be hard for your paths to cross with all the new high-tech security in your office."

When Bea didn't reply but took a sip of her coffee, Granny continued, "So. Does this mean that for the most part, your turmoil edged feelings happen after you leave for the day?"

Bea looked down at the floor and started laughing. "Oh, it's happening at home as well. Look!" She stuck both feet out for inspection. "One navy blue high heel and one brown and I have on a black suit today."

Granny smiled and sipped her own coffee.

"Now *you* look marvelous," Bea added. "You've been shopping with our dear friend, Tressie, haven't you?"

"None other."

"Both of you always make such a fashion statement."

When Granny looked a bit embarrassed, Bea continued, "Come on! You look stunning in that shade of summer gray," motioning to include Granny's suit with matching hat, heels and gloves.

Hesitating momentarily, she turned in her chair and asked, "My hair is starting to gray too. Could I wear that color?" Bea asked.

"Of course you could. But green is definitely a great color for you, as well." Thinking it would turn Bea's frown into a smile, Granny asked, "Why don't we go shopping?"

Shopping was the last thing on Bea's mind, but she couldn't concentrate anyhow, and before she talked herself out of playing hooky, she replied, "Oh, why not? Are you driving?"

"Of course I'm driving. How soon can you be ready?"

Bea looked around her office at the stack of work on her desk. However, her calendar was clear, thanks to her secretary. She grabbed her briefcase and declared, "I'm ready now."

"Good," Granny declared as she latched the layered desert carrier and rinsed out their coffee cups. "Why don't we stop at Sadie's first? I'm buying."

"You know we could walk," Bea suggested. A distant rumble of thunder caught her attention. "Or take a car. Did you drive Doc's old station wagon?" she asked as she locked up her files and punched in the security code.

"Yes. But be careful how you refer to my lifetime neighbor and veterinarian. We may look old, but we're not ready for retirement yet!" They were soon walking towards Doc's vehicle like they had dragons to slay and were not about to step aside for any army of fools.

They slid their parcels in the rear of the vehicle and wasted no time getting in and locking their doors.

"You may not be ready for retirement, but this old girl is," said Bea, indicating a torn section of upholstery.

"Don't let Doc hear you talk about his pride and joy in that tone of voice," Granny commented.

"Oh, I know you said he had the engine replaced and when opened up, it can really get out and scoot," Bea added.

"That's only part of it. He's partial as to whom he allows drive it as well."

Granny checked her rear and side-view mirror. What a shock! To see a man standing in the shadow of the building next to Bea's was unnerving! No wonder Bea was so frustrated.

Not wanting to upset Bea further, yet needing more information if she was to be of any help, Granny smoothly pulled away from the curb and asked, "How long has someone been following you?"

"Oh," Bea replied, once again trying to act like it wasn't important, "Over a month. Honestly, I didn't notice until the flowers started arriving. But the real reason I called Will to install the new security system was partly due to the cards attached to the flowers."

"The new shopping mall is right next door to your building, but the only entrance to your office is the front stairs, right?"

"No. The city also connected the rear fire exit door of my building to the second floor of the mall, which makes the garage and our office more accessible."

Hearing the trembling in Bea's voice, Granny tabled asking if that had been when the flowers started arriving and drove on in silence.

"I wish you could have met my Autumn Blaze Winters," Bea said, her voice diminishing to a mere whisper.

"Might I guess that the name describes her personality?"

Bea smiled and nodded. "She was a little firecracker, that's for certain."

"Is that why you wanted to adopt her?" Granny teased.

"No, she just needed someone to love her," Bea said softly, a gentle smile lighting up her eyes. Remembering, she continued, "The last time I saw her, she was sitting in the Children's Services foyer in a huge green over-stuffed chair, her nine-year-old gangly legs tucked up under her long skirt which almost hid her skinned-up knees. She had the most vulnerable, beautiful blue eyes. Her nose was always covered with a scattering of copper freckles about the same color as her hair.

"Are we being followed now?" Bea asked suddenly, twisting around in her seat.

"I don't think so," Granny replied as she pulled into the lot behind Sadie's Diner.

"When did Sadie have new awnings installed?"

"Oh. I believe she spruced up the interior in red and white; with black and white tile floors the same weekend of the Sycamore at Main Street Mall's grand opening," Bea replied.

Once they were seated inside, Granny asked again, "How long has this flower thing been going on?"

"Four to five weeks, if you must know," Bea snapped, then covered her face with her hands, took a deep breath and calmly looked at Granny. "I apologize for being so short," she said. "I've just kept it inside so long. What else do you need to know?"

"No apology necessary. Have you saved any of the cards?"

"I left that to my secretary. I assume she threw them away."

"What about the vases? Granny asked. I've seen that pattern somewhere."

After some thought, Bea replied, "Most of them are antique."

Granny listened to Bea's descriptions and took notes about the vases and quickly tucked the list in her purse when one of Bea's clients stopped by their table with a greeting about the weather. She made a mental note to ask Marcie about the vases at her florist shop. Perhaps she could help identify the most recent ones. Granny knew, in her gut, they were antique and familiar.

It was Monday. A new day. A new week. One of those bright and sunny-type spring days that inspires one to open the windows after weeks of gray drizzle. Bea arrived at her office around 10:00 and asked her secretary, who had returned from her vacation without any mention of a new job, to hold all her calls so she could finish early. She couldn't believe the stack of messages that had accumulated in one morning just because she had stayed home to clear out her closet, discovering her favorite blue silk blouse hidden between two suit jackets in the process.

The Sunshine Bright housekeeping teams had brought some sparkle into her office this morning, which included the carefully arranged photos on her desk. Bea traced her fingers across the photo of her mom and dad and her when she was three years old. Then she gently brushed her index finger over the chin of her Abe. When they married, he had been an officer in the Marines. He died in World War II. Another trio of photos of the little red-haired girl, Autumn graced her desk.

"She was my last chance to be a mom," Bea murmured softly. "Be safe little one," she prayed.

As she fingered through her rolodex, her hand stilled—gripping a well-worn card, a reminder that Autumn would be 18 this fall. Why send an Easter card when her cards had been returned for the past five years, stamped, *Return to Sender—No Forwarding Address*? But she just couldn't give up.

Gracious, she thought. *I have to quit my fanciful imagining for a past I can't change. Focus on what I can, and collect the file I planned to pull.*

By noon, warm sunbeams had found the shadiest piles of snow in the nearby alley and left rivulets and dirty puddles in their stead. As Bea gazed out her second floor window down onto Main, she noticed someone leaning against one of the brick buildings across the street. It was hard to tell the gender, and Bea was wishing for binoculars when another person ran past the loiterer. They both ran down Cherry Blossom Alley and disappeared, their coat-tails flapping.

Two youngsters peddling their bicycles from the opposite direction failed to stop at the intersection, forcing the police cruiser to hit his brakes.

The sun was reflecting off an object in the alley. Did one of the men drop it? Was it stolen? Is that why they ran? More worrying still, she and her secretery parked in the city parking lot just two buildings north of the office, in the direction where the two strangers had disappeared.

"Megan," Miss Bea announced, "Grab your jacket and come with me. We're going to move our cars to the parking garage behind the mall. We'll just take an early lunch. I'll take care of your parking fees, and you can tell your hubby the enclosed parking garage has round-the-clock security."

Megan grabbed her purse and their tan suede jackets, then helped Bea lock up and turn over the sign from *Open* to *Closed*. The two of them rushed out the front door of the building, crossed the street, and marched down Cherry Blossom Alley to move their cars.

Bea was disappointed when the glittering object she had spotted earlier was only a broken bicycle mirror at the edge of the alley. She had half-expected an illegal copy of a key to her building or part of a fancy flower vase. However, just as she tossed the mirror into the trash barrel at the corner of the lot, her heel skidded on something.

She picked up a polished, sparkling piece of pyrite, or fool's gold, in shades of red and yellow gold. It was heart shaped and encircled with an etched interlocking rope design. The other side was flat with lettering almost worn smooth. *Abe loves Bea.*

Her hands trembled. She had searched for this worry stone for years.

They returned to the office very quickly and Bea wondered if the heart shaped nugget was working for her or against her. Yet it fit into the palm of her hand like it belonged there.

When she returned to her office just under an hour later, her apparent secret admirer, as her secretary had preferred to call him or her, had left Bea a long-stemmed pink rose outside the office door with a card signed with the initial T this time.

Hiring a private investigator was no longer a possibility; it had become a necessity to her peace of mind. "Megan, I'm going to bounce some ideas off you. Feel free to interrupt at any time."

"Okay, Miss Bea."

"Do you think the flowers could be from the landlord who decided to purchase one of my rental houses?"

"Well not really, because he personally delivered six lovely carnations with a thank you note, not just one rose. Plus, he asked you to join him for dinner," Megan added, "and I doubt he would have done all that if he was unhappy with the way you handled the purchase of his new home."

"True. If it weren't for the attached cards signed with a different letter of the alphabet; I would probably be getting more sleep."

"And the carnations were the only ones with a thank-you note attached. Correct?"

"Yes."

"And wasn't that the same day I heard you pacing your office while you were on the phone with one of your former colleagues? The one who had refused to do business with you because you were a woman, who laughed at you and had apparently called for no other reason than to tell you to find another line of work?"

"It takes all kinds to make the world go round," Bea said distractedly. She wasn't used to having to deal with something so mundane as sexism when all she wanted to do was help people find the property that was exactly what they had been looking for, the way her dad had taught her.

"But the roses have been arriving every Monday since that day," Megan added.

"You're right. But I've done nothing illegal for someone to go to such lengths to have me followed! What do I have they could want?"

Bea's private phone rang. She automatically cradled the receiver on her shoulder while she continued to glance over a dated form, and replied, "Longacre Graham Real Estate, Bea speaking."

"Bea?" Granny began. "The Shadow Angels are having a re-organizational meeting this evening at 6:30. I think it would be a good time to present your request. Where shall I pick you up?"

"At my house."

"I'll stop by about half past five."

That evening Bea was still fascinated by the way Granny maneuvered through traffic, and then began to wonder about her sanity when she pulled into an alley and then into a huge garage, waited a few minutes, then backed out and headed out of town.

"Why the subterfuge?" Bea asked. "Were we being followed again?"

"I just wanted to be certain we weren't. Apparently, I've absorbed some of Deputy Brandi's training. Did you know that she boarded her German Shepherd, Pepper, at my place while the two of them trained for the Sheriff's Canine Corps?"

"Yes, but we don't have a dog with us now," Bea chuckled. "I just thought you were driving around town showing off your new vehicle. I like intrigue and mystery, although—momentarily mind you—I was curious where we were until I recognized the fencing on the Welby Woods Lane."

"We're at Willi Roberts's home," Granny confirmed. "Are you ready to go inside?"

Bea nodded and took a few deep breaths to calm her insecurities and excitement at finally getting the chance to meet the members of the locally famous, yet mysterious Carpenter Aunts' Card Club, presently known as The Shadow Angels, in a business setting. Of course there had been times when she thought she knew each one of them, but it wasn't like they walked around with a name tag on.

Originally the Shadow Angels were known as the Carpenter Aunts' Card Club because meeting to play cards was an acceptable reason for a group of women to spend their free time one day a week. However, these ladies had other ideas.

Although Jewel's husband Henry Carpenter had continued to discredit her at every turn, she still acquired her degree in law and business in spite of him. And, although he thought he knew who the card club members were, no one could have proved to him that a woman could outsmart him.

Each Shadow Angel had her own specialty. Opal took classes in stained glass and welding. Tressie, already an excellent builder, continued advanced carpentry classes. Willi attended carpentry and creative writing.

Their respective classes had been the starting point in

their lady detective direction, when other students shared their fears, frustrations, and suspicions. Yet even the students were never quite certain how their problems were resolved or who was responsible. Numerous times over the years The Shadow Angels' knowledge and gut instinct had saved lives and had earned the respect of local law enforcement as well. However, their meetings were still held in secret.

A group of younger ladies, The Little Angels, gradually assisted in situations from time to time and joined some of their required physical fitness and specialized dance moves. The Little Angels included: Marci Warren, Shannon Donnelly, Wendy Fox, and Deputy Brandi Davies.

Everyone was seated in a circle as the meeting began. These women wasted no time on small talk but got right down to business. Everyone's time was precious.

"There has been a lot of talk about us retiring and passing the torch on to the next generation," Aunt Willi began, addressing the Little Angels in attendance, "but we aren't ready for retirement. Rather we would become more efficient by combining our experience and strengths with your youth and creativity."

The Little Angels were astounded.

"Why?" Marcie asked.

"Think about it," Aunt Willi suggested. "Will's Blue Fox Detective & Security Agency often takes on more than one client at a time and as a result is getting a lot of free publicity and getting paid to do it."

"That's true," Wendy agreed, "However there have been times when Will said they wished for the members of the Shadow Angels' anonymity because it is one of your greatest strengths."

"This is a business for Will," Brandi added.

"Whereas," Shannon continued, "For the most part, all of us have other obligations."

"The rest of you have been very quiet," Marcie said, facing the older Shadow Angels. "Apparently this is something you have discussed at length?"

"We have," Willi replied. "We want to see our work continue, but there have been some physical challenges in which your youth and creativity has made a difference."

"But we haven't lost our passion for helping others," Jewel added softly. "That alone reinforces our request. Too many times people feel trapped in situations they have no control over. And there have been times when our intervention has kept the issue from escalating into a full-blown crime. There is no feeling that compares."

The Shadow Angels knew Jewel was referring to the way her ex-husband, Henry had flaunted his trysts with other women, sometimes right in front of her. That behavior had come to a screeching halt when she finally followed some of her own advice and, against her Christian beliefs, divorced him.

Then, oddly enough, most women shied away from Henry publicly. He suddenly became an unwelcome representative in the community. Except for his illegal gambling and bribery, his income had diminished greatly.

"I have a request," Brandi began. "I've been trying to find my brother, Mason, whom I haven't seen since he left the Flat Rock Children's Home. I know, we're not brother and sister by birth, but our mothers are sisters. So we're still cousins, even though I still think of him as my baby brother. And he has an aunt and two other cousins he has never met in Sunrise, Ohio."

"Leave your file with me," Aunt Willi replied. "I'll see what I can find." She never shared the fact that her husband had worked for the FBI at one time. What she had learned from him had been helpful from time to time.

Bea and Granny watched the proceedings with excitement and more than a little awe. They felt honored to be a temporary part of this secret alliance, as well as finally having the opportunity to be invited to Willi's home. The house had been built in the center of a ten-acre wooded area where Willi wrote her spooky mystery novels. They recognized a few of the items she had used in her novels, including the desk with secret compartments and a china cabinet with hidden drawers beneath the bottom shelf.

"Isn't this exciting, Bea?" Granny whispered.

Bea merely nodded because she knew she had to make a decision. Should she ask the Shadow Angels or Will and his Blue Fox Detectives to investigate what had been happening at her office? Worrying over some stupid roses, a shiny heart-shaped gold nugget and the feeling that someone had been following her probably sounded like an overactive imagination.

Still, she needed help in finding something concrete before she lost more clientele. It was taking Bea weeks rather than days to get back to her new clients, due partly to the roses and partly to the amount of new homes built on the edge of town in the past three years.

She was getting further and further behind. She would never get a better chance than right now to decide whether to ask The Shadow Angels or Will for help.

And the sooner Opal's son, Jonothan, could join her, the better. She knew that bringing him in as a partner would turn out to be the smartest business move she had made in years.

Jonothan's Return
Turtle Crossing

Twenty-four year old Jonothan Carpenter, son of Opal and Roger, was returning to his home-town with a determined agenda. He circled Turtle Crossing Aviation and landed his Piper Cub in the morning sunlight. For eighteen months—since his Uncle Henry had threatened to destroy his family if he didn't leave town—Jonothan had landed in the evening, on a private grass landing field which was owned by his airport assistant manager, Byron Beasly.

During these months, he had acquired all the licenses Bea Longacre had said he would need to work for her at Longacre Graham Real Estate. He had also secretly visited his mom because she was dealing with the accidental death of his dad, and she encouraged him in his studies.

His meetings with Brandi, too, were more sporadic than he would have liked. He was ready to marry her, but she was undecided. And he could never repay Bea for all she had done for him. She was his mentor and coach, and today was to be his first day as her business associate.

He would keep his distance from Henry, which might be much easier now based on what he had learned at an emergency meeting with the Shadow Angels on Christmas Eve. To their knowlege, Henry no longer resided in Turtle Crossing.

However, unknown to Bea, they were following up on some leads without discussing it with her. "Jonothan," Aunt Willi had said, "we feel you would be the ideal person to protect her."

He had just parked outside his private hangar, when he spotted his mom waiting for him beside his vehicle. After a welcome home hug, he said, "Thanks for meeting me, Mom."

"You said you didn't want a big fuss made."

"No. I'm anxious to prove to Miss Bea that her belief in me was not wasted."

They drove a leisurely path through Turtle Crossing, past the entrance to Robin's Clay, Tile & Brick factory, The Farmer's Elevator, and over the B. & O. Railroad overpass. Neither spoke as he turned onto the curving three-lane and slowed down to a crawl near the very intersection where a stand of trees once stood—the trees his father's truck swerved into.

Jonothan relived the crash now and then, but like the scars on his forehead, the emotional scars from the crash seemed to be healing over with time. Today he felt he could face the memories of his father's untimely death which continued to haunt him.

Despite the horrible way the day had ended, he was still thankful for the few hours he and his Dad had spent together that day. It had just been the two of them.

However, I'm still struggling with how Dad could hurt Mom by marrying another woman under an assumed name while he was still married to her, and had another son and a daughter with this woman.

"Jonothan," his Mom asked softly, "are you okay?"

"Thanks, yes. Much better. Shall I drop you at the school or home?"

"Home will be fine. Bea is as excited as you are," she added before he pulled away.

Ten minutes later, Jonothan cruised up Main Street toward Bea's office. Midtown Turtle Crossing hadn't really changed. Each store front was easily recognized by its unique awning designs.

Taking a deep breath, and minding the speed limit so as not to give Deputy Brandi Davies any reason to arrest him, as she had attempted a year ago Christmas. The memory softened into a smile. It had been her first night on patrol, his first Christmas home for a while and their first private meeting in a long time.

Jonothan turned into Apple Alley behind Sadie Hopkins' Diner. On their last date, Brandi had accepted his grandmother's engagement ring, but to his knowledge she hadn't told her friends or co-workers.

He pulled from the alley into Sadie's private garage. Out front, the diner sported candy-apple red and white awnings and, above the front entrance, etched in stone, *Est. Ginger & Charlie Hopkins, 1908.*

It is so good to be home, he thought as he entered through the back door of Sadie's Diner, waved at Sadie in the kitchen, left his usual order, and slipped into the back booth to read the midweek *Turtle Crossing Journal.* He removed his hat, tousled his sun-bleached blonde hair, and carefully placed his hat on the shelf behind him.

He settled into the booth with the newspaper. He was concentrating on an article in the paper and consequently missed the shuffle of feet as three men squeezed into the booth ahead of him. But when they jiggled the backside of the booth, he slid closer to the wall and put his hat back on, pulling it low over his eyes. He wished he had been more observant when the welcome bell above the front door jingled, announcing the arrival of more than one set of lumberjack type boots.

The new arrivals had been brusque with the waitress, Sadie Hopkins's daughter, Julie. Even before they were all seated, one of them ordered, "Bring us a pot of black coffee—on the double, Miss. Anything has to be better than the mud the Double-Circle Motel put out this morning."

Pretending to be disinterested in what was happening around him by holding the newspaper in front of his face; he listened closely and was astonished by one of the men's aggressive tone of voice, "You'll never pull it off. It's too *risky!* That redhead should have minded her own business and done as she was told!"

Jonothan's first daytime appearance in Turtle Crossing was supposed to have been a new beginning, but he hadn't expected it to start like this. He crumpled a corner of the newspaper thinking quickly. Brandi was the only redhead in town, except Miss Bea—unless the Find the New Woman in You Beauty Shop has decided that half the women in Turtle Crossing should try being a redhead for the next few weeks or months.

He was torn between rushing out and finding Brandi or sticking around to find out more about these brash braggarts and what they were planning. Julie saved him from doing something really foolish when she casually set his breakfast plate on his placemat without her usual smile and moved right on past him as though he wasn't even there. The men in the other booth fell silent until after she took their order.

"You've met her a time or two, Slim. It will be up to you to make the initial contact," one of the men said.

Jonothan wished he could see their faces. Remembering a game Brandi had taught him when they had visited the island cottage in Canada on a fishing trip; he closed his eyes, took a few deep breaths, and tried to fit the faces with the voices, including the sound of their heavy footsteps when they had blustered their way into Sadie's Diner.

He noticed he wasn't the only diner who appeared to be uncomfortable with the sexist comments these braggarts had made to Julie when she took their orders, and thought, *Just in case they have plans to follow through with their crude suggestions, I'm not leaving until after they leave, even though I promised Bea to expect me by nine o'clock sharp.*

Jonothan ate cautiously, wondering why the men were staying at the Double Circle Motel. His Uncle Henry had been infuriated when the new highway had limited immediate access to his motel, but apparently Henry hadn't closed it after all.

The famous private investigator Jonothan knew, Will Fox, would at least find out who owns it now.

Notes, he thought. Will was big on notes.

The men's choice of hotel had to be important; so he folded the edge of his placemat over and started writing.

However, by the time he had written the name of the motel, their comments were muffled while each of them shoveled down a Paul Bunyan Special. The only time he had come close to eating that much at one sitting was when he and Brandi had shared a Special after an all-night Canine-Corp training session with her dog Pepper.

The arrival of a Deputy Sheriff's car in front of the diner resulted in the immediate exodus of the men in the booth beside him. They threw money on the table and rushed out the back without a backward glance, he noted. Why would the appearance of a police car be cause for them to exit out the back when they had arrived by the front? This alone solidified his concern that they really were up to no good.

The front door jingled, announcing the arrival of a new customer. He had recognized the sound of the Sheriff's car, followed by her unmistakable footsteps and aura which announced the arrival of Deputy Sheriff Brandi Davies.

She never fails to take my breath away. I would love to

pull her into the booth with me and kiss her senseless. But of course she is in uniform and on duty and just might consider arresting me if I gave her cause. So, instead, for now I'll have to settle for breakfast with her at Sadies.

Unless one looked closely it was hard to tell if her hair was brown or red because she wore it swept up and in a bun inside her officer's cap. She slid into the opposite side of Jonothan's half-circle booth to be in a position to see the front door and keep an eye on the back door in the overhead corner mirror. Julie automatically set a mug of black coffee in front of her, smiled, and asked, "The usual?"

Brandi nodded and immediately asked Jonothan, "Where have you been the past two weeks?"

"Me? Running errands." The errands were for Bea, but he wasn't at liberty to discuss it with anyone else yet.

Brandi held the mug in her hands for a moment before she made eye contact with him as she tipped her head back to take small sips of the steaming black coffee. As Jonathan had expected, she made no effort to show him whether she had his ring with her at all.

My stomach feels like I just gobbled down an entire Paul Bunyan Special, he thought. He just wanted—no he *needed*—to see her alone. "Brandi, are you free to go out to dinner and a movie this evening?"

It took her an entire minute to respond. He saw disappointment sparkling in her eyes, but misunderstood. How could he know she was keeping secrets from him, and she feared he would never forgive her before the end of the day.

"That's it?" she said distractedly.

"I thought you loved the movies." he replied, surprised by her response.

He knew, but had forgotten why she had only been half-listening to him. It was a habit of hers to keep a running scan inside the diner and across the street whenever she ate at Sadie's.

His fear for her safety overruled his patience and he blurted out, "What are you mixed-up in that would make a couple of goons say, 'a certain redhead should have minded her own business and done as she was told'?"

"I'm not mixed-up, as you call it, in anything that should worry you. And just which goons are you referring to?" When he didn't answer, she said, "Jonothan!"

"Deputy, will you please keep it down out here," Sadie ordered as she set a large pitcher of cream and a pot of coffee on their table. Then she looked at Jonothan and added, "Please? Just tell her what she wants to know so we can all have some peace and quiet and I will bring you a big slice of cherry pie warm from the oven, topped with a double dip of Harvey's Vanilla Ice Cream."

He nodded, smiled and winked at Sadie, then, lowering his voice began, "Alright, *Deputy*," putting emphasis on the word, "Deputy" which usually riled her, but instead merely brought a frown on her forehead. He also noticed the gray shading in the soft tissue under her eyes which was probably the result of lack of sleep and stress. His stomach tightened as he was gripped with an unexpected sense of protecting her, and at the same time knew she was not the kind of woman who could be protected.

"The goons I'm referring to rushed out the back when you parked your Deputy Sheriff's vehicle in front of the diner."

Ignoring his comment, she replied, "I'm not the only redhead in these parts and besides, Miss Bea is in trouble and needs our help," Brandi said softly. "Someone broke into her office."

"Are you saying that she is missing?"

"No, doofus. She is not missing. She tried to get Will to do some investigative work for her but he said it would be a conflict of interest."

Brandi quit talking when the waitress brought her usual—a large glass of water and apple juice, coffee, one plate-sized blueberry pancake, two eggs and two slices of bacon.

When Jonothan wasn't forthcoming with an immediate reply, apparently hoping to make a point he would listen to, she pointed her blueberry laden fork at him and continued in a conspiratorial whisper, "We, the Shadow Angels are investigating."

"I see. And please explain what *my* involvement would entail," he replied softly, thinking about a stop he had scheduled before he started his new career.

What a tangled web, he thought. *I hate not telling you but I can't spoil Miss Bea's announcement.*

Brandi stopped eating, took several sips of her cream-laced coffee and reached out her other hand to grip his. "For now just stick close to Miss Bea and keep your eyes open," she said softly. "But you have to promise, we don't plan to tell Miss Bea that you are working with us."

Now this ought to be interesting, he thought.

"You realize I work for her now. Should I lie to her or do you suggest I post available real estate at my Airport Kiosk?" He failed to mention he was already licensed. Pretending had just turned into an almost full-time acting job.

"So you'll do it?" she asked.

"Yes," he replied as he reached for her hands.

She pulled back, her eyes full of apology, and scribbled a message on the white border of her place-mat. Just then her radio bleeped. She drained her coffee, motioned a curt goodbye, and went out the front door to take her call. A moment later, Jonothan heard her cruiser pull away from the diner.

Julie came by and Jonothan flagged her down. "I'd like two of your mom's apple-rhubarb muffins to go. My new boss loves them. If you're too busy I can stop by the kitchen on my way out."

She knew Jonothan always stopped in to have a few words with her mom, but those men had made her so nervous the coffeepot was slippery in her hands. "No. That won't be necessary. Here are your muffins, sir. Now don't forget your cane," she added as she handed him her mother's just-in-case-cane and pointed to the place-mat that Brandi had been doodling on.

Jonothan read Brandi's brief message, *I expect a full report.* Folding the place-mat inside his newspaper, he took his time getting out of the booth, and went into the men's room that was close to the alley entrance. He scrunched his hat down over his forehead, put his sunglasses on, rolled one pant leg up and limped towards the checkout display case just inside the front door. He even managed to bump into the sign standard, which read, *Please Seat Yourself* on one side and *Wait to be Seated* on the other.

When he righted the sign he noted that one of the men apparently hadn't left with the other three, or had he not been sitting with them in the beginning? Julie rang up his ticket, smiled and said, "Thank you. Come again. Have a nice day, sir," she added as she turned and cleared his booth, pocketing her tip.

The man at a front table left right behind Jonothan but left the diner briskly without so much as a glance at Jonothan. Whoever was at the back-alley-door had left as well.

Jonothan wondered who the goons were and what they were doing in Turtle Crossing. For certain he would check that out with Brandi later, assuming she was at liberty to share the information with him.

In the meantime, he slipped into Lady Ern's Mercantile on the corner of Main and Walnut Street and into Allen Ern's Dress for Success men's store that adjoined the Mercantile. Twelve minutes later, Jonothan had changed into the clothes he had purchased a month earlier and left for alteration and stepped-out onto Main in a slate gray blazer, black dress slacks, pale gray shirt and tie – plus a pair of black wing-tip shoes. Having re-shaped his hat, he strode out the door looking like he had just stepped out of a men's fashion magazine.

He placed the folded cane and take-out from Sadie's Diner into the Lady Ern shopping bag and slipped on a pair of aviator sunglasses, which he soon realized he didn't need. The wind had picked up and low-hanging gray clouds were chasing each other overhead.

Just like I feel, suspended between the need to protect Brandi and spending every waking hour pursuing her until she agrees to marry me, and soon.

Instead of walking to the crosswalk, Jonothan headed for the only jewelry store on Main Street. Using the storefront-glass as a mirror he scanned the area behind him, and up and down the street, and saw no one who looked suspicious. He wasn't ready for his Uncle Henry—or anyone who might report to Uncle Henry in jail—to know he was back in town, yet. He opened the newspaper to the want-ads.

Keeping up the pretense, he entered one of the double doors of Turtle Crossing's recently finished street mall. The town council, in their efforts to keep up with malls in the bigger cities had roofed over Sycamore Street at Main Street and added a parking garage in the rear.

A sudden clap of thunder was followed by a cluster of young women rushing into the entrance bringing the scent of rain with them. The street mall was busy. He had heard talk about the concept of combining the historic family-owned businesses with the upscale appeal of a shopping mall. While the roof kept out the rain, the skylights gave a feeling of space and light. Shopping had never been one of his favorite things to do, so this was the first time he had ventured inside.

Easter holiday sales banners drifted overhead. Numerous terra-cotta colored benches all along the brick street-mall encouraged shoppers to stop and rest their tired feet. Trees covered with colorful lights shared space with tubs of white lilies and huge baskets of spring flowers of every color imaginable.

The original brick street remained, with a paved area added around the escalators. Every storefront was occupied. There were two restaurants: a western-style steak house and a soup-salad-sandwich counter near the garage entrance plus a five and dime; a Ms. and Mr. Hair Salon; a pharmacy; a shoe store; department store; a quick stop that carried newspapers, magazines and tobacco products; plus a new grocery. The upstairs was filled as well.

He knew Miss Bea's office had upstairs access to the mall, and although taking the stairs from Main Street had always been quicker; he didn't want to draw attention to himself and casually stepped onto the escalator behind the women who had brought in the scent of a gentle spring rain.

He had picked up an advertising flyer just inside the Mall Entrance which listed Miss Bea's office number. So why couldn't he just rush to the office? Nerves? No, he thought as he stopped in at a gift and card shop, and continued wandering around. Trying not to act too suspicious and praying he didn't run into anyone he knew, he slipped out of the mall and headed towards the Graham Building entrance.

Signs on the wall read: *Left to the enclosed walkway, and the Parking Garage—Right to Business Offices Suite A, B, C, and D.*

Once he stepped inside the quiet business atmosphere, he took a deep breath and had a feeling the step he was taking today would change his life forever. The Shadow Angels had officially voted him in as the first full-fledged temporary male member. When he questioned if they were certain, he had received their unanimous 100% stamp of approval.

Then when he read his name on the door next to Miss Bea's—*J. A. Carpenter, Suite B*—he swallowed his banked excitement and whispered, "Hey, Dad, are you in charge of the applause meter up there?"

Bea had promised he would have his own office and had given him his own key, but he still had this little feeling of pride when the key unlocked the door. Telling the Shadow Angels he knew next to nothing about the real estate business was an echo of what he had said to Miss Bea over a year ago when she had said she would teach him all he needed to know.

He hated hiding the truth from them, but Miss Bea thought it best that no one needed to know he was fully-licensed to take over her office in an emergency. The fewer people who knew about this the better. From past experience, he knew she was referring to his Uncle Henry. She had assured him he would learn the business by accompanying her on a few appointments.

He turned on the light, placed his shopping bag on a side-table just inside the door and froze. There was someone else in his office. He turned and was stunned.

What a morning! My girl is out chasing the foolish law

breakers and I have to deal with a half-brother who could pass for me—in appearance only of course.

"What are *you* doing here?" Jonothan asked.

"You and I are going to take advantage of our situation," Jace began, hesitantly. "Please, Jonothan, don't leave until you hear me out," his lookalike, pain-in-the-neck, half-brother replied.

"I'm listening, but this had better be good or I won't be the one leaving."

"This was Marcie Donnelly's idea," Jace added.

"You've got to be kidding me. How do I know I can trust anything you have to say?"

"You don't. But surely you believe in second chances, don't you?"

The door that adjoined Miss Bea's office opened. "Jonothan, I see you have met your temporary new partner."

So much for pride in having my own office, he thought. *Now I have to share the air I breathe as well.*

Bea continued, "Granny insisted that I need a full-time bodyguard. Of course we'll have to be careful. But remember, only a few people in Turtle Crossing even know about Jace, let alone have ever met him. You, Mr. Jonothan Arden Carpenter, are about to be in two places at the same time."

Jonothan did a double take when he looked in the mirror behind his desk. He and Jace were dressed exactly alike. Their likeness in the mirror was unsettling. "I see Marcie's handiwork in your new hair style and color."

Privately, he thought, *Marcie had better have a very good reason for setting me up with a half-brother who once threatened my life. No, I will be extremely cautious.*

Just then, Marcie entered his office through the door that adjoined Miss Bea's. "Someone mention my name?"

Jonothan was so angry with her he wanted to spit. "You set me up!"

"Please. We have to talk."

"No kidding." He knew she was trying her best to smooth the waters, but he felt the betrayal like a recurring tooth ache.

"Jonothan," she pleaded, "I'm sorry, but our plans went awry not only when Brandi received that call but also because of the bruisers that were in the booth right next to yours."

"Yeah, well I was doing just fine until she pulled up out front. Then they beat it out the back door. Is Sadie okay?"

"She's fine. But *you* slipped away from one of Brandi's best men," she added, a tiny smile lighting up her eyes.

"Oh, you mean that was one of Turtle Crossing's finest who followed me out of the diner?"

"She didn't have anyone *inside* the diner. Hers was across the street from the diner."

Jonothan smiled. "I had planned to stop in at Erns to suit up for Miss Bea. You know, look like a successful business tycoon and maybe fool the jerk who was doing a lousy job of shadowing me. Now you're saying there was another one?"

"Will the two of you quit your sparring and listen to what Jace has to share with us?" Miss Bea intervened.

Something crumbled inside of him at the sound of her shaky voice. Bea looked like she hadn't slept well for weeks. It was apparent she had lost weight by the way her clothes hung from her drooping shoulders. The dark circles around her faded eyes were proof she really did need his help.

For as long as he could remember, his mom had always said he had a heart-full of understanding when it came to defusing complicated situations and making them simple. He immediately went to Miss Bea, gave her a hug and whispered, "I'm ready to go to work. What do you need me to do?"

She gave him such a hug he questioned if the sunglasses in his breast pocket would ever be the same.

He turned towards Jace, keeping his arm around Miss Bea's shoulders. "I'm listening. What have you cooked-up now, Mrs. Marcie Warren?"

He sat and removed the muffins and coffee he had brought for Miss Bea, and was pleased when she absentmindedly took a sip of the coffee and started picking at one of the muffins.

Marcie swallowed hard as moisture filled her eyes. She turned her back on Jace and signaled Jonothan, *I'm your Shadow Angels messenger.*

He nodded, managing not to heave a sigh. "I'm listening."

Wrecked
Marblehead

    Autumn began to regain consciousness in increments. Rubbing her arm, she questioned, *Why am I so cold?*
    Opening her eyes, all she could see was a wall of swirling white. But she was so sleepy. Her eyes drifted shut.
    Where am I? she wondered as something cool, yet light as a feather kept tickling her face. Moisture trickled down her neck. It must be snowing—the white outside was snow?
    This was followed by something warm and slimy. She wrinkled her nose. Something smelled like dog. The lighting was dim as she opened her eyes again and stared into the concerned reddish brown eyes of a mixed-breed Irish Setter.
    She motioned the dog away. "I want to sleep," she murmured. "You interrupted a won'erful dream."

Not to be forestalled, the dog barked. "Oooh, hush," she whispered.

When she attempted to cover her ears to block out the sound, only one of her arms responded. *Where is my other arm?* she wondered. *I—my body feels like I'm waking up in slow-motion increments, like waking up after tonsillectomy anesthesia.*

Frustrated, she shifted around in the seat and attempted to push the dog away, but her fingers were tangled in the straps of her duffle bag. When she finally freed her hand, her bag rolled onto the floor. Sharp needles of awakening were the catalyst that brought her more fully awake. She tried to wiggle her toes and frowned. Her legs were just there.

"Is this a dream? Whose car is this?" she murmured. The dash lights cast a greenish glow throughout the interior of the car. She struggled to keep her eyes open.

I'm in trouble, she thought.

Having always been a person who acted before she thought something through, she had gotten into trouble more often than she cared to admit. Thus she patiently took several deep breaths; however even that didn't help this time.

As her eyes adjusted to the semi-dark, she noticed a flashlight sticking out of the glove box. Awkward as it was, she squirmed around until her toe nudged the flashlight closer to the edge. One more nudge and it fell on the floor and blazed before stuttering on then off, on then off. The red light through her eye lids reminded her of a neon sign from her childhood, but she ignored the memory. Almost unconsciously, her hand rose to her throat to finger the tiny diamond stud she had fashioned into a necklace so long ago.

"Okay, dog. Where did you go? I'm sorry I sent you away. I'm afraid I just might be in trouble here."

She could still smell the dog. Then she heard a mewling whine followed by a friendly bark.

Autumn tried to reach the horn, but once again, pain enveloped her. "Help," she called out, but wondered if she made any sound at all. A brilliant light flashed in her face and she squeezed her eyes even more tightly shut.

"Are you hurt?" A deep male voice demanded. He was close now, speaking through the driver's side window, and his billowing trench coat blocked the blowing wind, allowing only a few snow flakes to drift inside the car. "Where's your coat?" he growled, his clipped demanding questions sounding like that of a teacher or matron, but with more of the edge of a military officer used to having his orders acted upon.

"I don't know," she replied in a whisper, her teeth chattering.

"Are you hurt?" he asked again.

She laid her arm over her tummy but felt no pain there. *My baby is fine, aren't you little one?*

She had never been one to accept assistance, because somewhere—sometime—that someone would demand payment. So rather than admit she was in pain, she hesitantly replied, "I'm cold."

"Is this your first time to drive in a blizzard?"

Normally, she would have responded in kind to his

accusatory tone of voice. But, although part of her mind was foggy, she was pretty certain she hadn't been driving because she didn't even have a driver's permit yet. No one wanted to assume the responsibility for her and anyhow her foster parents always insisted she could ride the city bus if she had any errands or school functions to attend.

"I have a sweater," she said, hoping this would ward off a lecture.

She was reaching towards the passenger door, when he yelled, "Don't open that door! I can hear the water crashing against the shore. We're on solid ground here."

Now she was really frightened and hurt because he kept yelling at her. She felt a tear slither down her cheek, to her outrage. She almost never cried, and certainly not in front of anyone—especially this jerk!

"There's room inside this overcoat for two, so turn around if you can," he said gently, and I'll help you out this side of the car, okay?" he encouraged as he helped her maneuver out the driver's door.

She would have been out of the car minutes sooner, but once again she grabbed hold of her bag which appeared to be stuck or caught on something. When she jerked on it, she almost fell out of the car headfirst. Then when she finally got out and attempted to stand, she collapsed in his arms.

"Perhaps it's just as well," he murmured, as he gathered the slicker around her and lifted her more securely in his arms. "Bring the bag, Bo," he ordered. Thus man and dog set out, single file at times, the dog leading, and sometimes side by side, until they reached a big old Jeep.

"You've got to stay awake," the man said when she closed her eyes as soon as he propped her up in the front seat of his vehicle.

Her head felt as heavy as her eyes. She wasn't afraid of him but felt safe for the first time in over eight years. Still, she shouldn't fall asleep. His chest had been rock hard and somewhere in the recesses of her mind, she just knew she would have bruises where his hands had clutched her tightly against him.

"Hey!" he barked, sounding more like his dog than a man. "You stay awake now, you hear?"

She wished he would speak to her in that deep soft voice like he talked to his dog, but she managed to hold her eyes open until the vehicle stopped. Once again all she could see was a swirl of white. The snow was so thick it was like trying to look through the Jeep's ice encrusted windshield. When the man opened his door, snow gusted inside the cab, lifting Autumn's hair and catching in her eyelashes.

"Bo!" he demanded, proving he could shout at his dog too. Bo turned and followed. "I've heard of people getting caught in a blizzard and walking in circles for hours, missing their destination by merely a few feet." He had tied the 50 feet of rope from the door of the keeper's house to the old hitching post. A heavier rope connected the keepers-house to the lighthouse because in fog as dense as pea soup—or a windy swirling snow storm—it would have been taking unnecessary chances to walk back and forth between the two without some sort of plan.

Autumn had been drifting in and out, fighting to keep awake despite the icy wind which forced her to close her eyes. She was starting to believe she needed a doctor, but so far she didn't have the kind of pain one of the girls had described when she had lost a baby. She just wanted to get where it was warm.

Inside, the crackling fireplace was almost her undoing. She stretched towards its warmth, until she looked at her rescuer, who was over six feet of muscle and clearly too handsome for his own good. She didn't even know his name—but not to worry. *I'm off men for the rest of my life,* she thought as she drifted into a broken, troubled sleep. Broken because, every couple of hours during the night, the man roused her enough to get a response from her and then moved back to the lazy boy to allow her to rest.

Men! Her mind kept zeroing in on the recent events that had shattered her trust in the opposite sex for a lifetime. From the moment the father of her baby had driven her away from the Home for Unexpected Births—in a rental car, so that he wouldn't be recognized—she had still hoped there was a reasonable explanation about why their baby still had to be kept a secret.

But now she knew why. His parents had wanted their grandchild so much that they had driven her to the Home for Unexpected Births, and were paying for her stay. They had meant to force her to stay there until her baby was born.

She was so embarrassed when he responded, "You've got to be kidding me! Stay married to you? Where did you get such a foolish idea?"

"From you when I refused to let you touch me unless we were married," she replied, still not understanding why he was so angry with her.

"You believe everything a man says to you? Don't you know a man will promise just about anything when he is trying to get a woman in the sack? Grow up!

"But why can't we stay married—other than the fact that you apparently don't love me?"

"I already have a wife!" he yelled. "Melody and I are very happy."

"Melody?" she repeated. The realization that he had used her settled around her chest. "Then our marriage was just a sham—and illegal."

"Where do you want to go now? Do you know anyone in the area?"

"No. I'll need to get a job, so anywhere that looks promising. If anyone asks, you could just say I walked away and you couldn't find me."

"You would do that?" he asked, surprised by her response.

"Forgetting you should be easy," Autumn added, acceptance just starting to sink in.

"You would just walk away? I don't know how to thank you, but I've put together a few thousand dollars here that should help take care of your...situation."

"Situation? This baby—*my* baby—is not a 'situation.' It is real and alive."

"What is all this?" he asked, peering through the windshield. He seemed not to have heard her last comment.

She looked out too. Something like a white wall, tall as the sky, was coming off Lake Erie like a winter nightmare. Within seconds they were enveloped in the sudden fury of 50 mile per hour winds and white-out snow. Of course, he was driving too fast for the unexpected conditions of the road in an unfamiliar car, and suddenly it was like someone else had taken charge of the steering wheel.

Spinning. She felt like she was still spinning. Her head hurt. *I feel like such a fool. I don't know what my next step will be, but don't worry little one. I love you. Maybe tomorrow, we can...*

"Go away," she said, shoving the cool washcloth off her forehead. "Leave me *alone*."

"Sorry, young lady. I can't do that. You've got to try to wake up. Are you thirsty?"

"I don't..." she began, drifting off again.

"My name is Mason," the man said loudly. Autumn tried to focus on his face. "I am a boatswain on leave from the Coast Guard, and I'm working on a novel about the life of a lighthouse keeper who was responsible for the care of the 65 foot high limestone Marblehead Lighthouse."

"That's the most boring idea for a book I've ever heard," Autumn mumbled. "I thought you wanted me to stay awake."

Mason grinned and continued, "No, it's really good. I mean, yes, I want you to stay awake. See, the lighthouse no longer needs a full-time keeper due to the light becoming electrified in 1923. The last keeper of the light left in 1946. I was in awe of this handsome historical masterpiece. It is still the oldest continually operating lighthouse on the Great Lakes."

Autumn coughed, shivered, wrapped her arms around her tummy, sat up a little straighter, and pulled the quilt up to her chin. "You're a real chatterbox, aren't you, Mason? Okay then, tell me about yourself. I'll do my level best to try to stay awake."

"You know, I might not have found you, if the Lake Erie snow squall hadn't held off until I finished my daily routine at the lighthouse. Some lighthouse-keepers of the past weren't always that lucky. Soon I have to decide whether I will stay in the Coast Guard, which has become a way of life for me, or look for employment elsewhere."

Autumn's head started to droop like she was falling asleep, and in concern for her and her baby, he quit talking. His momentary hesitation and silence resulted in her popping her head up—she sat up straighter and gave him a half-smile. "Continue, Mr. Chatterbox. Tell me about yourself. I'll try to stay awake. Promise."

"Well, except for a weather-glitch like today, my life is mostly quiet and solitary. I don't have to deal with people except by radio or during a rescue. My mother taught me at a very young age just how important I was to her. She never hesitated to tell me that I was her second accident—my sister was her first."

Mason paused when Autumn stirred a little. "It's nothing," she said. "Go on."

"The day our mother sent us to The Flat Rock Children's Home was the last time I saw her. A few years ago, I made inquiries, but a neighbor said the entire family had left in the summer of 1948."

That got Autumn's attention. "You grew up in a Children's Home?"

He nodded. "There have been times when I've felt like a nomad as I took up residence in different places, unaware I was looking for a place to call home.

"Okay, so I believe there is a God. And I still say my prayers as I was taught at the Children's Home; however when I was younger, sometimes my heart wasn't in them. It had become more like saying nursery rhymes—something I memorized but the words didn't always touch my heart.

"I left the Children's Home when I was fourteen with a family that was planning to adopt me. That's when the habit of my prayers changed and became more real and personal. Being alone, hungry and scared can do that to you. That's also when you realize that God doesn't always answer your prayers to suit you; but his love is always there for you."

"You said you had a sister," Autumn prompted. "Did she also grow up in the Children's Home?"

He nodded again. "Brandi. We spent as much time together as we could. We ate in the same dining room and attended church and school together but we lived in separate cottages at the home—well, they were called cottages, but they were huge. The building where my sister lived had three floors plus a basement. The only thing I remember about the girls' cottage was that there were at least twenty beds in each of the two dormitories. The boys' cottage dorms were on the second floor but in two separate buildings.

"Our personal family time together was usually confined to the ten-minute walks from the Children's Home Main Building to the church and back; three times a week. The last time I talked to my sister; we sat outside on the girls' fire escape steps—near the dormitory door of the girls' cottage, sheltered from view of the Main Building by branches of the nearby trees—and talked about our dreams. I wasn't afraid of getting in trouble, but I didn't want her to be punished for being there with me, even though I was her brother."

Mason was no longer looking at Autumn. His eyes had gone distant and hazy with memory. "She cried when I told her I was leaving, but I couldn't stay with her. I was going to have a real family. What a farce that turned out to be.

"The day I turned fifteen, I overheard a conversation. My family had changed their mind, and were surprisingly expecting a child of their own.

"I didn't want to go back to the Children's Home. I was tall. Big for my age—and could pass for eighteen. I've been on my own ever since."

A shadow of his earlier smile returning, he added, "What a sentimental slob I'm turning out to be. But you are still awake, so I wasn't too boring."

Autumn was wide awake. When he finished telling her his story, she wondered at the similarities of their childhood. Except for his orderliness and strict adherence to prayers, which appeared to be as much a part of him as eating and breathing—it appeared to her he was forever thanking God for watching over him while he slept, thanking God for furnishing each meal and again thanking God for another good day at bedtime—and the weather. He was always praying about the weather.

His schedule was so tight that each and every hour was accounted for and noted in his practice journal. She wondered how he accounted for the time he had spent rescuing her.

Well, as soon as the weather cleared and she was on the mend, she would have to leave. The last thing she could ask of him was to take her on as a charity case.

Perhaps his routine was catching, she thought, as she prayed silently that she was carrying a little girl.

The following morning, Mason asked gently, "Does your head still ache? Miss? Or is it Mrs? Do you know your name? Is there anyone I should call?" She didn't look like a runaway to him, but yet she had been very protective of her bag, and the car was a rental.

"Yes. My head still aches a little, but not enough to take a pain killer. My name is… my name is, uh…"

Thinking he just might be getting himself into a boatload of trouble, he saw something familiar in her eyes: fear and loneliness. He also noted a look of confusion in her eyes which would account for her being un-steady on her feet. Similar to when he had suffered a concussion aboard ship.

"Do you think you need to see a doctor?" he asked gently as he took her hand in his. He'll need to know your name, as would I, and how far along you are. I was a medic's assistant for awhile, so I'm not *too* worried about your health, but what about your baby?"

"My baby? But, how could you know?"

"When I was carrying you, the little bundle you have inside there kicked me."

She smiled, put her head down for a moment, sipped the tea he had set in front of her and said, "Just call me Red. My baby is due in a little over four months. While I was at the Home for Unexpected Births, the girls and the medical staff informed us about what to expect during our 'time.' My baby is still active and I have not had any unusual pain."

"I think your duffel bag and bed pillow cushioned both of you during your unexpected spin."

"I'm going to miss my poofy pillow," Autumn grinned, but it faded almost as quickly as it had come. "But not my foster parents or their son. I was foolish enough to believe that someone really thought I was special. That's a mistake I won't make again!"

She turned away from him and stared into the fireplace recalling the reason why she had walked away from the Home for Unexpected Births. She had double-checked the file folder three times to make certain it was her file. She *had* to get away. That's why she'd called the father of her baby to pick her up at the Home for Unexpected Births to begin with; only a family member could sign the release to get her out.

If it is a little boy, I'll want to adopt it, her foster dad and terminal grouch had told her caseworker. *If it's a little girl, my wife will insist on adopting her. She always wanted a little girl.* Thinking about her child growing up in that household chilled her to the bone.

"This family took me in as a foster child," Autumn began, deliberately not using their names, so if asked he wouldn't have to lie to protect her. "To help the cook and housekeeper. I made the mistake it sounds like you made—of thinking they might like me if I did my work and studied real hard. As usual I messed up again." She sighed and bowed her head and continued, "I pray my baby is born on or after my eighteenth birthday. My baby is due on Labor Day."

"But my foster family weren't the only ones who wanted my baby for themselves. My baby's grandfather wanted an heir to carry on the family name which is why he took me to the Home for Unexpected Births. I was not allowed to leave until after my baby was born. But what that crusty old business owner didn't know was that his one and only son, while dating a woman they wanted him to marry, had eloped with me. And his tutor," she added with a humorless laugh.

"What a mess! And I foolishly landed right in the middle of it all. He had flirted around with me to keep his parents from finding out his secret. But I just wish he hadn't used me in the process. I would have helped him had he told me right from the start instead of making me believe he loved me. Why did I believe him?"

She didn't want to think about it anymore and scooted lower under the blankets. What seemed like moments later, he was once again prodding her to wake-up. "Chicken noodle soup. Just what the doctor ordered," Mason said softly. "Come on, sleepy head. Does your head still hurt?"

He didn't expect an answer but chuckled when she replied, "I'll try to eat a little bit."

The girl fell asleep shortly after she ate the soup, and Mason curled up on the Lay-Z-Boy to read for awhile. As before, he set his alarm clock so he could check on her during the night.

He had noticed the swelling and the slight laceration on her forehead had gone down some. He knew next to nothing about pregnant women, but this young lady seemed like a strong pioneer similar to the type who raised their families as lighthouse keepers.

Mason was at a loss to understand how the previous keepers raised a family and still kept the lighthouse spotless and in tip-top order. It was apparent they had to have had a deep, abiding faith, tremendous courage, and a powerful sense of the importance of their profession to have survived this lifestyle.

He woke with a start and looked at the clock. Twenty minutes had passed so he heated up the tea kettle for some herbal tea.

After an hour of fiddling with the ham-radio; he was surprised when she joined him in the kitchen.

"Amazing, look." She stared out the window. "It's stopped snowing."

Sure enough, the wind had died down during the

night and had drifted around the lighthouse deep enough to cover the layers of stepping stones down towards the water, reminiscent of a Christmas card. The snow led her to thinking about Christmas and how she had planned to spend her first Christmas as an adult in Turtle Crossing with Miss Bea. Of course that wasn't about to happen now. Miss Bea would be disappointed in her. As usual, she hadn't thought ahead much at all or she wouldn't be in this predicament.

Just then she felt a little flutter and was immediately contrite. *I know little one. I suppose you would be better off with a family who has the money to raise you, but you know what, I'm not like my mom. I already love you and you're not going to be ditched just so I can go on my merry way. I'll find a way to take care of both of us.*

When she opened her eyes she saw his reflection in the window. That was one thing about this man, he was not judgemental. He was kind and courteous but she was still afraid to depend on anyone. *I'm going to have to find another place to stay,* she thought.

"Are you and the baby okay?"

"Yes. Yes. We're fine. I was just thinking, do you know of a place where I could get a job? A few hundred miles away from here would be preferable of course."

Her question felt like a kick in the gut. He didn't want to see her go. Now wasn't that a surprise from one who liked the isolation and privacy he had acquired. "What's your hurry?"

"I'm used to taking care of myself, that's all."

A loud knock on the door caused them both to turn.

"Mason?" A voice called. "It's Sheriff Boswell. You have a minute?"

Autumn instinctively snatched her bag off the floor and slipped into Mason's bedroom. Mason waited until she was out of sight before he opened the door.

"Sheriff, what can I do for you?" she heard him ask as the sheriff stepped inside. Coffee?"

"Love some," the sheriff began, "We're canvassing the area for a runaway named Autumn. I know this photo isn't very clear but if you see her, give my office a call okay?"

A photo? Autumn felt another flutter in her tummy that had nothing to do with the baby. As friendly as he was, Mason was a stranger. Would he turn her in? She risked peering around the edge of the door. She could see Mason and the sheriff standing at the kitchen table, mugs of coffee in their hands. Mason stared at the photo for several moments and then shook his head.

"Didn't think so," the sheriff said. "Have any trouble getting home when that blizzard blew in?"

"It took me longer to get back but I'm certainly glad I got the chance to stock up while I could because the weather report suggested this snow storm could last for three days and special caution driving along Lake Erie."

"Oh, you've been listening to those ham-radio buffs. Good," the sheriff replied as he set his empty mug on the table, replaced his hat, and said, "I suppose I'll be seeing' you around."

"No doubt. Thank you for stopping by." Mason stood by the door and waited until the sheriff's car turned onto the highway and disappeared.

He was glad he had followed up on a comment in one of the keeper's journals and had filled the wood box with enough to last for several weeks. While it was still daylight, he went back outside and pulled his Jeep up closer to the back door and out of the wind.

Back inside, he closed the curtains in the kitchen, drew the window shutters closed and checked to make certain all the doors were locked before he moved toward the bedroom where he was certain Autumn was hiding.

She met him at the door. "Would the fact that you are hiding a runaway have anything to do with shuttering the windows?"

"No. The shutters are to help keep out the cold. And, a runaway? I haven't seen a runaway."

"Come on, Mason. I don't want to get you into trouble. And I still haven't seen a doctor."

They stood in silence in the doorway. Bo materialized at Autumn's side and snuffled at her fingers.

"Bo's taken a liking to you," Mason said.

"He probably thinks he is protecting me."

"From me?" He inquired; smiling with genuine amusement and innocence.

"From anybody, silly," she giggled.

Neither spoke for a few moments.

Oh, he could see how she might have left a trail of broken hearts in her wake when she looked at Bo and smiled. And he couldn't help but wonder if she wasn't just a little bit in love with her baby's daddy, no matter what she said.

But what about the two families she had told him about—the ones that wanted her baby for themselves. Could he keep her safe? And why should he care? After all, he had his own plans.

Jonothan's Surprise
Turtle Crossing

Jonothan's head was spinning. Since he had been old enough to make some of his own choices, the only time he wore a suit and tie was for weddings and funerals. Today he had added Realtor to this list, just for Miss Bea. He loosened his tie and unbuttoned the top button of his new shirt—running his fingers around the inside of the starched collar. He had worked so diligently towards his new career. He refused to believe his entire day would continue to match the gloomy dark clouds after the sunny way his morning had started.

Marcie, possibly feeling obligated to help defuse the sparks that hovered just below the surface between Jonothan and Jace, rose and gave Jace a meaningful look. "Jace, I sure could use your help," she suggested. "I have some floral arrangements that need to be delivered before midday. See you later, Jonothan."

The silence in his office after Marcie and Jace departed was stifling. Jonothan slowly walked over to his desk, and ran his hand over the beautifully polished cherry wood. Then to the windows that looked out onto Main Street and downtown Turtle Crossing. But he still felt like an intruder until he sat down in Mr. Longacre's chair, which would now be his. Then he opened each desk drawer, closed them, and pictured each filled with files. He imagined his certificates framed, and hanging on the wall.

"Jonothan," Miss Bea began, "you look right at home. Can you come into my office? I would like your opinion on how you would approach a couple of subjects."

Jonothan threw himself into the work, and found it an easy fit. He had prepared arduously for this, and the next time he looked at his watch he was astounded. Where had the morning gone?

"Jonothan, you have brought back the excitement I thought I had lost and your noted ideas are compelling," Bea told him, looking more like her usual happy self than she had all day.

They ate soup and sandwiches from Sadie's, after which Bea took Jonothan on his first tour of homes with a client. When they returned, Wendy and Will Fox greeted him at his office door. It was good to see his old friends.

"Would you like to see my new office?" he asked.

"We would indeed," Wendy replied.

When Jonothan opened his office door, he was astounded by the party transformation that had taken place while he and Bea had been out. His desk was piled high with gifts that overflowed onto the floor.

"Surprise!" his closest friends cheered.

Jonothan turned to see Bea standing in the doorway of her office. "You knew about this?"

She nodded her head and said, "Go on in. The rest will be here shortly."

His mom hugged him and whispered, "Congratulations! Your dad would've been so proud."

Most of the gifts were items that he could use daily: an electric Royal typewriter plus a box of business cards from Bea, matching lamps, a leather-bound desktop monthly calendar, pens, paper clips, a daily planner, and a set of antique car bookends that had always set on his dad's desk in the family dining room.

He had saved the gift from his mom for last and read the card aloud: "'From Mom and Dad.'" He removed the tissue paper and exclaimed, "Dad's briefcase! You had it repaired! Thanks so much, Mom," he responded as he hugged the briefcase close to his chest.

Jonothan noticed that Jace had the grace to look away. Jace knew he was partially responsible for the damage done to their dad's briefcase and their dad's fatal accident. It would have surprised Jonothan to learn that there were moments when Jace's heart ached, but he hoped some day to repair some of the pain he had caused Jonothan and his family. But it wouldn't be as easy as repairing their dad's briefcase.

"Jonothan," Will began, "Wendy finished a painting for Bea's office, and thought you might be interested in seeing it before we hang it. She has had some restless nights putting this collage together."

When Bea removed the wrapping, she acted like her worst nightmare had come to life. Except for her lipstick and blush, her face had lost all its color. Jonothan instantly looked at Will and saw that he had not missed her response either.

"Bea," Wendy asked, "don't you like the painting?"

"Oh, yes. The painting is beautiful and so real. The street scene in the center is exactly like Turtle Crossing was when I was a little girl. I dream of it this way sometimes too, but those dreams are…" she trailed off, still pale. "Thank you. You have a marvelous talent for details."

While everyone filled their trays, they also studied Wendy's painting. "Wendy," Jonothan asked, "I can see that most of the pictures on this collage are from old postcards of Turtle Crossing but where did you acquire the ones in the upper left and bottom right?"

"I dug them out of the *Winthrop News* and *Turtle Crossing News* archives."

"It's all beautiful," Jonothan added, pointing to her signature, Wendy S.W. Fox, as well as the painting. "You approve of the way I signed the painting?"

"You don't need anyone's approval. I'm certain acknowledging Tom Sands, the man who raised you as his own, and Winthrop Warren, your birth father, is something they both would be proud of."

"Jonothan," Marcie said behind him, unfolding large sheets of paper across his desk, "take a look at these maps that Will found for us. The first is of Miss Bea's building and the new Sycamore at Main Street Mall. The second is Jewel's Emporium, the two nearby Five and Dime Stores and the Red Brick Bank. The third is of Turtle Crossing proper about fifty years ago. Do you notice anything?"

So this wasn't just a welcome party, Jonothan realized. He had work to do as well. He took a few minutes to look at the maps. Something was either out of place, missing, or hidden, but he couldn't quite put his finger on it.

Addressing Bea, he asked, "Have you looked at these maps?"

Miss Bea glanced at them and replied, "Something doesn't look right to you either?"

Ever the private eye, Will had been eavesdropping on their conversation and joined it now. "They're legitimate, Jonothan. So what is it you're questioning?" He sounded unusually agitated.

Noting that Wendy probably was tired and Will appeared a bit testy, Jonothan rolled up the maps, and suggested, "These maps can wait. Thank you both for the daily planner and for coming."

Bea looked at Jonothan with relief in her eyes. "Later suits me fine too."

As Marcie prepared to leave, she asked, "Bea, aren't your lights usually off by 7:00?" She then turned to Jonothan and said, "Call me if you find anything?"

His Mom, as the emissary for the Shadow Angels, had forewarned Jonothan about Bea's numerous rose deliveries which had her so spooked, she took as much work home as she worked on in the office.

"Thanks for putting this party together, Marcie," Bea replied. "Have a good evening," she added.

Will still seemed troubled by the conversation about the maps. Jonothan couldn't decide whether it was the maps themselves or some recent falling-out between him and Bea. But his first commitment was to Bea. After his dad had died she had offered him a backup career plan.

She had said, *I'll hire you, help you get licensed and field train you.*

Then when the Shadow Angels had asked him to *pretend* to be Bea's associate, he wasn't certain what their expectations entailed, plus he still had an airport to run.

Ten minutes later, Jonothan's office was finally quiet. He drew out the maps and brushed his fingers along a seam in one of the maps that had been repaired and wondered where Will had acquired it.

He heard a light tap on his door that exited into the hallway. He quickly hid the maps in a drawer behind his desk, spun around in his executive-type maroon leather chair, and opened a file folder before calling out, "Come in."

The door opened so slightly he thought it might be an apparition. She was dressed all in black—the apprentice uniform of the Shadow Angels. Her partner, a German Shepherd, named Deputy Pepper, entered the door beside her. Both on alert.

Over the years, Jonothan had seen his mom dressed in similar garb.

Brandi closed the door and turned to remove a calf-length black hooded cape which she removed and draped over the back of a nearby chair to dry. The rain had left a chill in the air. Pepper waited at the door as ordered, while Brandi approached Jonothan's desk.

It had been weeks since he had seen her alone and it was grating on his nerves. She circled around behind his chair. "You feeling a little tense?" she asked as she kneaded his shoulders.

"Are you suggesting that I don't have a reason?"

"No. I'm just sorry you got this dumped on you without warning. Believe me, that was not our plan." Changing the subject she asked, "What do you think of your office? It suits you, you know?"

He looked around the room. The décor was old world. He pointed to a bust in the corner. "Is that a real Remington sculpture?"

She nodded. "That's why it's locked in a glass case," she said softly as Jonothan slowly turned his chair around.

"There's never any time for *us*," Jonothan remarked as he lightly drew his index finger in delicate patterns over the back of her hand, then up the inside of her wrist and watched her eyes darken.

"I know. Marcie filled me in on her way out," she whispered. "I thought you might like some company."

He gently pulled her closer until she ended up in his lap. Time ceased to exist as he gently held her close and then away so he could look into her eyes. Had they always been so blue?

"Are you really committed to this? And whose idea was it that we cannot be seen together? After all, if Jace is supposed to be a around acting like me, surely—"

"It was my idea," Brandi said.

"What? Why?" he said, genuinely surprised.

"Whatever is happening to Miss Bea is big enough to affect us all. Our relationship has to be kept in the shadows until Miss Bea's mystery is solved. I can't tell you why just yet."

"So, until this investigation is finished and Bea is safe, I'm also stuck working with Jace, of all people," he said bitterly.

She looked like she wanted to say something else, but before she could, Bea's voice drifted through the wall from the other room. "Jonothan, are you ready to go?" Her voice sounded hoarse, like she had been crying.

Pepper left his post, paced the circumference of Jonothan's new office, then turned back and stared at the Remington.

"Give us two minutes." Jonothan reluctantly lifted Brandi off his lap and whispered, "Have you lost weight? You haven't been sick have you?" he asked slightly alarmed.

"No. You're just used to seeing me in uniform."

"True. We do need to schedule some off duty time for *us,* though. I suppose we could neck in your squad car," he teased.

She thumped him on the arm. And although she didn't use her full strength, he still felt it. "You need to spend less time in the gym," he said as he rubbed the spot where her fist had connected.

However, she didn't even smile. "Now Jonothan, snuff up that tie. You are to escort Miss Bea to her car. You know why she is so special to all of us, don't you? She helped Marcie's mom get her own place when Henry was on a sabotage mission to get legal custody of Marcie and David when they were just children."

"And what or whom are we fighting against now?" he asked.

"That's the problem, we're not certain yet," Brandi replied.

"But you have your suspicions."

Brandi leaned forward and gave him a brief kiss before replacing her cape. "I have to meet Jace. Sorry about your arm."

Jonothan watched her go, hating this part of their plan. A few minutes later, he watched from the shadows as two men got out of their cars and followed Brandi and Jace. He wanted to rush down and warn them, but he just gripped the new window frame and prayed for their safety. He didn't notice two Shadow Angels across the street, and would have been surprised how quickly Marcie had changed and joined his Aunt Tressie.

Jonothan retrieved his briefcase from under his desk, and slid the rolled maps inside. "Miss Bea?" Jonothan called. When she joined him, he bent his arm in gentlemanly fashion, smiled and said, "Shall we depart?"

She chuckled as she locked the door and set the alarm.

"Miss Bea, do you happen to know our destination?"

"Weren't you listening? We're to meet at your Aunt Jewel's Emporium. If I wasn't so frustrated and furious, I would say this is exciting. We will be going in the back door?"

"I thought we were supposed to keep your schedule as normal as possible. Since when did you start parking in the mall garage?"

"About two weeks ago."

They walked down the hall and into the glassed in and well lit skyway to the garage. He wished he had checked out the garage when he first arrived just as he had the mall. Strange, he thought, how spending time with Brandi and Marcie had changed his way of thinking about the years his mom had spent with the Shadow Angels. They made it to the car and out of the parking garage with no surprises.

"Why all this cloak and dagger stuff if we're just going to Aunt Jewel's Emporium? No matter how many stories Henry spread about the Shadow Angels, he still doesn't know a thing. He would never admit that some stupid woman should get credit for putting him in jail."

They arrived at the Emporium a few minutes later. He pulled in to park near the side door as was his habit. "Here we are. Now where did they say we should park?"

"Downstairs."

"Downstairs?" As soon as he repeated her directions, a metal grate that covered the incline into the basement garage rose up, the garage door opened and he drove in. He had been down here as a child, but couldn't recall the reason. The garage door closed behind them and he faintly heard the grate close.

Jewel's car was parked in its usual reserved space beside the Emporium. As usual, Aunt Willi and his Mom had parked their vehicles on either side of Jewel's. It was apparent they knew something they hadn't shared with him. Willi, Tressie, and his mom were waiting for them in Jewel's back office.

Before anyone else could speak, Jonothan said, "Do you have time to look over these maps and photos Wendy dropped by my office this evening? Something either looks out of place or is missing. When Bea and I were discussing what didn't seem quite right, Will got a little testy and said they were legitimate."

Bea looked at Opal and asked, "And, do you know when the old map of downtown Turtle Crossing was removed from the Courthouse Lobby?"

"I just remembered," Jonothan began. "Mom, didn't you write me that a crew had been brought in to clean the vaulted ceiling and walls a few years ago?"

"Yes," she replied. "I wonder why it was never replaced."

"All in due time," Willi replied. "Now what else are the two of you losing sleep over?"

Autumn & Bo
Marblehead

Lake Erie was calm with barely a ripple, yet Autumn woke feeling full of energy moments before the morning sun peeked through the trees. The keeper's house was quiet—almost too quiet.

Why?

Then she remembered. Bo's usual snoring day and night was as comforting as the ticking of the Big Ben wind-up alarm clock; but she couldn't hear it now, which meant Bo went out early this morning.

Autumn had become more cautious since the day the local Sheriff had stopped by, and as of today she had been Mason's guest for over a week. Finally, her head had started to clear up and her sleepy nap-time moments had finally passed.

The hall light was off and the bathroom door open as Autumn made her way to the kitchen. Through the window, she saw Mason standing up on the catwalk of the lighthouse—his attention focused some distance out on Lake Erie. The water was still as glass.

Reflecting, she thought, *This is so like my life. Stormy, then calm, but never quite happy.*

She recalled a word Mason had used in a game of Scrabble the night before—*serene*. That was what she saw in Mason when he played the part of the lighthouse keeper, when he was writing and when he was praying.

Autumn knew it was time to make a decision about where she would go next, and she knew Mason had been thinking along similar lines. Because sooner or later someone besides the Sheriff would be looking for her. Not only that, but since her arrival, Mason had found one excuse after another why he was too busy to visit his neighbors. She didn't like being in the way.

She wanted to surprise him, she thought as she made her way to the bathroom for her morning shower. He had done her laundry, cleaned the lighthouse keepers' home, went without sleep to care for her, kept the wood-burning fire going, and cooked their meals for over a week. And day dreaming had not appeased her appetite.

After taking a quick shower and preparing their breakfast, she was certain her day would be just fine.

When she emerged from the house, showered and refreshed, her smile of accomplishment distracted him from his journals.

Mason had been reading another one of the lighthouse keepers' journals. He held it up to show her. "Judging by the temperature, the moon still visible this late in the morning, the keeper would already have put in several hours of journal logging and cleaning of the light. *I* spent half my night writing."

They heard a vehicle out on the road and turned toward the sound at the same time. Bo had even stopped his usual morning inspections of the lighthouse grounds.

Mason lifted his binoculars. "Out of state," he said tensely. "They're coming up the drive."

By the time the car pulled into the drive, Mason had exited the lighthouse and was raking stones out of the nearby grass.

Autumn, in her customary hiding spot in Mason's back bedroom, heard the car in the drive, said a little prayer she had copied from Jonothan, and decided it was time to jump-start her departure plans.

Breakfast was in the warmer and she was in Mason's bedroom hiding when he and Bo came back inside. "Autumn you can come out and help me eat this scrumptious looking omelet. Thank you."

"Our visitors?" she asked.

"Lost. Although I wouldn't say the gentleman who introduced himself as Will looked like he ever needed anyone to give him directions. They had a map, but the address he was given was non-existent."

"You don't suppose they were looking for the Home for Unexpected Births, do you?"

"I didn't ask. He gave me one of the flyers he has been

leaving at local businesses. Do you recognize any of these young ladies?"

Of course Autumn recognized them—especially the ones on either side of her. That day they had been pretending they didn't have a care in the world. But that was miles away and months ago when they were barely showing, except the one hiding in the back row.

"Mason, I have to leave as soon as possible."

"Why? Don't you like my company?"

She couldn't possibly tell him that her best friend had delivered her baby the day after this photo was taken. She never got to see her baby. It was gone when she woke after the anesthesia. She had wanted to keep her baby, but her family had insisted it be adopted out. She could go back to school and no one in their community would ever have to know—but her.

She cried in my arms every night until her mom arrived to take her home. I never knew her name or where she was from.

Fighting the tears, she replied, "You've been wonderful. And I can't forget Bo, now can I?"

Bo whined and lay down at her feet, looking at her like he was not too happy with the way their conversation was going.

"What did this Will person look like?" she asked.

"He was tall and lanky—black hair and real dark brown eyes. I didn't like the way he looked me over either."

"Who would be looking for you?" she asked in surprise. "The way you talked you don't have any family or friends who might have hired someone to find you, do you?"

"The only person who might do something like that is my sister but I can't see her hiring someone to do something she could probably do herself. We'll have to be leaving soon anyhow."

"We? That's the first time you have referred to us as 'we.'"

They finished breakfast and washed the dishes in compatible silence. The sun was shining through the sparkling clear windows Autumn had cleaned the day before.

At last Mason said, "I don't know what kind of plans you have been dreaming up inside that pretty little head of yours, but I don't think it's safe for you or the baby to just take off to some unknown destination—alone."

The old Autumn would have fired right back that she had been referring to her and her baby. But the hopeful look in Mason's eyes stopped her, and she replied, "You also know we can't stay here. You have another option in mind?"

"I can resign from the Coast Guard and …"

"But, you love the Guard."

He gave her a pained look. "I was offered a job as grounds-keeper at a golf course in Winthrop, Ohio. I have to let them know today."

"Today? That's great but what does that have to do with me?"

"As a kid, did you like to play dress-up?"

Was he saying what she thought he was saying? "I'm very good at pretending," she said cautiously.

"The job comes with lodging," he said. "I could live on site in what the owner called the Carriage House. You could be my overweight brother or cousin."

"Overweight!"

"Well, you can't play the part of my pregnant brother."

Mischief sparkled in her eyes. She felt a small smile forming on her lips. "No one is looking for a guy. It might just work." The smile faded. "But you love living on the water," she said softly.

"The golf course has a pond," He grinned. He didn't do it very often, but she loved it when he did.

She shook her head. "I have to find a job. I can't continue to take advantage of your hospitality, not even as your fat cousin."

"Would you consider staying as my guest?" he persisted. "Look at it this way, whoever is looking for you is looking for a young pregnant woman, right? This would take the pressure off you and give you a chance to relax and decide what you want to do after your baby is born."

She considered asking him to be honest with her, but right then her baby kicked her so hard in her left rib that she straightened her shoulders and took a deep breath.

Misunderstanding the expression on her face, he was immediately contrite. "I'm sorry if this plan doesn't seem feasible, I know there are dozens of other options. What I'm saying is I haven't committed to anything on paper yet."

"I understand that you're not trying to run my life, but what I'm not used to is someone offering to take care of me—for me. Well this time it's for me and my baby."

"But—" he started.

"You mistook my gasp of surprise. Here." Not knowing quite why she did it, she took his hand and placed it high up on her abdomen. And at that precise moment, her baby once again responded with an even sounder jab.

"Whoa. Doesn't that hurt?"

She shook her head no. But as soon as he gently massaged that exact spot with light concentric circles the baby calmed. She reluctantly released his hand, feeling something more than a friend's kindness.

"Autumn, do you trust me?"

Trust was not something she was comfortable with. She had learned at a very young age to trust no one but her mom. And even though social services had told her that her mom had died, she had this feeling she kept close to her heart: *Mom, I pray every night that someday we'll be together again.*

It was very difficult to bring herself to say yes, but she also couldn't say no to his proposal to accompany him to a town called Winthrop. Obviously this lighthouse was not a good hiding place; too many people had already come looking for her here.

Autumn wished she could pack her mixed regrets away as easily as she gathered her miniscule belongings and folded them neatly in her duffle bag. While she packed, Mason left on a brief morning shopping trip. When he returned he handed her several packages. As soon as she buckled the straps of her new bib overalls and looked in the mirror, she saw that Mason had been right; she really could pretend to be a guy.

When she returned to the kitchen to show him how the overalls fit—pant legs trailing after her feet, a good six inches too long—she couldn't help teasing him about his purchase. "My legs are not what's growing," she announced and couldn't help smiling.

"Oh, I've made allowances." He handed her a pair of sturdy workman's shoes, heavy duty socks, plus a strange looking rigging and a small pillow.

"Why should I wear this?"

"The Bibs will already be filled out, thus allowing room for the baby to grow and you can just remove the pillow when that happens," Mason revealed. When she looked doubtful, he said, "At least try it. I was looking through an old catalog and remembered when one of my bunkmate's wives was carrying triplets. She wore one of these slings to take some of the stress off her back during her last trimester."

"What about my hair?" she asked.

"Ah, I forgot." He reached into the bag on the table and pulled out a tall, striped Railroader cap. "I thought you could, you know, kind of pile your hair up inside it." He reddened. "I can do a passable braid."

She felt color rising in her own cheeks as she accepted the hat. "Where did you learn to braid or … perhaps that's none of my business."

"One of my classmates was in the boy scouts and challenged us to learn to tie a lot of different knots."

"Knots? That's not very encouraging."

"Sit!" he commanded.

Beside him, Bo sat back on his haunches at once.

Mason and Autumn looked at each other and burst into laughter. She turned the kitchen chair around and sat with her back to him. He did a fine job of braiding, and several minutes later her cap fit her nicely with her braids coiled on top of her head.

"How soon before we leave?" she asked.

"Are you packed and ready to go?"

Her eyes lit up, and Mason thought her smile alone could melt snow off a mountain top.

"Aye, aye, Sir. The sandwiches are packed plus I baked and filled two coffee tins with peanut butter cookies. The thermos is also filled with hot coffee."

"I see you even mopped the kitchen floor. You were supposed to leave that chore for me."

"You can empty the scrub bucket."

While he did so, she finally figured out the pillow rigging, and had just tucked in the long sleeved blue and white pinstriped dress shirt when she heard a car pull in the drive. "Oops, I almost forgot. Your hands would be a dead giveaway because they are so graceful and feminine," he added as he peeled the tags off a pair of gloves and stuck the tags in his pants pocket.

"Here we go," Mason suggested as he carefully perched a pair of sunglasses on her nose. I'll be introducing you as my cousin, Andy. Do you like the name? It's the closest I could come with the initials A.B.C. on your duffel bag."

She merely nodded.

"Playtime, honey. Are you ready?" he asked as he opened the kitchen door and greeted the sheriff.

"My wife heard you were leaving when she talked

to you at the grocery," the Sheriff began, "She insisted I bring over a batch of brownies for you to snack on during your trip. I know you're a bachelor and all, and we all know how costly it is eating in restaurants all the time."

"Please thank your wife for me, Sherrif," Mason said as he accepted the brownies. And when the Sheriff looked expectantly at Autumn, he added, "This is my cousin, Andrew Coolidge. He's helping me move."

In as low a voice as she could manage naturally, Autumn replied, "My friends call me Andy, Sir," she replied, briskly shaking the Sheriff's hand, and sending a silent prayer of forgiveness for their first step in subterfuge. Protecting her baby had become her ultimate goal.

"Andy," the Sheriff acknowledged, and dismissed Autumn as though she wasn't even in the room. "I'll get out of your way. I can see you were just loading up. You know where to leave the keys?"

"That I do, sir."

"Oh, nice meeting you Andy," the Sheriff added as he went out the door.

"It worked," she whispered and rushed to the refrigerator to finish packing their basket of food and the new cooler Mason had set on the counter.

She wanted to rush outdoors but curtailed that joy for stops along the way. "Our trip may take longer than expected," she commented as she gathered up the box of dreamy smelling brownies.

"Why is that?" he asked, and he shook his head no when she started to lift up a corner of the brownie box. "Patience. You have to wait until our first stop."

"Well that might be sooner than you planned. I'm not only eating for two, I'm emptying for two as well!"

It was almost two o'clock by the time they pulled out of the drive. She had told Bo goodbye when Mason dropped him off at his real home, the neighbors' next door, who had just returned from vacation.

She glanced at the map and the directions he had written and then became engrossed with the houses they passed, the traffic whizzing by, the huge blue sky, the lovely shades of the trees. But she never once turned the map over. Had she taken more notice, she could not have missed the town of her birth, Turtle Crossing, which was less than sixty miles west of Winthrop.

Jonothan's First Appointment
Turtle Crossing

Jonothan and Bea returned to the office following an evening appointment because she wasn't ready to call it a night. He was pleased to find a note she had left on his desk earlier in the day, *Hey Partner, tomorrow look over these files and get back to me ASAP.* With a satisfied smile, he cleared his desk, and latched his appointment journal in his briefcase.

Feeling restless, he knocked on Bea's door and asked, "Are you ready to call it a night or would you prefer to join me at Sadie's?"

"Sadie's? I suppose we should debrief after our appointment this evening."

"How else am I going to learn? I can't read your mind."

"Oh, you wouldn't want to do that right now," she replied, her voice husky as she choked back angry tears.

This was yet another side of Miss Bea he had never seen. But she agreed to go to Sadie's, and he kept quiet on the way, knowing she would discuss whatever was bothering her when she was ready.

He was still full of excitement. This had been his first appointment. Initially, he had expected to feel intrusive when asking the clients just enough personal questions to assist them in finding just the right home, but Bea had taught him well.

He wasn't even nervous walking in to Sadie's without disguising himself.

Henry. That name or face didn't even make him shudder. He knew it should, but he was now a Turtle Crossing business owner. Henry would have to tread softly. Or would he?

Sadie's daughter, Julie, led them to a quiet but well-lit corner table. "Mom just made a fresh pot of coffee, Jonothan. Miss Bea, your special tea will be right out. If you want anything else, just let me know. The special today is peach cobbler."

Jonothan pulled a pad and pen out of his inside jacket pocket, loosened his tie and the top button of his snowy white shirt. They were the only customers in the diner as they had arrived between the evening meal and the late night shift. Jonothan wasn't even encouraged to wake-up the juke box because he couldn't think of a song that fit whatever had upset Bea.

When the squeak-squeak of Sadie's sneakers broke the unusual silence, Bea jumped; then looked around like she had forgotten where they were. Her eyes lit up when the scent of her special tea stirred her senses. Bea nodded her thanks. Meanwhile Julie placed a decanter of coffee on the table, plus a plate of cookies. "Are these the cookies you were working on earlier this morning?" Bea asked.

"Yes," she responded, shy that Bea had asked in front of Jonothan.

Bea tasted the cookie like it was the most delicate and delicious experience ever. Jonothan however, had already started on his second before Miss Bea had eaten half of her first one.

"I'll take a couple dozen of these to go," Jonothan said, but he was focusing on Bea. He was puzzled about how relaxed Bea had become after her second cup of tea.

"Mind if I try your special tea before I move on to coffee?"

Begrudgingly, she obliged by pouring him barely enough to cover the bottom of his cup and plunked the tea pot down with a thump.

"I see you're not willing to share much are you?"

She nodded in his direction and waited. He downed the contents in one swallow. His eyes watered. His ears were so hot, he was certain they must have turned beet red.

When he had gathered his senses, he said, "This isn't like you," he gasped. "Especially since you know I've steered clear of drinking alcoholic beverages since I was old enough to understand how it can ruin people's lives. Since when and how often do you indulge?"

"I do not need a lecture. Anyhow, this is Sadie's homemade cherry dinner wine. Her daddy had a winery and distillery right below here in the cellar during prohibition, which is just one of the many secrets this town keeps under wraps." She stared moodily into her cup a moment longer. "I guess you deserve an explanation as to why this evening bothered me."

He waited. She held out her mug and he poured it full of black coffee. Taking a deep breath, she sat up straighter, and appeared to be gradually gathering her thoughts. After Bea took a few cautious sips of coffee, Julie returned with bowls of clam chowder accompanied by a basket of fresh-from-the-oven sour-dough dinner biscuits. Bea waited until Julie had moved on to seat the group of contractors who had just entered the diner.

"Today was the anniversary of when I met my little girl."

"So, is there a connection between your little girl and the family we sat with this evening?" he asked cautiously.

"Yes. Their son and daughter-in-law adopted two children at about the same time I tried to adopt my little red-haired girl. I didn't fit the mold because adoptions were for two-parent households. Unfortunately, my husband was killed when his plane was shot down over the Pacific.

"The son of the couple we talked to this evening was married. I argued that I had been married—that I was just widowed and could take care of a child just fine. But that didn't matter. However, a year or so later, this couple had a child of their own and didn't want the adopted children anymore. Thus, the grandparents are raising them."

"But what truly infuriates you," Jonothan guessed, "is that you have no idea what has happened to *your* little girl. Would that be a fair assessment?"

"Now young man, you sound just like your mom."

"Thanks. Now the real question is what Sadie's wine cellar full of secrets has to do with your little girl. Did you really think I wasn't paying attention when you mentioned town secrets alongside Sadie's wine cellar? Does it still exist?"

"Nothing! No one! It's just that, ever since Wendy dropped off that painting, old memories have been—well, distracting me.'"

"I know those feelings all too well," Jonothan agreed.

"Are you referring to your dad's accident last summer?" Bea asked.

"Yes. But how can I help now? What is it about that painting?" Jonothan asked softly, hoping in a way she could shed some light on why he had been waking in the wee hours of the morning. "And maybe at this point I should tell you that I've also been having some sleep-robbing dreams lately."

"Did I mention dreams?"

"No, ma'am. But I can tell by the look on your face that I am on the right track. Right? Is that why you insisted the painting should stay in my office instead of yours? Even though you have more free wall space than I do?"

She folded and unfolded her hands so many times, that Jonothan was undecided as to how aggressive he should be with her, but then something Wendy had said made sense. "Do you remember what Wendy said when I removed the wrapping?"

"She said it had come to her in a dream. She had worked on it for weeks."

"And something else," he encouraged.

"That Will said it reminded him of an old photo he had seen recently of Turtle Crossing at the turn of the century."

"Who do we know who would have such a collection?" Jonothan asked as he motioned for Julie to bring two dishes of peach cobbler.

"There are old photos plastered on all the walls in the train station."

"True. However, his photos are on a much smaller scale. You know I haven't really studied the photos that Sadie has hanging here in her diner."

Jonothan looked up to where she was indicating and saw photos of the town's first train station, the old creamery that had been replaced with Harvey's Ice Cream Parlor, the livery stable that was replaced by the Johnson Garage.

"But what was in the photo behind the cash register?" he wondered aloud.

"I'm not certain but it was there the day Wendy delivered her painting to the office. Which reminds me, how much have you told the Shadow Angels?"

"Not much. We'll check out the high school, the newspaper and Aunt Jewel's Emporium; but for now I think it's time for us to leave, don't you agree?"

While Bea paid at the counter, Jonothan was mesmerized by the interior photograph of a garage that hung on the wall behind the cash register near the front door of the diner.

What memory is buried here?

Goosebumps ran up his spine. It took all his strength to not whip around and see if anyone was watching him.

And, he mused, *what does Sadie's wine cellar have to do with secrets?*

Starting Over Together
Marblehead to Winthrop

Mason drove away from the lighthouse and his past with mixed emotions. He would miss the life that had kept him on track for the past five years, but for the most part he would miss his U.S. Coast Guard family. Extended leave had also given him the opportunity to write for longer periods of time than an hour or so between assignments.

And Autumn had surprisingly been a welcome distraction. She had brought sunshine and hope and a reason to change the direction of his life. More specifically, she had given him the courage to call Captain Richard Warren.

He and Captain Warren had crossed paths one evening while the Guard had been in port. The captain had been attending a military reunion and had invited Mason and his buddy to join him at his table.

Warren had overheard Mason discussing his lack of family and had picked up on how bleak Mason had sounded when he mentioned that without the Guard he was undecided about his future and it would soon be time to sign-up for another tour of duty or opt out and start a new life outside the Coast Guard.

Warren had said, "I have a son and daughter about your age and I would hate to think they wouldn't have a place to call home. You ever need a job—anything—don't hesitate to call me."

Mason had carried that business card in his billfold for nearly a year. It had been a long time since anyone had looked at him with such understanding and sincerity. He had practically worn the print off the card with his indecision about even dialing the number.

He had prayed daily, asking God for his help in making a decision about his career and finding his family. His hands had perspired and even trembled when he dialed Warren's number. The first surprise was that the captain had answered the telephone.

When asked if he remembered Mason, he had enthusiastically replied, "Of course I remember you, Mason. How have you been?"

"I, well, Sir, I've been reconsidering signing for another stint with the Coast Guard and wondered, that is, do you know anyone who is hiring?"

"I most certainly do. I am looking for a full-time groundskeeper for our golf course. You would start out mowing greens, but …"

"I'll take it," Mason had said at once. "But I'll have a relative with me." They were still talking when Autumn walked into the kitchen.

He had prayed for direction and all he had needed to do was get up the courage to dial the telephone. He prayed God would forgive him for the less than truthful lifestyle he was committed to, assuming that Autumn would want to go with him. She needed someone—and no one had needed him in a very long time.

"How soon can you be here?" Richard had asked.

"If all goes well, two days," Mason had replied, trying his best to contain his excitement.

And here they were, two days later, within fifty miles of Winthrop. Mason stopped at a service station and used the pay phone to call ahead. "Captain Warren, I apologize for not calling you earlier. We had a couple of construction detours, but plan to arrive before dark. You said the gate keeper would need the make and model of my vehicle and the names of any passengers. I am driving a blue 1950 Jeep. I have the relative with me I mentioned last time we spoke."

"That's fine. The Carriage House has been aired out and is ready for your arrival. Oh, by the way, if your relative needs a job, there's room for another strong back on the groundskeeping team. You take the weekend to get settled in and plan to start Monday morning at six o'clock sharp in my office at the Club House. I'm looking forward to seeing you again. Drive safely."

Mason was abnormally quiet after his telephone call, and he could tell Autumn's patience was starting to wear thin. It surprised her how quickly she had become attuned to his moods.

"Are they still expecting us?" she asked.

"Yes. Everything is fine," he replied brusquely. Not understanding why the closer they came to their destination, the more nervous he became. A new start was what I was looking for Lord, but a real family too?

Can we really be a family?

"If your new employer thinks I'm a problem, you can just drop me off in the next town," said Autumn. When he didn't respond she continued, "Look, it was your idea for me to pretend to be your fat relative."

When he didn't even nod his head, she questioned softly, "At least tell me what you're worried about."

"I'm not worried. Just apprehensive. And stop calling yourself a problem. Please?"

"I will try very hard, but you've got to be up front with me. I know you're not used to sharing your feelings, let alone your life with others; but this is me. You can tell me anything."

They were both silent for several seconds. "I'm just concerned. Our new landlord and employer has offered you a job as well. He said he needed another strong back."

"Oh. I see. Well, I can handle landscaping and flowers as long as I...well, as long as the job doesn't require a lot of digging, lifting heavy bags of mulch and topsoil..." The sentence hung unfinished. "This isn't going to work, is it?"

"Do you have a better idea?" he added a bit gruffly.

Mason saw a sign that read, *Sunrise*. He hadn't planned

to take yet another detour delay, but the uncertainty had been gnawing at him for weeks. When they turned off the highway they were immediately in a traffic backup.

"Why don't we stop and pick out a couple of men's suits—you know something a bit more dressy and light. And you'll probably need a pair of suspenders too."

"Or we could go there!" Autumn said excitedly and pointed through the windshield.

Mason drove to the store she had indicated and pulled into the first parking place he found, directly in front of *Lady Ashley's Alterations and Costume Shop.*

The alterations department wasn't just about clothes, but flowed into the masquerade department with before and after photos that focused-on the use of makeup. Two hours later, they loaded their purchases—along with a shopping bag full of rhubarb from the Lady Ashley, shop-owner—into the back of Mason's Jeep. Autumn eyed her new face in the side mirror. "I barely recognize myself. I could *really* pass for a grandpa. You know, once in a while, I faintly remember a grandma and grandpa."

Autumn and Mason were eating sandwiches and sipping on bottles of chocolate milk out of the cooler as they left the little town of Sunrise behind them. "Do you want another peanut butter cookie or a big chunk of brownies?"

"Whatever you hand me will be fine."

"Ahh, because you know that sooner or later you will get a big chunk of those brownies anyhow," she teased.

"Something like that. I'm also glad that you made an appointment with Doctor Ashley for next week."

"Yes. So am I. If Lady Ashley's husband is as nice and

competent a doctor as she is a seamstress, I know it will be easy to put my trust in him," she said with a deep sigh. "I was surprised when she called and made the appointment for me to stop in his office after hours. I was picturing myself as Andy—dressed in men's clothes, sitting in the doctor's office with all those other women. But I'll do whatever I need to do because I want my baby to be healthy and get a better start in life than I had."

After about ten minutes of silence, he glanced over to see she was sound asleep. He let her sleep for about thirty minutes and then woke her. "We're almost there."

"Sorry I conked out on you. How much further?"

"About five miles."

"Good. At least the sun hasn't set yet."

"I didn't think it would be a good idea for you to be asleep when we stop at the Warren Security Gate House."

"Security? So that's why you had a false I.D. made up for me? Isn't that illegal?"

"I don't like it any better than you do," he growled thinking that he had broken a lifetime of laws since he had decided to protect Autumn and her baby.

"No," she replied softly. "I'm very appreciative of everything you are doing."

"Then I don't want to hear another apology either, okay? It's only temporary. We're going to take this one step at a time. These are good people. If we do get in a jam, I'm sure they'll help us."

But as Mason glanced over at her, he wasn't sure at all. Being with her seemed so right, yet not-so-right—and it was the last part that worried him.

Mason turned into Shannon's Haven Golf & Country Club drive off of Summerville Road just east of Winthrop, Ohio, and followed the drive marked *Members Only.*

"Good evening, Mr. Mason Davies. Good evening to you as well, Mr. Andrew Coolidge," the caretaker greeted them, dressed in a striking blue blazer and matching cap. After he perused their I. D.'s and compared them to the ledger marked *Special Guests staying at the Carriage House,* he returned their identifications with a small map. "You'll be staying at the Warrens' Carriage House. Turn left at the sign marked Private Drive. Enjoy your stay."

As they pulled away, Mason heard Autumn breathe a deep sigh of relief. The tall iron gate opened and Mason drove five miles per hour as posted.

"Wow," Autumn gasped. "This is quite a place." She continued looking right and left, right and left at the well kept grounds and golf course; then suddenly burst out, "There's the *Carriage House Parking* sign."

Mason shut off the engine, and they sat in the car watching the sun set. A low lying fog was moving into the dips and valleys of the golf course. A light breeze played with the flag on Hole 1. When they got out of the car, they pushed their car doors shut rather than swinging them closed.

"It's so quiet," she whispered and off in the distance they heard murmured voices and the hushed sound of tires and quiet running vehicles as their headlights flashed a golden path out through the gate to the highway.

Mason retrieved the key Richard Warren had left for him and just as he turned the key Autumn whispered,

"They even left a light on." When she saw the kitchen she sighed and added, "Can we stay here forever?"

He wondered if she was aware she had said "we." The concept of the two of them together forever sounded good. However, the feeling was swiftly followed by the thought that she might have been referring to her and her baby, not him.

She disappeared into the lavatory, and when she returned he was struck by the way she looked at him with tears in her eyes. "I'm fine," she said, as she struggled to collect her composure. Blowing her nose on the tissue, she added. "I feel like I've just come home from a lifelong journey."

Mason swallowed hard to get *his* emotions under control. He cast around for something to say and saw a letter sitting on the kitchen counter.

"How could we already have mail?"

He pulled out a kitchen chair and motioned for her to sit down. He then opened the envelope and began reading.

"*Mr. Mason and Guest. Welcome. Take the weekend to get acquainted with our growing town of Winthrop. The enclosed map is self-explanatory; however, no matter where you go on the premises, please wear the enclosed Badges. This is for your safety as well as ours.*

"*I would like you to meet my family. Please join us Saturday, at my Daughter Shannon's house which you'll find marked on the map as The Artist's Loft. We'll eat at around 6:00pm. Dress is casual.*"

He looked up. "You said it first, Autumn. This must

be what *home* feels like." She gave him a watery smile. He stood. "Well, it appears we have a big day tomorrow. I had better unload the car."

"I can help. Honest."

"I know, but you rest a moment."

He threw a switch by the back door which lit up the back patio and the parking area. They didn't have much luggage, so he unloaded the car quickly and placed their bags in the two downstairs bedrooms. He found Autumn sitting quietly in the dining alcove off the kitchen, sipping iced mint herbal tea.

"Well," she said, sounding much more like herself, "for certain, our first paychecks will go towards restocking the refrigerator, pantry and freezer."

The following morning, Autumn couldn't quit talking about the privacy fenced-in outdoor garden. "I can get all the fresh air and sunshine I want right here," she declared, raising her arms up to the sun.

"Does this mean you are backing out on me this evening?"

"Do you mind? I need more practice with the makeup and wig."

"I understand, but we need a more normal excuse for why you are not attending."

"Well," she began as she took forever getting up out of her chair. "Could be my arthritis flares up at the most inopportune times, and guess what?"

"This is one of those times?"

"Partly duc to our long trip."

He chuckled and reached across the patio table to smooth out an extremely dark line that was supposed to imitate crow's feet around her eyes. "You definitely need more practice. Eating breakfast this morning in the garden was a fantastic idea. It's so peaceful and quiet and—"

Just then a golf ball hit the fence. The cracking sound was more like the echo of a gun shot, which was followed by voices just outside the fence.

Neither of them moved, and before they had time to investigate they heard someone just beyond the fence say, "Hey mister, this is private property. Forget about looking for the ball and drop another where it went out of bounds."

"Who are you?"

"Security, Mr. Jones. Your partner knows the rules."

"Well, what if I don't like your rules."

"You can leave," the security guard's voice grew deeper and sterner.

"You can't do that. I paid my money. After all this is for charity, right?"

"Come on, Jonesey," his partner cajoled. After the men moved on, the security guard phoned in the incident and melted into the copse of trees a few feet down the hill behind the Carriage House.

Mason and Autumn looked at each other and Mason whispered, "Andy we're going to spend part of today working on your temporary appearance and your voice."

Autumn had found use for the rhubarb the Costume Shop owner had given her the night before. Lady Ashley had saved all she needed for a pie and insisted Autumn take what was left.

That evening Mason arrived at Shannon's home with a warm-from-the-oven rhubarb cake Autumn had baked. The moment Captain Warren introduced his daughter Shannon, Mason was certain he had met her before, however he had never met anyone by the name of Shannon.

"Welcome to our home," Shannon greeted as she accepted the warm cake. "I don't believe I have ever tasted rhubarb in cake."

"It doesn't sound good at all," her three-year-old daughter, Lily Anneé stated. Her twin, Lauri Rose said, "If it has cinnamon on top, it has to be dee-licious."

"You see, Lily, things aren't always what they seem," Shannon added as she placed a display of condiments for the burgers and hot dogs on the table.

Mason was glad Autumn had decided to wait at least one more night before appearing as sixty-year old Andy. One thing for certain, Shannon's family had better be off-limits until Autumn became more adept and comfortable with aging her appearance. The wig added male dignity to her otherwise milky skin. Perhaps they could find her another Andy Outfit tomorrow in Winthrop.

Shannon's husband, David, and her brother, Sheldon, were out of town on business. Mason and Captain Warren carried trays of food to the patio.

As Mason passed by the foyer he couldn't miss the family portrait hanging in a place of pride, and was immediately ready to leave the Warren Estate and find another place to live.

Shannon had married David Donnelly, who had lived in the Big Boys' Cottage at the Children's Home while Mason had been stuck in the Little Boys' Cottage. Would David remember a kid who was too scrawny and tall for his age? Mason knew he had filled out in the face, and his hair was no longer white/blonde but had darkened to a chestnut brown. Would that be enough of a difference, though?

Here he had been worried about protecting Autumn's identity and he might be the one to blow her cover. He decided not to tell her what he had found. She didn't need any more stress. It wasn't good for her or the baby.

Now, if we can just pretend until September, he prayed.

The Angels Investigate
Turtle Crossing

Brandi reflected as she sat, waiting for the Shadow Angels' meeting to start, that she was becoming totally frustrated with the turn of events that continued to keep her and Jonothan apart. She had left his office with a heavy heart. Okay, she was still questioning her feelings for Jonothan, but thinking about him was also interfering with her job as a Deputy Sheriff.

She had been in high school the first time she had fallen in love—or what she thought was love—but quickly found when love wasn't returned, the result was sadness not happiness. She had worked very hard to get that young man to change his mind; however he had been in love with someone else.

Heartbroken and wanting revenge, Brandi had foolishly married a man who planned to use her to help him destroy the Warren Family Business.

At first, when her husband demanded they spend all their time with each other excluding her friends, she thought that meant he really cared. But gradually her marriage turned into a real disaster. Her husband had taken over every aspect of her life. Every decision from what she wore to what she ate—plus, anything she purchased had better have a receipt and meet with his approval.

After his accidental death, his personal junk had been stored in an attic, and only recently, while in search of something else, Brandi had found a packet of letters sent to her from her brother, Mason. They were post-marked in the first year after he had left the children's home, and had been addressed to her under her maiden name, Davies. Even worse, they had been opened and apparently read because some of the pages were stuffed back in the envelopes out of order.

Each letter from Mason was a precious treasure. Tears fell as she read his letters and immediately stepped-up her on-again, off-again, search for him. However, the day after she found them, Miss Bea and Granny Oates had requested the Shadow Angels' assistance; thus putting her search for Mason on hold once again. Protecting a life was their number one priority.

Because Will's wife, Wendy was expecting their first child, the Shadow Angels' would not consider scheduling her in the field. And Brandi knew Wendy would not want to be totally left out of the loop, thus Brandi asked her to make a few telephone calls. Wendy reluctantly agreed.

And here they all were, waiting for Jonothan's new information. He had brought the maps as well as an enlarged copy of Bea's painting.

When he had laid them all out so everyone could see, he began, "I accompanied Mom and her grade school class on their yearly field trip to visit James Tea, the Station Master at the Railroad Depot. At first I thought I would be bored with his stories about the railroad. After all, I had heard them since I was a kid. But with all that has been going on, I listened more carefully, trying to determine what he was *not* saying.

"He was telling mom's grade school class about the military troop trains that had passed through Turtle Crossing during the wars. But suddenly two burly looking men entered and stood just inside the door like they were waiting on a train.

"From then on the station-master's voice, his demeanor, and story lost their intrigue. The children even noticed.

"Mom?" he continued, "You obviously picked up on it too, because you encouraged the children to move on so they would have time for their ice cream cones before their field trip was over."

"Yes. I noticed," Opal agreed.

Jonothan nodded. "I waited around, pretending to be working on papers from my briefcase and looking at the clock until the men left."

He looked at Brandi, clearly expecting her to come to his rescue because he was new at this undercover stuff, but she thought he was doing just fine, so she didn't say a word.

"Did you recognize these men?" Aunt Willi inquired.

"Are they local?" Aunt Tressie asked.

"They're not local," he replied.

"But you've seen them before," Marcie said softly, "What aren't you telling us?"

Brandi knew it was time to intervene and said, "He got dumped into the middle of an ongoing investigation and that's why he is being careful of what he says."

"Alright, let's move on," Aunt Willi suggested. She turned to Bea. "What do you think we are dealing with here? What really has you puzzled, Bea?"

"Something is happening in our town and none of it is good."

"Anything specific?" Jewel asked softly. Everyone knew that she had lived in Turtle Crossing most of her life and was certain that she knew most of what had ever happened in Turtle Crossing, which included some of her ex-husband, Henry, and his shady shenanigans. One could write a series of books about his escapades.

"You're going to think that Jonothan and I are crazy," Bea said, "But we agree on one thing—the entries to a few of these buildings are not where they used to be and there hasn't been any major construction recently that we're aware of."

"No," Jonothan agreed. "Not major stuff, but look at the differences in the brick on the alley side of the Woolworth building." Showing them an enlargement of a specific area of the store frontage, he added, "Now compare these two photos."

"Well," Jewel pointed out, "That one is easy. New management replaced the windows."

"Look closer. While they were replacing the showcase windows, they closed the alley exit door and enlarged the rear delivery entrance," Jonothan noted.

"That was about the time my father died and I started working in our Turtle Crossing office full time," Bea added. "I never talked to them personally, but the story about town was that they made the changes because it allowed better access for delivery trucks."

"No one had a problem with Marcie and me taking photos for my painting," Wendy added. "As a matter of fact, several businesses were excited that I planned to feature privately owned businesses in Ohio for the rest of the year in the Business Section of the *Winthrop News*."

"I thought Will asked you to slow down on your field interviews," Brandi said.

The corners of Wendy's mouth turned down in a grimace that communicated very plainly what she thought. "I'm expecting our baby, but—"

"If she needs help," Marcie intervened, "she promised to call me."

Brandi nodded her thanks to Marcie, whose help would make Brandi's return call to Wendy's anxious husband, Will, so much easier.

"Why don't I see what I can find out before anyone asks any more questions?" Bea suggested. "It is well known that I plan to be involved with some renovating in Donnelly's Travel office downstairs, so my asking shouldn't be out of line since management of that business has also changed."

Looking at her watch, Tressie pounded her gavel on the desk and announced, "It's time to adjourn. Everyone take a packet and report back on Tuesday or sooner if the need arises."

As scheduled, Opal and Jewel joined Brandi in Willi's private office. "Your team has two hours to report in," Jewel stated.

The general population of Turtle Crossing had never seen Deputy Brandi Davies and Pepper work as a team. And only one or two members of the Sheriff's Department were aware of the fact that Pepper had passed all the required tests that made him a *bona fide* officer of the law.

Brandi had wanted to tell Jonothan her plans for later in the evening; however, that was not how the Shadow Angels or the Sheriff's Department worked and she had felt keyed up all day because tonight was her first assignment to work as a Shadow Angel. She was dressed in black. Even Pepper was wearing a lightweight black coat designed and patterned just for him. In uniform, they were ready, on the alert.

They had arrived at the Sycamore at Main Street Parking Garage about ten minutes before she was expected and two minutes before her Angel partner was due. However, as she approached Miss Bea's building, she felt the air around her change. Someone was coming.

She waited—every muscle ready to spring into action—regulating her breathing. But then the approaching figure signaled the all clear and she relaxed; Marcie was right on time.

She felt Pepper's head brush her fingertips. Good. He had also sensed that the slight movement was Marcie, but still they waited. The seconds ticked in her head like Miss Opal's antique metronome. Finally, the two minutes were up. She inserted the key in the slot, listened for it to catch and the three of them slipped inside.

They hadn't worn any fragrance this evening and from their hand and body movements, no one would have known that this was their first assignment as Shadow Angels. They had studied the floor plan of the entire building, knew when the cleaning crew left and where every desk, chair and file cabinet were located in each office.

Within minutes they were inside Jonothan's office, scanning it for bugs and anything else that appeared out of place. But they were not alone. There was someone in Miss Bea's office and they were not being quiet. The beam of a flashlight appeared and disappeared under the door that connected Jonothan and Miss Bea's offices.

Marcie, Brandi and Pepper were standing close to Jonothan's connecting door to Miss Bea's office when they heard a key being jiggled in his door. As the Shadow Angels moved around the perimeter of the room into the far corner, they blended in with the dark walnut paneling.

Unbeknownst to either of them, Pepper's hindquarters bumped against the book that released a button hidden behind a book titled, *You Too Shall Be Free.*

Brandi felt the floor move and suddenly, *whoosh!* One moment the three of them were backed into the corner of the office, and the next they were enclosed in a silent, dark space. Afraid to move and afraid to speak, this trio of rookie Shadow Angels didn't know where they were or whether or not they could return to Jonothan's office. Except Pepper. He didn't appear to be all that bothered.

Brandi knew that wearing some of her deputy gear inhibited her agility in tight spaces; however she was glad now that she had. She carefully squirmed around until she could loosen her flashlight from her belt without knocking Marcie or Pepper from the platform on which they stood.

The surreal silence and the lack of fresh air were suffocating. Light. It was surprising how much difference it made. As Marcie's flashlight scanned the area, they felt confident to step off the platform. The curiosity of the unknown was stronger than the fear of being trapped. They scanned the bookcase door for a clue as to how to return to Jonothan's office.

The entire corner of Jonothan's office was apparently on a turntable of sorts. The room they had been spun into was a storeroom about five feet wide by twelve feet long, and it didn't look like it had been opened for several years. Yellowing photographs, old newspapers, magazines, books and memorabilia covered the walls and file cabinets. Drapes the same crème color as the walls were drawn across the far end of the room.

When Brandi gently tugged on the cords, they were surprised to find a door, painted the same color as the wall with a padlock hanging open. Brandi slipped on plastic gloves and gently lifted the padlock.

Pepper sat and waited while Brandi worked to open the door. When the latch released, she opened the door, ever so slightly and shone her flashlight. "Marcie, look! A stairway."

"Maybe you should lead the way," Marcie said, her voice shaking.

Brandi said, "Heel, Pepper." Then she tipped the light towards Marcie. "Come on. From now on, the three of us stick together."

The stairs, which were wide enough for the three of them to descend side by side, appeared to be untouched by age.

When they stopped on a landing half way down, Brandi said, "Wouldn't you say we are at street level?" Without waiting for an answer, she shone her light against a tall door to her left. Strangely, it appeared to slide open rather than swinging open like a regular door. "I wonder what is behind this door."

"It has to be Donnelly's Travel," Marcie noted. "This door just has an old-fashioned skeleton key lock. Finally, maybe we can get out of here," she added. Brandi quickly unlocked the slide to the side door with a gismo that Marcie had never seen before. However, when they had the door half way open, they were disappointed. The door opening had been walled over from the inside. Pepper sat on the landing watching with disinterest almost like he knew this was not going to be their way out.

Brandi cautiously scanned her light back and forth and straight ahead as they continued to descend the stairs. After what had happened in Jonothan's office they didn't want to get spun into yet another surprise. Marcie pointed out the loose moulding on the floor directly in front of them. She backed up cautiously and stepped back up on the bottom stair.

Pepper stayed close to Brandi while she tugged gently on a section of hinged oak moulding which opened towards her with a squeak. It revealed recessed curved handholds at floor level. Lightly brushing her fingertips into the recessed curve, Brandi's finger nail caught on the latch just above floor level. She got a firmer grip and tugged on the latch.

Nothing happened.

Brandi noticed a vertical track that had been grooved into the fancy wall moulding. Pictures raced through her mind. She had seen tracks like that before when Opal had invited her to tea; and retrieved a fancy glass serving dish from her antique kitchen cupboard. It had doors that slid around in a track from open to close; and Aunt Willi had a roll-top desk that rolled up and down, front to back.

Brandi placed her flashlight on end to light the space where they needed to work, motioned Marcie to join her and suggested, "I don't know if I can lift this by myself, so we're going to try this together, okay? Feel inside the groove, then we'll try sliding the latch to the right with one hand. On the count of three, we lift."

The two clicks released the door and it began to slide up easily. However, still being cautious, they only raised it about three feet. They went down on their knees and stared in amazement as they scanned the opening with the flashlight which revealed stairs that went down further. The air didn't smell musty but as fresh as Opal's back yard.

There was a wide landing just through the door, but beyond that they seemed to be peering into a dark, empty chasm. A spiral staircase led down to the landing and disappeared into the darkness, where it was quiet as a tomb.

Before they could investigate any further, the hair on Pepper's back stood on end and he gave a long, low growl. Men were talking a short distance away. Their voices echoed like they were in a tunnel.

Brandi switched her flashlight off. They gently lowered the door partway and listened. They needed to know more.

"Junior, you're hearing things. Look, do you see any footprints beyond this point?"

"Let's get out of here," the other voice—"Junior"—said.

"Your cellmate knew what he was talking about though," the first voice went on. "This town has forgotten all about this place."

"As soon as we get what we came for though, I ain't coming back. It's spooky down here," said Junior.

"Let's go eat. See? That Diner has a lot going for it after all."

Marcie and Brandi waited a solid fifteen minutes before they lowered the door into its track, slid the latches back into place, scooted the loose moulding trim back into the slot and headed back up the stairs.

"We've got to try to get back into Jonothan's office," Brandi stated.

"I remember my mom telling David and me bedtime

stories about this secret magical town that was a part of the Underground Railroad years ago. That once in a while a few southerners hid out in a secret passage for days at a time. The elders of the church kept it so hush-hush that the majority of Turtle Crossing was unaware of their activities."

"Do you think that's what these passages are?" Brandi asked.

"I don't know, but I agree that we need to know what those men were looking for or planning."

"I wonder if we might find something in one of those file cabinets upstairs that might help us understand what has someone in such a tizzy? Maybe it's not Miss Bea, maybe she just happened to be in the wrong place at the *wrong* time."

When they returned to the file cabinet room, Brandi checked all six of the cabinets. The first file was boldly marked, *Deceased or Cancelled.*

"What about the books on top of the files?"

"No. It's just wallpaper. They're not real," Brandi replied. "But what is real, is my flashlight batteries are putting out a fainter light. Why don't we all step up on that platform and see what happens.

"While Brandi was jockeying for space, her knee pressed against something and like magic they were *whooshed* back into Jonothan's office.

"No one is going to believe us," Marcie whispered.

Before they could take a step Pepper pressed against both of them. Voices were audible through the door between Jonothan and Bea's offices. They had momentarily forgotten that they were still on the job.

"Well, Miss Bea," a male voice was saying, "I think you should call the cops. I saw lights up here in your office earlier."

"But I feel safe with you, Hector," Bea replied.

"*Night watchman,*" Brandi whispered. Marcie nodded.

Bea continued, "It appears someone has bypassed the security code, but it doesn't look like anything has been taken. I'll call it in right away and they will take care of it for me."

Brandi and Marcie waited until Hector's footsteps diminished.

Jonothan's office was partially lit by the street lights in front of the building, and they needed to let Bea know they were here without frightening her. She walked over to the door separating the two offices and knocked softly five times in a rhythm the Shadow Angels had taught Bea at their last meeting.

Brandi heard swift footsteps on the other side of the door. A moment later the door opened a few inches and Bea's anxious face appeared in the crack. She turned back to make sure Hector the night watchman had really gone before coming into Jonothan's office. Meanwhile, Marcie was busy checking Jonothan's office for bugs once again.

Brandi motioned Bea to follow her, pointing out where the oscillating cameras in the ceiling lights were still running. At Brandi's silent request, Bea keyed in the new code, closed and locked the doors and headed towards the parking garage.

Bea was seldom seen walking to her car alone, but this night it looked like that was exactly what she was doing. And she was marching to her car as though she was angry about something. She opened the back door of her sedan, tossed her briefcase inside, and appeared to fiddle with something inside her car door before finally sliding in and adjusting her rear view mirror. Brandi and Pepper had slipped into the back seat while Marcie crawled into the front passenger seat ahead of Bea.

No one spoke a word until Bea had pulled out of the parking garage into the street. "I don't suppose you ladies were skulking in Jonothan's office to congratulate me on finding my clients the perfect house tonight," she said. "The security guard almost caught you."

Brandi shook her head. "That wasn't us. You had more than one uninvited guest in your office tonight."

Bea took this news stoically. "Is that so?"

Marcie, on the other hand, spoke furiously from the passenger seat. "Bea! Why were you alone this evening? I thought either Jonothan or Jace was supposed to be with you."

"They are. But both of them were called out on other appointments this evening."

"In that case," Brandi said, "Marcie and I will escort you home."

The Two Autumns
Winthrop

Autumn and Mason waited for three days before she made her trial run appearance. They chose Winthrop because they weren't known here and it was time to get acquainted with the area and the businesses.

Mason had asked Captain Warren—who insisted on being called Richard—which grocer had the best cuts of meat, which one had a better selection of fresh fruits and veggies, and in general where the bank and restaurants were located. Richard had marked them with smiley faces for fantastic, X for great to good, and a red circle with a diagonal line through it for deliciously decadent to your health and pocketbook.

The town of Winthrop had become a shopping vacation for collectors of the arts. Autumn and Mason had driven around Winthrop and were impressed with how every home and business on Main Street had been refurbished. The Historical Society and Chamber of Commerce had managed to make the old look new and yet kept the charm of the early 1900's intact.

The street signs had recently been replaced and the history of each building was posted on a bronze plaque. Of course it was impossible to just drive by and read them.

Mason turned onto Chevy Alley and parked in the parking lot. Autumn had been studying the map and suggested, while marking it, "Do you suppose anyone cares that we parked a Jeep in the Chevy Lot?"

"No. Umm, Cousin—I mean Grandpa Andy, you forgot your cane."

"Oh, shoot. You know I'm beginning to like pretending to be someone I'm not," she added, lowering her voice to a mellow contralto as she withdrew her cane.

The parking lot was filling up fast. Mason saw eight adults exit a station wagon with flyers in hand. One woman dropped her flyer as she rushed to keep up with her companions.

"It appears we came on a special Saturday Sale Day. Half of these vehicles have out of county license plates. Including mine," he added.

"Maybe this was a good day to come after all. We can blend in with the out-of-towners."

"I totally agree," Mason replied. "Take your pick, Josie's Fabrics and Quilting, Art by Shannon and Wendy, or the *Winthrop News*. Shannon's twins told me to stop by and see their mom's art at the purple street light."

"I'll pretend to be interested in fishing lures if you'll

pretend just a little bit to be interested in quilts. Is it a deal?" she teased. Because she had watched him shape, then cut and tie-off the oddest looking lures, she knew he would have to at least be curious about lures in a different area.

But from the moment they entered the Quilt Shop, Mason reminded her more than once that this was not usually a man's hobby. Then to his surprise, they followed a couple of men down an aisle that led to the back of the store and entered a door marked, *Welcome! Quilters in Session.*

The spacious room was sectioned off so that visitors could follow the progression of the construction of a quilt. Bolts of fabric lined the corner wall behind several tables used for measuring and cutting the quilt pieces. Quilters were pinning and basting quilt pieces before stitching them together.

The center section featured three huge quilt frames, surrounded by chairs where at least six men and women were concentrating on poking their needle and thread down, then up through a fully pieced quilt, the batting and the backing. Autumn had to grip her cane tightly to keep from running her fingers across the lovely even stitches.

Mason leaned over and said, "Grandpa Andy, it's getting late. We can come back later to look for a baby quilt for your niece."

Autumn nodded and followed him out of the store, barely glancing at the display of baby quilts. Once outside, Mason asked, "Are you thirsty or hungry yet?"

"No. I'm fine. Where to next?"

"Art has always been a weakness of mine," he replied as he motioned towards a store across the street from them. *Shannon's Art Gallery* was boldly carved in walnut above the entrance, and Wendy's name had recently been added.

"Is this the same Shannon you met the other night?"

"Yes, I believe it is."

"Well, I enjoy *some* art. Do you think she'll be in today?"

"According to Shannon's witty twin daughters, she's in and out. She paints in the morning in her home studio and works in the office two days a week as needed or in emergencies."

Inside the gallery, the noise from the street was softened by the closing of the door. The air was cool. Dramatic lighting magnetically drew their attention to each piece of art. Visitors and enthusiasts alike were so in awe, they merely whispered now and then. The next room had a vaulted ceiling with a circle in the middle of the room sectioned off by a low fence.

Featured in the center was one of Shannon's most famous paintings. It was a painting of Shannon's mother, Summer, dressed in white leather. Another was simply titled, "Broken Arrows." The arrows had been broken but the detail of the ageless designs told the story of Shannon's ancestry, plus an empty frame titled, "The Unfinished Life."

When Autumn read the title, her baby kicked and she thought it told the story of both their lives.

Mason was quiet, yet attentive as they walked back to the car. Autumn felt certain if she didn't tell him how she felt she would be in tears. "Mason, can we go to church in the morning? Then later, I want to visit Winthrop's library and museum."

"Of course. Right now, though, I'm trying to decide whether you want a salad or ice cream."

She smiled at him, and nodded, "Both. And the next time we come in to town, I also want to purchase fabric to make a layette for our baby."

"I didn't know you could sew."

Autumn smiled and replied, "It's something I seem to have a knack for. And I found a sewing machine in the dining room at the Carriage House." When he only looked at her, one eyebrow effectively questioning her reasoning, she added, "I tried it out. It works."

"Does sewing take a lot of time?"

"I never kept a stopwatch in home economics at school or during the few projects my foster parents' maid invited me to help her finish. Why?"

"Because Richard asked me if my Grandpop knew much about accounting. It appears that their accountant is expecting her first baby and needs some time off but wants to come back to work a few weeks after her baby is born."

When she didn't respond, he went on more quickly. "It wouldn't be too bad, would it? You could walk from the Carriage House to the office. The money would be yours. I know you have been fussing about paying your own way, and well, I couldn't speak for you, so what shall I say when I call him?"

"Say yes. I'll be there. What time?"

"He suggested eight o'clock Monday morning."

Thus, on Monday her sewing plans were changed from early in the morning to after lunch. Mason stopped by to have lunch with her after she had worked her first eight to noon shift. He was hesitant to admit he missed her, thus his concern that she wasn't working too hard was a good cover.

He hadn't expected to see her in a pair of his old cut-offs and one of his old tee shirts that she had cut off into an interesting tank top. She was looking healthy and tanned and vibrant. Seeing her without her wig, but her aging makeup on, she looked like a little girl playing dress up.

Earlier that morning, Richard had visited Autumn's office and mentioned that his granddaughters had stopped by the Carriage House several times to meet Andy, but "he" was either taking a nap or was out somewhere. Thus, Autumn explained that she now kept the blue plaid Grandpa robe on a hook behind the kitchen door as a quick cover up.

Complicating matters, she was in her seventh month and running out of clothes that fit. But she had another checkup with Dr. Ashley on Wednesday, and afterward they stopped by Lady Ashley's, right at closing time as usual. They left her store loaded up with several new Andy costumes and a small sack filled with tomatoes from Lady Ashley's garden. But, despite the Ashley's hospitality, Autumn and Mason were both pleased to get out of the store.

"Did you notice that guy at the counter?" Autumn asked once they were safely inside the Jeep. "The one who picked up our receipt and gave it back after it fell out of the bag?"

"I noticed him all right. While you were in the dressing room, he approached me and said I reminded him of someone."

"And did you also see that after he returned the receipt he took out a little ledger and scribbled something down?"

Mason looked at her in disbelief. "You're kidding."

"I'm not." She rummaged in the bag, searching for the receipt in question.

"Sorry, I should have been paying closer attention."

But what really had Mason feeling shaken—and what he wasn't ready to tell Autumn—was that the tall, imposing man by the counter had asked him if he knew anyone by the name of Brandi Davies. His heart in his throat, a hundred questions that raced through his mind, the foremost being, *How does this man know my sister?* He prayed his casual response, "Can't say I do," when asked about Brandi had been believable.

Worst and most shocking of all, though, was that until now, he couldn't have imagined any scenario where his sister's need could overshadow Autumn's.

Suddenly Autumn burst out laughing.

"What?" He glanced over and saw her staring down at the receipt.

"It says, 'Grumpy and Gramps,'" she said, holding it up to him. "In the space where the customer's name goes,

Lady Ashley wrote 'Grumpy and Gramps.' I guess that makes you Grumpy."

"You're kidding! No wonder that guy was staring at it. Using such obviously false names alone would make him suspicious."

"Not if you look at her other receipts."

"What do you mean?"

"Lady Ashley puts fake names on all of our receipts. We've been Jack and Jill, Romeo and Juliet, and The Prince and The Princess. I think she must do it with all of her customers. You know, for fun."

"Oh." Mason was only half paying attention when she noted that he had double checked the rear and side view mirrors several times in one city block.

He jumped when Autumn softly asked, "Are we being followed?"

Without answering, he turned down a one-way street going the wrong way and pulled through a parking lot onto another road going the opposite direction. "Not anymore," he said at last.

Autumn was watching the mirrors too now. "Dr. Ashley mentioned that in special cases like ours, he does house calls. That might solve some of our problems. And Lady Ashley said all I have to do is call her and she could mail that suit I tried on today in a larger size."

"That might not be a bad idea," Mason admitted.

The Carriage House had a large parking area paved with flagstones. Since their arrival Mason had parked in the space nearest to the house so Autumn didn't have to walk as far, but after their experience in Sunrise today he parked his Jeep in the far corner that could not be seen from the drive or from the golf course as it was well hidden by evergreens and flowering shrubs.

It was only three o'clock in the afternoon, but the sky had darkened quickly as they'd pulled off the highway into Winthrop. They had just carried their packages inside the house when a clap of thunder was quickly followed by pouring rain. Autumn turned on some lights and set the kerosene hurricane lamp on the kitchen table just in case the power went off.

Within minutes, she had heated up some soup and grilled ham salad sandwiches while Mason dipped out fruit salad into dessert dishes, made a pot of her favorite herbal tea and shelved groceries in the pantry. He even hung her new outfits in her closet without hesitation.

Safe in the isolated Carriage House, it was difficult to feel too worried about a strange man taking an interest in the funny names on their receipt. Mason had called Autumn "Honey" three times today and she was beginning to like the way it sounded. However, once she had graciously hidden a smile when he caught himself and more loudly sputtered, "Hon—Honestly, Gramps, since when have you cared what color shirt you wear?"

Mason's teasing comment had resulted in a gray-haired lady blushing who also added, "You look most handsome in the blue. It matches your eyes."

"Thank you," Autumn had replied innocently.

As Mason entered the kitchen now, she asked, "Did you see the dirty look that sweet old lady's husband gave me?"

"Yeah, he was pretty intense," Mason replied.

"I know. He rushed her out of the store after that."

"We had better eat before the lights go out," Mason suggested.

"Good idea. I filled the thermos with hot tea just in case."

Outside the storm was growing worse with every passing minute. Thunder rumbled and the rain poured down in torrents. At one point lightning struck a tree on the golf course with a *crack* that sounded like the whole world had split in half.

But while the temperature dropped outside, inside the oven had taken the chill off the kitchen and their hearts.

"Your suggestion to come home and eat was a great idea," Mason said.

And much cozier, she thought, deciding she would treat every moment with him as a wonderful treasure.

A Convocation of Angels

Turtle Crossing

Once Bea pulled into her garage and exited the car, Marcie followed her into the kitchen while Brandi remained in the garage to take care of preparations. Bea turned lights on in the kitchen, down the hall, in the bathroom, the study and her bedroom.

As was her habit, when she brought home clients' papers she didn't plan to work on until morning, she drew her bedroom drapes closed and immediately filed her briefcase in her safe.

Marcie watched as Bea drew her bedroom drapes closed and approached her chest of drawers made of the same cherry as her vanity and bedside tables. When Bea opened the chest, Marcie learned the details of yet another Shadow Angels' design. The top two drawers opened fully whereas the others were merely false drawer fronts.

Inside the middle drawer façade, second row down, she removed a stack of ladies' handkerchiefs, slid back a panel and dialed the combination. The door opened on silent hinges. She slipped her briefcase inside the top sliding file drawer and smoothly closed and locked a Chester safe. Finally, she set one of the bedside lamps on a timer, and then turned off the other lights to give the appearance she was in for the night.

Out in the garage, Brandi had just finished moving various potted plants and lawn chairs away from the three-car garage's middle door which opened on the back side of the building as well as in the front. The door had not been designed for secrecy or concealment; in fact, Bea's mom had painted lively scenes on the inside and outside of what she always referred to as Daddy's Drive-thru garage. But tonight it made a handy emergency exit to avoid prying eyes. A car had already followed them through downtown earlier as they had left Bea's office—at least until Brandi had directed Bea through several turns that left the pursuer behind.

Bea entered the garage with a bag slung over one shoulder in time to help Marcie remove the truck tarp off Miss Bea's daddy's black Lincoln which she kept in tip-top shape. She always said she felt like he was beside her when she drove his car.

Brandi and Marcie raised the well-oiled back garage door. Smiling, Bea turned the key and the old Lincoln's engine purred so quietly that Pepper, lying on the front seat next to Bea, barely twitched an ear. She drove out the back just far enough for the car to clear the door.

As soon as they had lowered the back garage door and locked it, they clamored onto the running boards of the Lincoln, one on each side, blending in with the night and the car. Grass now covered the rear drive from lack of use, but it had been kept mowed and Bea knew where the drive curved around flowering honeysuckle bushes to an overgrown privacy fence at the back gate.

The alley at the back of her lot was so overgrown that no one used it but her because she was on a corner lot. It was like driving through a maze. She stopped. Marcie and Brandi scrambled off the running boards to unlock and open the impressive green steel gates. Bea drove into the alley and once again waited while they replaced the padlock and scrambled inside through the rear door windows.

As soon as Bea pulled out onto the street, Marcie finally broke the heavy silence that had descended upon them since arriving at Bea's house. "There isn't bug on this car, so we can talk freely as soon as we stop and get gas."

"And make a phone call," Brandi added.

"I'm afraid the attendant would remember two women in black dressed like they were up to no good stopping for gas and using the payphone as well," Bea chuckled.

"You just don't want to give up the chance to drive your daddy's classic," Marcie teased.

Bea smiled and said, "There's a black blazer and an A-line jumper in that bag I brought. I also grabbed a bag of your favorite peanut butter cookies to munch on for the road."

"You are a dream, Miss Bea," Brandi commented as she slipped on the blazer and tossed the jumper to Marcie.

"After we gas up and I'm driving, we would like to toss a few questions your way."

"I'll take notes," Marcie added.

Bea handed Brandi a twenty dollar bill for gas and drinks. Then she turned to Marcie and handed her two dollars in change for the payphone. Although Bea stayed in the car with Pepper, she kept looking around to see if they really had lost the car that had been following her for weeks.

As soon as they were back on the road, Marcie began with the questions. "Let's go back a few years. Did you ever spend much time in your father's office when you were younger?"

"As a child, not much – but as a teenager, I used to stop by his office. That's when I was showing off for my friends. Why?"

"Close your eyes, and picture his office back then," Marcie suggested.

"Okay," she began. "The foyer was different. His secretary would never let me in his office without an appointment, so I had to sneak in."

"How did you sneak in?"

"Well, remember, back then my office and Jonothan's office were all one big room. Part of the foyer and the secretary's desk space is now part of the optometrist's office."

"Okay, so where was his desk?"

"At the far end of the office. It was huge. There was barely room to get around the ends of his desk. He said when a client has to walk all that distance to talk to him; he had time to evaluate them."

"Why was it remodeled?"

"I'm not certain. He never liked his office being on the second floor. He talked about moving his office downstairs, but couldn't because the jeweler had a life-time lease and didn't want to relocate."

"But the jeweler did relocate."

Bea frowned. "Later. Yes he did."

"Then why didn't your dad move?"

"We only talked about it once. He said he was obligated to keep things as they were."

"He never mentioned what that obligation was?"

"If he did, I don't recall anything that made sense." Bea's frown deepened as she looked between Marcie and Brandi. "These are not the sort of questions I expected. I take it I have to wait until we arrive at our destination to find out the reasons for all your questions?"

"That will be sooner than you think," Brandi said.

Miss Bea had recognized land marks the moment they left the service station, but had kept quiet as she tried to focus on Marcie's questions.

The drive at Aunt Willi's country home was already starting to fill up by the time Bea, Brandi, and Marcie pulled in. Marcie's one phone call had resulted in an emergency meeting of the entire circle of the Shadow Angels except Wendy. Jonothan, Judge Oglethorpe and Granny Oates had also been invited.

Everyone was quiet as they hung their coats in the foyer guest closet and were handed a hot basket dinner consisting of hamburger casserole, yeast rolls, tea, coffee and choices of several cookies and fruits. Soft music was playing while everyone ate and watched a slide presentation of old Turtle Crossing newspaper articles.

After the last slide, Willi turned up the lights and Aunt Tressie began speaking, "It has been suggested that we have a situation that requires our attention as a group. Please allow Marcie and Brandi to tell what they experienced earlier this evening before we start with questions or suggestions. Take notes, doodle and draw pictures, whatever—but it looks like the date of our waiting window has just closed."

From their seats, Brandi and Marcie began describing the evening's exploits. Brandi took the lead, with Marcie occasionally contributing or simply confirming some of the more incredible details. No one was more surprised about the swiveling corner bookcase than Bea herself, and the moment she heard about it she started jotting down notes and drawing pictures of a day she remembered long ago in her father's office.

When Brandi and Marcie had finished, Tressie took the floor again. "This could have been so much worse," she continued. "Good thing you two don't freeze up in a crisis. But even so I shudder to think what could have happened if either of you had been alone in that situation. We'll all be teaming up until this mystery is solved, as usual."

They drew names from a hat. Jewel drew Brandi, Willi drew Marcie, Opal drew Jonothan, Tressie drew Granny and Bea. As the hat was passed around, Aunt Willi asked, "Before we get too much further, I'd like to know what any of you might know about these tunnels under Turtle Crossing that Brandi and Marcie found.

"I can tell you quite a bit about it," Judge Oglethorpe commented from the doorway. He leafed through his leather briefcase and drew out a paper-clipped set of documents, which he passed to Willi. "Read this and you will understand why it has been kept secret for so many years. And if someone is planning to use it to take advantage of anyone we love, then it's time to seal it up for another century."

All were quiet while they finished eating and listened to Aunt Willi read the document. The judge had also brought along photographs and a map of the hidden parts of Turtle Crossing, which he also passed to Willi when she had finished reading.

"Judge?" Jonothan began. "I remember going into the tunnel with mom one time when a tornado was supposed to hit Turtle Crossing. But there were lights down there then, and it was very dark between the lights. It was cold and I could hear water dripping somewhere. The walls were dark and wet—"

He stopped suddenly and glanced at his mother.

"What about stairs or doors?" Brandi prompted.

"I wasn't supposed to talk about it," he said, still looking at his mother. "I've just remembered that too. But, Mom, Brandi and Marcie could have been hurt or lost to us."

Opal looked at her son and his fiancée and nodded. "I understand. But I don't think either of us could share anything pertinent at the moment. It seems the most pressing matter is to find out who these people are and why they are here."

Marcie and Opal were both taking notes of pockets of conversation and keeping their eye on the clock. Special reports were usually kept to thirty minutes and their time was close to running over. The oven timer went off and Willi's husband, Brandon, wheeled the cart around collecting baskets of dirty dishes, utensils and napkins.

"Jewel, you know where *some* of these entrances are, don't you?" Willi asked cautiously.

Jewel had always been the quiet one and right now her expression looked as though she wished she could keep silent. But it was also apparent she did indeed know something.

"Yes. The house I grew up in was connected to the tunnels. And although our basement entrance wasn't the only one, I don't recall the tunnels being an issue before Henry donated my family home to the city of Turtle Crossing. However, due to some blasting at the Turtle Crossing Bridge that is under repair right now, is it possible that checking out these tunnels could be dangerous?"

"Jewel," Bea cut in, "did you know Isabelle and Marty are still taking care of the landscaping and housekeeping at the library in exchange for living in the Guest House Cottage behind the Carpenter City Library?"

"I heard it mentioned, but what does that have to do with what we're discussing?"

Bea calmly collected her thoughts. "Jonothan stopped by the Martin & Martin Landscaping and Nursery looking for something for his mom for her fall garden, and had a conversation with Martin. Previously, Martin had asked Jonothan to do some research about an empty lot near the nursery or an affordable house between the library and the nursery because Isabelle is *really* nervous about living so close to the library."

"Why?" Jewel exclaimed.

"Because," Bea answered slowly, "ever since a night when Isabelle heard men's voices echoing in the basement, she's been afraid to work there at night. She checked out the entire library and at first thought someone was still studying after hours in the reading room, however she found no one. She was certain if the voices had been clearer she might have been able to identify at least one of them."

Bea hesitated, not wanting to drag up any painful memories for Jewel, but she also felt it was important to repeat what Isabelle had told Jonothan. "She thought one of them sounded like your ex-husband, Jewel. She even went so far as to call the area prison to make certain that Henry was still an inmate there."

"It is possible to hear voices from the tunnels if you're in the right place," Jewel said. "But if the men were foolish enough to have been talking right outside the library basement door, it could not have been Henry because he is too sneaky and smart, not blustery and loud."

"But doesn't the fact that they were there at all bother you?"

"Yes, but that still doesn't mean they are aware of the library entrance unless we're dealing with someone who had dealings with Henry when the library was our home," Jewel concluded.

"Bea," Tressie asked cautiously, "did you know about

the stairs and old files that Marcie and Brandi found in your office this evening?"

"No. I just knew my daddy was hiding something though because the day before he died of a heart attack—I'm sorry," she said softly as she took a couple sips of ice water, cleared her throat, and continued. "That day—it was his birthday—I was sitting at his desk with my feet curled up in his chair to wait for him. I must have fallen asleep, because I was awakened by loud voices that seemed to echo from somewhere, like I was waking up from a nightmare. All I remember my dad saying was, 'You can't blackmail me anymore! Now leave! Leave me and my family alone!' I heard a rumbling and then my father's footsteps coming closer like from a long way off."

"Why were you in town?" Willi asked. "You were living outside Turtle Crossing at that time, if I remember."

"That's right; I was managing his real estate office in Lima. But my father wanted me to close up the Lima office and come back to Turtle Crossing to run the home office."

Willi nodded and gestured for her to go on.

"He woke me and said it was time to go home and apologized for being late. I didn't feel comfortable questioning him about what I had heard and the time to question him passed. I had just put it out of my mind until now."

"So," Marcie began as she took a deep breath and checked her notes. "You didn't notice that the book case looked any different?"

"Not really. He always had books stacked on the floor

all around that corner bookcase. And perhaps I didn't want to know because those childhood memories of falling asleep in his chair when I was a little girl are ones I want to cherish."

Willi shifted in her seat. "Brandi, how would you and Marcie feel about returning to the area below Bea's office to investigate further?"

"Since this involves their office, I would feel more comfortable working in teams of four—two inside the office and two in the tunnel entrance."

Bea looked at Jewel and asked, "Could the librarian be at risk when she is working there alone?"

Jewel considered. "I don't know who or what we're dealing with here. But if you know how and where, access to the tunnels from the basement is like walking out your back door to the garage. Simple. But," she added, "like the unknown or inexperienced—what you don't know—can be dangerous. Henry taught me that."

Brandi had been taking notes and without looking up from her notes asked, "Is there also an entrance from Sadie's Diner?"

Jonothan turned to gape at her. "Why?" he demanded.

Since everyone knew how protective Jonothan was of Sadie and her daughter, Julie, Marcie stated, "That's what one of those men said: 'Junior sticking around the diner sure was a good idea.'"

Jonothan looked at the Judge and when the Judge nodded his head and motioned towards the map, he continued, "Sadie has an extensive wine cellar. Her Grandpa used to make moonshine during prohibition. Later he just made dinner-wines for the locals; but now Sadie only offers his wine to her very close friends on special occasions. Anything you want to add, Judge?"

"No. Have you been down there recently?"

"No," Jonothan replied, "but when she remodeled the diner bathroom facilities, to make them handicap accessible, she closed off those stairs to the wine cellar."

"Is there another entrance?" the Judge inquired.

"Yes. But hopefully it is still non-accessible except through Sadie's private entrance."

"But what if they found the alley shipping entrance? I'm worried about Sadie's safety," Jonothan added.

"If Sadie really did wall off the wine cellar, there should be no outside access," Opal put in, but she looked uneasy as she said it.

"What amazes me is how these tunnels meander around under so many of these merchant's enterprises without the owners being aware of their existence," Brandi commented.

"I'll ask you your own question, Judge," Jonothan said. "How long has it been since you were down there?"

"Twenty years or so. This map belonged to my grandfather."

"But the notes on this copy look more recent," said Willi, staring down at the map in front of her.

"My dad headed up the city water and sewage crew who used parts of the tunnels to run proper lines throughout the city."

"Why only parts?"

"Because some segments of the tunnels go quite deep."

"According to the map key, the city sealed some areas of the tunnels."

"It appears this was for the safety of the city maintenance crews should a water line break."

"Jewel," Tressie said with some finality, "can you, Jonothan, and Brandi check out the library? We'll all report back here, unless there is an emergency. Granny and Willi will be your backup. Call any one or all of us if you feel the need."

"I have a request," Marcie suggested. "If this gets more complicated than we have the manpower to handle, can we call Will?"

Everyone approved with a nod of their heads.

"Then let's call it a night," Willi said. "Meeting adjourned. See you all in two days."

An Unexpected Visitor
Winthrop

Autumn's insecurities of the past were waging a vicious battle against who she had become—a mother focused on protecting her child—at any cost. No way would her child ever feel unwanted like Mason had. She wasn't used to someone—anyone caring about what *she* wanted and needed. So for awhile, perhaps she came off as unappreciative of all that Mason had worked so hard to help her accomplish, namely a safe environment for her and her baby.

Dr. and Mrs. Ashley had loaned her numerous books on child care which she had read cover to cover, resulting in her courage and anticipation of being the best mom ever.

She was in her eighth month, and as her due time came nearer, even though Mason had changed the direction of his life for her and her baby, the fear of her former foster parents showing up and grabbing her baby right out of her arms was a recurring nightmare. But this place was so safe. The Carriage House built of local stone, had withstood numerous storms, including a tornado.

Autumn cradled her arms around her unborn child. She wanted her child to look at her with the same loving connection she had observed between Shannon and her father Richard when Shannon had stopped by the office to talk to him about a business transaction they were involved in. Their love was so powerful she had stared at them like one does at a beautiful painting. Could love be enough? She knew her baby would recognize her voice the moment it was born. So if that were true then just their touching alone would be like no other, wouldn't it?

She was unaware of the tears that were streaming down her face when she felt a gentle touch on her shoulder. Mason. Even though he was standing behind her and she couldn't see his face, she felt something she knew wasn't proper. She wanted a real marriage with Mason and refused to settle for a marriage that had left her feeling used and unworthy.

He leaned around her and set a steaming mug of Ovaltine on the table in front of her. "Want to talk about what is weighing so heavy on your heart this morning?"

She knew she couldn't tell him what she had been thinking. "You said we had some decisions to make," she sniffled.

Mason pulled up a chair beside her and took a sip of his Ovaltine before he replied, which allowed her time to dry her eyes. "Thank you for including me," he said. "I can't bear to think of myself without thinking of you and I can't think of the baby as just an extension of you but of me as well."

"But, you're not the father. I can't expect you to pretend that you are. I know how you feel about honesty and how you have hated this pretense we have been living."

"Honey, do you honestly believe that other people in relationships don't have issues?"

She hesitated and then said, "I doubt that Shannon has had a problem in her entire life," Autumn continued. "She is the epitome of what a grand lady should strive to be."

"Yes. She is. But she didn't grow up here. It's not my story to tell, but things aren't always what they seem. This family has suffered more than their share of heartache." He stood and moved to the stove, where he began cracking eggs into a skillet and adding bread to the toaster.

"Mason, do you know someone by the name of Brandi Davies?"

Mason twisted around to look at her, eyes wide and full of an alarm Autumn had never seen in them before.

"Sorry," she said quickly.

They didn't speak for several minutes. He set the eggs in front of her and took a bite of toast before he answered, "Where did you hear about Brandi Davies?"

"In the office yesterday," Autumn replied. "Shannon said that Brandi was coming to visit this weekend. Whether she is family or someone from your past, I don't want to be the reason you can't see her."

A hundred emotions crossed his face. He had told Autumn once that his heart had been broken sometime in the past. Could this be his past returning?

Not now, she begged silently. *Not when we are so close to being a family.*

Mason reached over and took Autumn's hand and waited until she looked at him. "Unless there are two women by that name, she's my sister. A sister I haven't seen in over five years. She's coming here?"

Autumn breathed a deep sigh of relief. Mason squeezed her hands more tightly. She had a sudden and terrible intuition that he knew exactly what she'd been thinking about him when he'd come into the kitchen.

He waited again until he was certain he had her undivided attention. "I would have married you at the lighthouse, but you said you would never marry."

Her temper flared and she tried to tug her hands away from his but when he just gripped them tighter she let loose with, "Wait just a minute there, Mr. Mason J. Davies, I never…I never…" Her face flushed with embarrassment and he smiled.

"My first instinct was to protect you and your baby. But, the more I got to know you, the more cautious I became because I didn't want to spend the rest of my life—let alone a few months—without you. I told myself I could marry you so that your baby and you would have another name. Honey, look at me. Do you trust me?"

His eyes were so filled with emotion and caring, that she would have felt guilty not telling him the truth. "I do, but marriage?" she asked in disbelief. "You really mean it?"

"I most certainly do."

Suddenly she pulled out of his grip. "This has to be the real thing. Legal and official and everything. I've lived in too many places with too many people. I don't want my baby getting passed around from parent to parent, not knowing where they belong. But we also need a ring, a minister and a license. This has to be forever!"

"I have had the ring for months," he replied softly.

Her baby kicked her so hard in the ribs she gasped and had to lean back to ease the wonderful discomfort.

"Are you okay?" he exclaimed when he saw the expression on her face and the flutter of her gown. "May I?" he motioned. He took her hand and touched the place where her gown had fluttered.

She placed his hand on the place where the baby was continuing to kick raising a slight bump on her otherwise smooth tummy. "Wow! You don't suppose we've got a football kicker here, do you?"

When she failed to respond, he thought maybe his touch was uncomfortable for her and started to pull away. But she grabbed his hand and said, "Would you think there was something wrong with me for wanting you to touch me? I mean touch *me*, not just because of the baby?"

He ran a finger down her cheek and across her lips. He watched her pulse jump into overdrive. "I've been a fool not to notice," he said softly as his lips followed the same path.

His lips were like velvet and she was on fire. He held her face in both of his hands and kissed her. She felt the want and the need and leaned closer. Then, feeling guilty for having feelings about a man she wasn't married to, backed away.

Before either could say anything more, they both jumped at a loud pounding on the kitchen door.

"Honey, I have to go, but we're not finished here. Remember that." He kissed her lightly one more time, but had no choice but to answer the door when the pounding got louder and he heard Richard yelling his name.

She raced to her bedroom to get dressed as a grandpa. She left the door open, just a crack, and heard Richard call out, "Mason, come quickly. I need your help. One of the new workers was fishing this morning, lost his footing and went into the deep end of the pond. I was out for an early morning run and threw him one of the life preservers from the maintenance shed. But every time anyone tries to swim out for him, he just starts thrashing around until they back off. Sorry to call you out on a night like this, but with one arm in a sling, I knew I wouldn't be much help."

Mason had grabbed his rain jacket off the coat rack by the back door, retrieved a bag with his rank and name from the Coast Guard emblazoned on the side and hopped onto the work golf cart.

It seemed like hours before the fire department arrived and parked in front of the Carriage House. She knew by looking at the clock that it had taken them all of twenty minutes, but in that time she dressed and put on her makeup and wig.

The firemen arrived just in time to carry the worker

to the waiting ambulance which turned around in the Carriage House parking lot and headed for the hospital. Autumn was still standing at the window when two men who were supporting Mason between them stomped into the kitchen. She was stunned. Mason was soaking wet. "Mason! Did you fall in too?" Her voice came out scratchy and low because she was so frightened.

"Fall in?" Richard questioned. "You've got to know about his rescue training with the Coast Guard. He did what he was trained to do. He took off his boots and coat, put this rigging on and went in and rescued a man who didn't know how to swim and panicked. He needs to get out of these clothes and in a hot shower as soon as possible."

Mason took one look at Autumn and realized he had to say something before she panicked and said something that might blow her cover. "Come on Richard, I can walk on my own. You'll scare Gramps into having a heart attack."

One of the firemen asked, "Sir that was quite a rescue. May I call you later about a training program for our men?"

"I'll get back to you on that. Richard, I'll see you in the morning."

And needing to reassure Autumn, he looked at her and said, "I'll be right out after I shower and get into some dry clothes."

She merely nodded.

The fireman left to join the rest of their crew. In the recesses of her mind; she heard the fire truck leave and removed her dark sunglasses. She hadn't noticed how she looked until she passed by the wall mirror by the back door and squealed. She didn't even recognize herself and momentarily clapped her hand over her mouth to keep from screaming, thinking one of the firemen had been left behind. She had been so worried about Mason; she had put her wig on backwards.

The following afternoon Brandi stopped by Richard's office. Autumn's office was across the hall and she couldn't help but eavesdrop. Although she couldn't really see Brandi, Autumn picked up an accent similar to Mason's. Brandi hinted about a case she was working on but as a Deputy Sheriff, she couldn't say much.

However, when Brandi crossed the room, Autumn caught a brief reflection of Brandi in a trophy display case. She was nearly as tall as Mason with a similar military stance. And if she was as beautiful as he was handsome? Wow!

Feeling guilty for eavesdropping, she started to close her door when Brandi asked Richard who was living in the Carriage House. Autumn held her breath.

Richard hesitated for a moment and then said, "He is a young man who just mustered out of the Coast Guard and didn't have a place to call home."

"Well, I'm not surprised that you offered him a place to stay. Is he looking for work?"

"I hired him. Of course you're most welcome to talk with him. I'm having my usual on-the-grill stuff this evening. He knows he has a standing invitation for Friday nights. His grandfather is with him, but he never comes to the social stuff."

"A Grandfather too?"

Autumn closed her door when she heard his comment and hastily wrote a note to Richard that she wasn't feeling well and would be out for the remainder of the day. She was so nervous she had to rewrite it because she automatically signed her given name.

When she stepped out in the sun, she leaned on her cane for a moment and readjusted her sunglasses. One of the maintenance crew was returning a golf cart for repair and offered Autumn a ride to the Carriage House. She didn't dare refuse and held onto her hat and wig all the way.

At least the young man was cautious with his driving, because, he admitted, he didn't figure a man his age was used to getting bumped around. She wanted to shout, *I'm not a fat old man—I'm a young woman expecting a precious baby!*

But she still had to stay undercover until her eighteenth birthday. At least then she would be of age and hopefully it would take a court trial for her foster parents to possibly be allowed to force her to give them her baby. She didn't know where she would get the money for a trial, and she surely didn't want to take advantage of Mason that way.

Back inside the house, she removed her navy blue blazer and hung it on a hangar just inside the back door. Her hat and wig followed. She finger-combed her hair, poured a tall glass of cold milk and headed for her favorite spot, the indoor garden. Her tomato plant was doing well, as was her double border of green beans. She was tempted to remove her navy blue suit pants, but was hesitant just in case someone decided to stop by and check on Grandpa Andy.

The last thing she expected was that her nap would be cut short by none other than Mason when he came bursting through the back door yelling, "Andy? Andy! Where are you? Are you okay?"

"I'm fine. I'm fine," she mumbled, struggling for a moment to make sense of why he would be so upset.

"Richard was worried about you after he found your note and that one of the maintenance men had given you a ride. He said that the young man was worried about you because he thought you were stumbling about as though something was wrong. Why didn't you call me?"

Trying to defuse Mason's anger and frustration and worry about her, she finally calmed him down by just plain kissing him. He immediately calmed and held her like a precious treasure, then kissed her back with a passion she realized was banked due to her condition or his constant questioning of her feelings for him.

When he finally released her, he motioned for her to sit down and gently lifted her feet onto the footstool and asked, "You're certain you are okay?"

Only when she nodded did he ask, "Then pray tell why you wrote Richard that ridiculous note?"

"I overheard Richard talking with an early afternoon guest. Brandi Davies stopped by his office. I didn't want to chance her asking me a lot of questions about you, so

I thought it best to leave. I think they expect you to stop over to Richard's home for the evening meal."

"I know."

"What are you going to do? If you come up with an excuse, he'll want to know the reason why."

"I already have an excuse if I need one. Richard said I should take the rest of the day off and take care of you."

"And what happens when this Brandi figures out who you are and wants to meet her long lost grandfather?"

"I hadn't thought about that. I just wish I knew if I could trust her. You know sometimes people *do* change."

"But not that much. Didn't you say that honor among the children at the children's home was very strong?"

"Yes. I can't remember ever having to worry if someone was going to tattle on me."

"Well, then why not feel her out tonight? Give her a chance to talk about what she is doing with her life. Maybe the answer will come to you. Did you know that she is a deputy sheriff?"

"No. How can that be?"

"I would assume she qualified, or she wouldn't have the job."

"I didn't mean that to imply she wouldn't qualify, I just remember that she was always afraid of guns."

"Oh." Changing the subject, Autumn asked, "Well, what do you want me to fix for you to take this evening?"

"Richard said I should waive bringing anything this evening, but I figured I could dip into our stash in the cookie jar. I don't want you doing anything the rest of the evening. And before you tell me you need to eat dinner,

I'll bring you a plate full of food from the party. Shannon will insist anyhow."

Mason thought he would stay in the shadows until he could check out this Brandi Davies and hopefully he wouldn't have to do anything that would jeopardize his new job and home in Winthrop. However, Shannon's twin girls called to him just as Brandi walked out on the veranda.

Brandi turned at the sound of his name. He stared at her like she was some alien apparition, and she in turn stared back. He had been a kid of fourteen the day he left the children's home and lost the only real family he had known because another family wanted to adopt him. The part of his heart that had frozen that summer had only recently melted with the appearance of Autumn.

Mason and Brandi approached each other like wary opponents, although neither would have admitted they were afraid of rejection—a pain that would have cut like a knife. Mason was the first to speak. "Are you the same Brandi Davies who left the Flat Rock Children's Home in May 1956?"

She cautiously replied, "And are you Mason Davies, my once scrawny little brother who promised to write?"

"I wrote. You never replied," he stated bluntly.

And then they were hugging, hard and tight and a bit desperate, neither wanting to let go.

"I'm sorry, Sis."

"I'm sorry too." She took his hand and led him over to a lawn swing. They sat, still holding hands. "My only excuse is that I married a guy who I thought really loved me. But what I took for love was his need to be in control. He died two years ago. We had lived in his parents' home.

"A few months ago, I found a couple of bundles of letters you sent me packed away in their attic. I had never seen them until that time, but they had been opened and the letters stuffed back into the envelopes. That's when I hired someone to find you through those letters, but by that time you were long gone."

Shannon's girls were watching them, curious because they loved their Auntie Brandi and concerned because she had tears in her eyes, but so did Mason. Brandi noticed the twins watching, and, not wanting to upset them, stood and walked out on the lawn away from the house to talk in private.

"It's so good to see you," she said as she continued eye contact and took his hand in hers. "What's going on? You look happy, but wary for some reason. Guarded. Please believe me when I tell you that you can still trust me."

Mason hesitated. "I heard you're a Deputy Sheriff now. You've taken an oath to uphold the law."

"Yes," Brandi replied cautiously. "So…have you done something against the law?"

"Let's eat before the steaks get cold," Richard announced from just a few feet behind them, startling them both. They hadn't heard him approach across the soft lawn.

But had he heard *them*? If he had, he gave no sign. Mason watched Richard take the path back to the house and knew he was going to have to trust someone soon. And he had two logical choices now: Richard and or Brandi.

When they all returned to the veranda, it became clear at once that the twins had shared what they had seen and heard.

"You are Brandi's little brother all grown up?" Shannon exclaimed. "I can't believe it. Dad has said you remind him of—" But Richard gave her a look that very clearly said, *Now is not the time.*

So, maybe Richard had overheard their conversation after all, Mason thought. "That's right," he told Shannon. "It's been a long time since we've seen each other. Lots to catch up on."

Shannon's twins ignored the stilted moment they'd caused by rushing to Mason's side.

Laurie Rose asked, "What do you have in the basket?"

Mason had forgotten the basket and replied, "Ah. A little birdie told me that you two have a sweet tooth and if I want to keep my friendship with your mom, I had better put these with the desserts."

"Can't we peek?" Lily Anneé asked jumping up in the air as Mason held the basket high over their heads.

"You heard him," Lauri Rose admonished, tugging on Mason's shirt sleeve, hoping he would tell her first.

"What have you been up to these last five or six years?" Brandi asked as Mason handed the basket to Shannon.

"He's a hero," Lily Anneé said.

"A hero?" Brandi asked, looking from one twin to the other.

"Yep," Lauri Rose continued. "He saved a fisherman from drownin'."

"That's 'cause he was in the Coaster Guard," Lily Anneé added.

"You mean Coast Guard," Shannon corrected.

"Yeah. That too," Lily Anneé agreed.

While everyone filled their plates and found a seat on one of the benches or chairs, Mason noticed that Brandi was following him everywhere as if she was afraid he might disappear.

"Before those two little munchkins join us," Brandi began. "If you don't believe anything else, please remember that if you ever need anything, call me," she said, her eyes bright, her heart overflowing. She remembered the times she had promised herself she would write—would look for him—and hadn't followed through.

Then the realization hit her: if not for Richard Warren, she might never have seen Mason again. "It kills me to say this, but I have to leave. I'll be in touch," Brandi said. As she slipped one of her business cards in his shirt pocket, she repeated, "You need *anything,* night or day! I mean that with everything that is in me. Call!"

She stood on tiptoe and kissed him on the cheek. Then quickly turned and headed for her car, lest he see the tears she was barely holding onto.

"Be careful what you offer, Sis. I just might take you up on that," he replied softly. He watched her drive away and thought, *Thank you Lord for such a beautiful memorable day. Keep her safe.*

As Brandi pulled out of the drive, a memory from the past whispered, *The Lord works in mysterious ways. Thank you Lord for this marvelous chance to reconnect with my brother after all these years,* she prayed. Once again Shannon's family had unknowingly been instrumental in helping her family.

Jonothan Remembers
Winthrop

Jonothan didn't know where his mom got her energy. It had been around midnight when they had pulled in to the drive and she couldn't quit talking about the evening's events, whereas he was tired and felt drained from lack of sleep and this unrecognizable emotional cloud that dogged his heels night and day.

After his mom had gone to bed, he was still upset from all he had heard at the Shadow Angels' emergency meeting. Just the revelation that Brandi and Marcie had been locked out of his new office, with no way to return rippled through his chest.

He also felt jittery as he paced back and forth from the front parlor to the dining room and back, where his mom had displayed several photos on her writing desk. But he was drawn to the photo of him and his dad. It was his first-day-of school picture—taken a day late. His last thoughts however were of Brandi, but he couldn't call her at such a late hour no matter how much he missed her.

Plus, something about the tunnels was still nagging him. Why had someone gone to so much trouble to make certain they hadn't left behind so much as a cigarette butt or candy wrapper—nothing that might lead anyone who might accidentally venture into the tunnel to believe that they were not the first to discover it.

He had acquired the habit of sleeping in his dad's chair, especially when something was bothering him and he was asleep the moment he kicked off his shoes and shoved the chair back into the lounge position.

Of course, his mind wasn't as ready to go into sleep mode as his body was. But he had made some very important decisions by mulling over unanswered questions at bedtime, praying for some divine intervention.

Mom and I were running and I had to take three steps to her one. Is that why I was so out of breath? Could a tornado really suck the oxygen from the air? That combination of surreal silence right at sunset, the greenish-gold of the sky and the sound of a train bearing down on us where there were no tracks was eerie.

So this must be the Tunnels I've heard the men at Donnelly's Hardware talk about as secretive and frightening, he thought from within what might or might not have been a dream.

Once inside the tunnel, the roaring subsided and Mom

said, "Jonothan, we're safe. Now you stay beside me in case the lights go out."

Then the lights went out and it was darker than a moonless night. At that very moment, Mom was digging in the paper grocery sack for a snack for me. I immediately reached for her hand, and panicked when the hem of her shirt slipped out of my fingers. I kept trying to call her name but I couldn't make a sound.

I remember hearing a story about how people who spoke a different sounding language were led to freedom on a trail known only to a select few. There was a tunnel with a rope the thickness of my wrist fastened onto the wall and once inside they followed it.

I could hear mom calling me. Sometimes she seemed closer and sometimes further away—sometimes on my right, sometimes on my left. I'd always been cautious about the reality of angels until that night when a soft voice said, "Don't cry little one. You just follow me." My legs felt like rubber and my feet felt like they weighed as much as the bowling balls at the alley on the edge of town.

Then when the lights came on mom was still standing where we had stopped. I fell at her feet but still remembered the soft encouraging voice, her warm breath on my neck.

My voice returned several days later and by that time the scratchy rope burn blisters on my hands were starting to heal as well. The knees of my trousers were torn and my knees were scraped and bleeding from the numerous times I had stumbled and fallen on the uneven rocky tunnel floor.

***

He woke with a start, cold and shaking, questioning how far he had walked. He'd heard voices in those tunnels, he now remembered, reminiscent of the rhythmic ebb and flow of the tide crashing water on the shore and then withdrawing. But he couldn't find a door that would lead him back to his mom. It was like standing outside a door that was ajar, behind which you could hear people talking but not see them.

Just as it had been with those thugs in Sadie's Diner the other day. He'd heard their voices but couldn't see their faces.

He shook his head, focusing on the real question for the moment: what did this childhood memory of the tornado have to do with what Brandi said about her and Marcie's surprising adventure? They had heard one of the men say, "Hey, Junior. It looks like the diner was a good choice after all."

He was ready to call her until he looked at the clock. *It's only three o'clock in the morning, so starting the shower would wake mom, but that doesn't mean I can't study the maps.*

He made a pot of coffee, grabbed a pecan roll and a rhubarb muffin, and started comparing notes from his dream with what had been revealed thus far.

Two hours later, his mom woke him. "Sorry, mom. I must have drifted off. Talking about the tunnel last night brought back that recurring nightmare. The lights went out and I was frightened because I couldn't find you."

Opal smiled. "You always woke in a chill and then couldn't fall asleep unless I held your hand."

"I don't like the dream much better now than I did then," he said, rubbing his palms against his eyes.

"And this morning in the hours before sun-up, the memory came back in full?"

"Yeah. I woke up around three and try as I might, I couldn't go back to sleep."

"I see you raided my pie safe," she teased. "I've got another pot of coffee brewing. What do all these notes have to do with your dream?" she asked as she brushed his hair back off his forehead. Her motions automatic even though there wasn't any hair to sweep away because he kept it shorter since Miss Bea had hired him as her associate.

"I'm working on that. But, Mom, haven't you lived here since you were a little girl? Was my dad a member of the Good Ole Boys Association?"

The cup Opal had just retrieved from the cupboard slipped out of her hand and crashed to the floor. Her face was pale when she turned and the two just stared at each other.

"Dad took me with him one night didn't he? I'm not making up that memory?"

She nodded but said nothing.

"Is that why Uncle Henry has tried his best to keep me away from Turtle Crossing? Is he afraid I will remember something?"

Brandi knew she was scheduled to meet the Shadow Angels this afternoon, but she hadn't slept much during the night. She had been startled out of a sound sleep around 3:00am and fought with her pillow for over two hours before deciding it was a waste of time. She wished she could remember what it was that had awakened her. She had had assignments before but they hadn't kept her up all night.

She finally rolled out of bed to complete a mountain of paperwork she'd been avoiding, which served the dual purpose of distracting her and eating up the hours leading up to her appointment.

She arrived at Jewel's Emporium around 2:00pm. The Angels had planned today's exercise for early afternoon on the theory that they might learn something during working hours that they had not learned in late-night snooping. Brandi parked her old pickup truck at the delivery entrance, unlocked the back door, and slipped into Jewel's back office.

Once inside, Jewel greeted her. "My two employees think I'm out of town for the weekend on a shopping trip. My car is parked in Opal's garage." All the while she was talking so softly that Brandi had to read her lips.

Jewel placed one finger on her lips and Brandi watched in amazement while Jewel used the knot in the paneling as a handle to slide and lift a latch which released a hidden panel. A pocket door here shouldn't have surprised her, but it did. Brandi wondered if all business had secret back entrances.

She joined Jewel on a landing. The stairs on her right went up to Jewel's apartment, and on her left the stairs went down to the basement level. However, when they reached the bottom of the stairs, she realized this was a segment of the basement she had not seen when she had been officially enlisted into the Shadow Angels.

Jonothan was already on the landing, dressed in black, wearing what looked like a camera lens on his forehead. He nodded in greeting and Brandi nodded back. They both understood that this was not the time for chit-chat.

"Remember to keep one thing in mind at *all* times," Jewel continued, addressing them both. "Do not make the mistake of trying to figure out directions by the usual North, South, East, or West. The tunnel turns and curves around and back. You're thinking has to change once you enter the tunnel. A compass is useless down there."

"Then you've been in the tunnel before?" Brandi asked.

"It's been years. But even then I depended on Hen— well, someone *else* to get me back. Whoever designed this code used the alphabet and numbers. They had to be simplified and complicated at the same time so as to identify the proper locations.

"However, that has been a few years ago, and there may be changes I would be unaware of. You and Jonothan are our emissaries, so to speak. You are there mainly to observe what these tunnels consist of. The maps you studied are just a skeleton of what it feels like to be in total darkness.

"Can we take photos?" Brandi asked.

"As long as you do it without flash," Jewel responded. "And with the amount of light down there, that means very long exposures, and you still might not come away with a usable picture."

"I understand."

"Sit down here and let's get you ready for your journey. Pull on these steel toed boots and buckle them snugly. Next, fasten this headband around your head like Jonothan's got his on, with the visionary light in the middle."

Brandi slid the headband down her forehead so that it sat just over her eyebrows. A heavy-duty insulated wire ran from the light fixture in the headband down to a thick leather belt in Jewel's hands. Brandi accepted the belt, which was even heavier than her deputy's belt and featured round fittings that reminded Brandi of the ammunition belts John Wayne wore in the movies.

"Now this is a very special belt. It has brackets that hold the batteries for your light, which are usually good for an average of twelve hours."

"Okay. We're ready to go, right?" Brandi asked, the excitement and anticipation had her as anxious as an athlete at the starting blocks.

"Not quite. We're anxious for you to try out a recent innovation of the Shadow Angels. It's a shepherd's hook type cane which has the capability of doubling as an emergency flashlight. The only difference being, that the light is projected out and towards the floor."

Brandi took the cane and activated the light before shutting it back off again.

"Now. I do believe you're ready," Jewel pronounced as she drew the door open just far enough for them to step out onto the landing. "Be back in one hour. I'll be waiting," she said as they checked out the landing with their special lights and carefully closed the door.

Noting that the landing had room enough for them to turn around, Brandi and Jonothan marked the door Jewel had just closed. She aligned her cane beside the door, felt for the groove closest to the bottom of the door, then mentally marked the distance from the door to the first step.

Using a soft black cloth, Jonothan gently brushed the panel lightly and read the letters CH*2E with an arrow below it pointing towards the door. *This is too easy*, he thought. Then remembered he was supposed to keep communication with Brandi open, and repeated his thoughts aloud.

She nodded and said, "Just so we're on the same page, what do you make of the code?"

"I would say it is a pretty good bet that 'CH' stands for 'Carpenter, Henry' and the '2E' could be second entrance or 'E' for 'Emporium.'"

"How did you determine the location of the panel? By the first groove from the top of your cane?"

"Yes. And the arrow points to the left," he replied.

"I noticed that too. Anything else?"

How could he admit that being in the tunnels was right on the edge of revealing some sort of memory that he'd kept shoving away for the last several years?

He shook his head no and then replied, "No."

They had progressed about twenty feet from the door when she pointed out a black wire running along the ceiling and said, "Why would anyone run a communications cable down here?"

"I have no idea, but our orders are to find three doors,

go no further, and return." He leaned forward, put his arm around her and whispered, "Brandi, we're being followed."

She pulled away from him and said, "I know. I wish I had Pepper with me."

"I wish you trusted me as much as you trust Pepper," he muttered.

She was surprised by his tone of voice and let the comment pass. But she wondered if encouraging him to enter the tunnels had really been a good idea. He seemed edgy down here.

"I suggest we stop for a moment, turn out our headgear, and try using the low beam of the cane lights. The floor and ceiling are closer together just ahead, even though the space widens to allow enough room to drive three semi-trucks through side by side."

They had memorized the maps and expected the curve ahead and crossed to the opposite side of the tunnel taking the time to mark the wall beforehand.

"According to the diagram, door number three should be just beyond the curve; but something has been changed. I don't see a third door."

"And it's good we moved when we did. There appears to be some activity ahead and behind us. It wouldn't be good for us to get caught in the middle," Jonothan observed.

"I've been looking forward to some time alone with you, but I hope this doesn't turn into a long stakeout," Brandi added.

Jonothan chuckled. "I'm in total agreement," he

whispered. "Do you suppose we could short out our night vision if we tried to kiss in this tight corner?"

"That's all we would need. We're supposed to be observing, not revealing—"

She broke off suddenly as two men and one woman appeared from another tunnel barely fifty feet across from where Brandi and Jonothan stood. Two more people joined them almost immediately from a different direction.

"Apparently *they* weren't following *us*," Brandi said, as she loosened her camera from inside her vest and took several photos.

"I know. Hopefully, they didn't see us," Jonothan replied. "Wait, isn't that…" Brandi felt a sudden change in Jonothan's breathing, followed by his urgent statement. "It's time to leave." When she didn't move as quickly as he thought she should, he added, "Move! Now!"

When they turned their backs on the group in the central area of the tunnels, they turned on their headlamps being careful not to look at each other which could have not only revealed their location, but blinded each other in the process.

They had no trouble carefully retracing their steps and were back at Jewel's entrance in nearly half the time it took them going out. Jonothan slid the latch open an instant before she got to it. Her hand was on top of his when Jewel opened the inner door, ushered them inside, and closed it before turning on any inside lights.

They moved away from the door, unfastened their grungy boots, and carefully removed their headgear and placed them in the suitcases in Jewel's mirrored closet.

Meanwhile Jewel threw the locks on their tunnel entrance and closet, pulled the pocket door into place and joined them in her state of the art conference room.

The Shadow Angels were waiting for them, sitting facing the five by five foot screen. Jonothan and Brandi looked at each other.

"Did you send out backup?" Jonothan asked.

"No," Opal replied quickly, "but a team was ready just in case."

Jonothan and Brandi breathed a sigh of relief.

"Congratulations! Let's get down to business," Willi announced. "Everyone has pad and pencil. You may already have drawn some initial conclusions, but remember appearances can be deceiving."

"Door number three at the curve wasn't where these blueprints show it," Brandi stated.

"And the people you saw meeting down there?" Jewel prompted.

Brandi and Jonothan shared another quick look, and both understood the same thing at the same time: they both knew exactly who had been meeting down there, and they could not reveal that information to anyone. Not yet. If the Sheriff and Jonothan's half-brother, Jace, had matters to discuss in a hidden tunnel under Turtle Crossing, it would be more than her job was worth to blow the Sheriff's cover.

"As a Deputy Sheriff of Turtle Crossing, I cannot reveal who I saw without discussing it with the Sheriff first. I will share it with you if given permission."

The Angels stared back at her, more than one wearing an expression of consternation.

"However," she added quickly, "I can tell you that walking in the tunnels is like trying to stand up on a muddy slippery slope." Pointing to the map, she continued, "If we were to go to this curve and then straight, there is an opening to the outdoors big enough to drive three semi-trucks side by side inside the tunnels. So this is probably why no one appeared to notice our cane-lights turned on low beam. I also noticed tracks in the floor and ceiling, as if for sliding doors like you might see on a barn, except massive."

Opal knew exactly where those doors were. This was the same entrance she and Jonothan were led to wait out a threatening tornado. Even knowing this; she prayed he never, ever remembered seeing his dad that day as well.

"Our compliments to the Shadow Angels' cane light," Brandi continued. "It isn't nearly as bright as the headlamps but at least you can see where the undulations are in the floor of the tunnels. Although, where this group was standing, the floor looked smoother and possibly has had more traffic than the section outside the Emporium."

"I second everything Brandi has reported," Jonothan added. "And, I am certain someone followed us, almost from the time we left here, but for some reason I didn't feel we were at risk. I felt this someone was just observing. But what could be their reason?"

Brandi turned to Jonothan in surprise. She had felt it too. Little did they know they were both in for a surprise.

***

Had Ariel Ern Jamison, the new owner of the Welby Mansion Bed & Breakfast, known that anyone had been aware of her presence, she would have rushed back out of the tunnel immediately.

This was the first time in the three years since she had returned to Turtle Crossing that the Emporium Tunnel entrance had been used—which was about the same length of time since Jewel had kicked Henry out and filed for divorce.

Henry Carpenter was a master bricklayer who at some point had grown too lazy to work. But, just because he was in jail, didn't mean he would hesitate to pay someone else to continue to harass the good citizens of Turtle Crossing.

Ariel knew firsthand how Henry manipulated people's lives. She had pretended to be asleep a few times when her husband, Jamie and Henry had talked, which was how she found out who the Shadow Angels were—that they kept fit and sharp and were not afraid to cross Henry because they knew his weaknesses as well.

And now that Ariel had returned to Turtle Crossing, she occasionally fed information to Sadie, who passed it on to Jewel or Opal. From what Ariel had heard, Deputy Davies and Miss Bea were both walking a very fine line.

Sadie was anxiously awaiting Ariel's usual morning arrival and had unlocked the door off the Diner's pantry which led further on through the intricate twists and turns in the unused part of the wine cellar, and into the tunnels.

Ariel removed her hooded cape and Sadie remarked,

"You look fantastic. I think I'll try being blond for a while."

"Trust me, it feels great to have that wig off momentarily," Ariel replied.

"How are you doing with the Boarding House?"

"I had visitors again today. Nice couple looking for somewhere peaceful and quiet to retire."

She took a bite of one of Sadie's warm-from-the-oven cinnamon rolls and added, "I just thank you, and Bea, and God for this opportunity to start a new life."

Sadie poured two cups of coffee for her usual eight-minute break and joined Ariel. "It's right that you're at the Welby. No one has any idea who you are. But do you really feel safe?"

"So far, but if Henry ever gets out of prison, sooner or later he will figure out who I am.

As both women knew, Ariel still carried the scars from the night her husband, Jamie and one of Henry's hired goons nearly beat her to death. She'd tried to run several times before that, but Jamie had always found her. That last time, she'd woken up days later in the hospital only to learn that Jamie had been killed at a train crossing.

Gruesome though it was, she had been free after that. However, her sister had disappeared the same day. One of the nurses had told Ariel a lovely young woman fitting her sister's description, had admitted her to the hospital as "Ariel," which was not her true name at all, but her sister's. But with her jaw wired shut, she had not been able to correct the nurses or ask after her sister. In the end she understood she would have to change her identity to survive whether her husband was gone or not, because her husband's old cohorts might still come looking for her someday.

It was this fear that motivated Ariel to travel almost exclusively by the tunnels under Turtle Crossing.

"Well, I'm so glad you survived all that pain and fear and returned home safely," Sadie replied. "You have been a tremendous help feeding us information but now we're both going to have to be more careful."

Ariel nodded her head and added, "Well, anytime I can help someone else get out of a situation like I was forced into; I will gladly step forward. Thanks to the Shadow Angels' help, that young woman and her kids are in a safe place now.

"And, if I have to sell the Boarding House, one of the real estate developers said he would put me in a managerial position if I sign with them. But, you know, they are really getting pushy, almost like they have a deadline themselves. Thus, my deadline isn't far off. Sadie, I may need some advice."

"Go see Miss Bea," Sadie suggested. Sadie had been one of Bea's father's secretaries when Ariel worked part time in his office as well, and was certain there was tunnel access somewhere. At the expression on Ariel's face, she quickly added, "Or not. Perhaps that was just me looking for easy possibilities."

"I knew exactly where the entrance was," Ariel recalled, "however I have no way of knowing if Miss Bea or Jonothan or any of the Shadow Angels are aware of the hidden entrance or what had been happening right under their noses off and on for years. Let sleeping dogs lie? Why not? So far it has been working."

"But are you happy?" Sadie asked.

Ariel shrugged. "Ever since returning to Turtle Crossing I've kept to myself. Existing and bored is better than worrying about staying alive. I have an old car I seldom drive except to church but never in Turtle Crossing. Instead I drive a few miles away to a little town called Sunrise. And when I need to get around in town, the Welby keeps me connected."

The Welby Mansion Bed & Breakfast was southern in style. Ariel's regulars liked the ambiance of Ariel dressed in Victorian to Pioneer period clothes. It was easy to make the transition from long skirts which covered her black trousers for the tunnels and then slip into a wrap-around jumper or skirt to keep on schedule at The Welby. Of course, she always wore long sleeves to cover up the scars on her arms, which saved her having to answer questions.

She also wore a small gun tucked into a harness that she had made out of an old billfold and the belt that still had Henry's initials on it. She carried a small knife strapped to one ankle as well. Singing the song, *God Will Take Care of You* just isn't enough. Her memories, painful though they were, keep her alert.

No one will ever beat me again, she thought. *I lost my daughter and almost lost my life because I trusted the wrong man and the pain of losing my little girl is an ache that even prayer hasn't healed.*

Ariel's dream was to someday ride her sister's stallion, Night Whistle, into the tunnels, just for fun. But she didn't see that ever happening. Even if she ever got up the courage to try it, the poor animal would probably break its leg in the dark.

Ariel and Sadie had just finished their morning coffee when their visit was cut short by the unexpected call from the back of the Diner. "Sadie? This is Deputy Davies."

Ariel's heart pounded as she slipped through the pantry entrance, praying they had not seen her, and waited exactly two minutes before stepping down into the wine cellar entrance to the tunnels.

Jonothan, Brandi and Pepper had arrived at Sadie's just before dawn. They had been on watch since midnight. They had watched the lights in Sadie's upstairs apartment come on and off followed by a dim shaft of light that streamed from the all-white kitchen into the back hall of the diner. One hour and eighteen minutes later, a milk truck pulled into the alley. Jonothan and Brandi waited in the doorway of another business and watched. Sadie's schedule was already on record. They were looking for out-of-the-norm activity.

When the milk man drove on through the alley to his next stop they noticed that he hadn't secured the back door of Sadie's, so they slipped inside and left the door as they found it—unlocked—and left Pepper at the door on duty.

They were close enough to the kitchen to hear the soft laughter of two women. The laughter was followed by the sounds of oven doors being opened, large baking sheets being removed and placed out to cool and others replacing them, followed by the sound of the oven timer she had reset.

Brandi and Jonothan knew Sadie had mirrors placed in strategic positions so she could spot anyone entering her kitchen. They didn't want to frighten her but knew it was time to alert her that something might be amiss.

Brandi backed up a few steps between the kitchen and the back door and called out, "Sadie? This is Deputy Davies." The moment Sadie turned towards the door Jonothan watched someone move like lightning and disappear into the pantry. He stayed out of sight and waited patiently while Brandi switched into her deputy personae.

"Sadie, remember when I told you not to be alarmed because we would be keeping a watch on your diner?"

"Yes," she hesitantly replied.

"We stopped in because your back door was left ajar. Other mornings your delivery man has closed it, but if you're expecting another delivery, we'll be on our way."

"No, the milkman must have made a mistake! Please lock it for me."

Brandi noted the two cups of coffee at Sadie's corner table near the telephone where she took takeout orders, but said nothing. "Sadie, you would tell us if you were being threatened, wouldn't you?"

Sadie was still trembling from Ariel's close call and merely nodded in agreement.

They left the diner and climbed back into the old truck. "Brandi, did you see a blur slip into Sadie's pantry?"

"Why, Jonothan, you are really getting good at this. Just let me know anytime you would like to join the force. You've known Sadie all your life. I don't think she's afraid for herself, but—"

"But she's protecting someone else?" Jonothan suggested.

"Exactly! Do you think we should stick around for a bit? If we didn't see anyone enter or leave Sadie's, how else did they get there?"

They looked at one another and then said, at the same moment as if they had rehearsed it, "The tunnels."

Secrets Revealed
Winthrop

Mason and Autumn had been at the Carriage House for four months. She was still afraid to go out alone just in case someone recognized her as a runaway or possibly figured out where she and Mason had moved to and were just biding their time. Mason walked her to and from the office; otherwise she stayed indoors until time for their evening walks on the golf course.

Walking had resulted in a double blessing because she felt stronger and more resilient than when she had played high school volleyball and basketball.

Her baby was due in six weeks. All day she had felt crampy and achy and just plain under the weather. When Mason asked her if she wanted to join him for their usual walk, she declined.

"If your discomfort hasn't subsided by the time I

return, I'm taking you to Sunrise for a checkup."

"If I'm not feeling better by the time you return from your usual walk, I will call Dr. Ashley," she replied.

Mason had just left when Autumn heard a knock on the back door. Thinking that Mason had forgotten something, she was a blink away from opening the door before checking her appearance in the oval mirror between the kitchen window and the back door.

She peeked out and saw it was Shannon. She tucked the freshly pressed men's dress shirt into her navy dress trousers and buttoned one button of the over-sized matching vest, readjusted her wig and opened the door with a smile on her face. She was looking forward to the day when she could talk to Shannon one on one as a woman. But that couldn't happen for a few weeks yet without her Gramps persona in place.

"Good evening," Autumn greeted in her best froggy voice. "Please come in. Would you like a glass of ice-cold lemonade? Would you like ice with a bit of lime frost or plain?"

"Just plain, no ice," Shannon replied brusquely.

Autumn had noticed the briefcase on Shannon's arm and, thinking Shannon might enjoy a relaxing moment, suggested, "Please join me in the garden room."

When they were seated, Autumn was curious as to the reason for the visit, and it was apparent by the fiery light in Shannon's eyes that she had something to say.

"Thanks," Shannon said as she relaxed and nibbled on the half-dollar size buttermilk sugar cookies that Autumn had set on the table.

Autumn sipped her lemonade and waited for Shannon to get around to stating the reason for her visit, and hoping Shannon didn't notice that she was still feeling some discomfort.

"Gramps," Shannon began, "Brandi said she is worried about Mason. We don't know who you are, but we know you're not his Grandpa." Autumn's glass slipped through her fingers and hit the glass topped table harder than anticipated. "Please don't be alarmed. No one is asking any questions you don't feel free to talk about. It's just that Mason is Children's Home Family and you have to understand—we may have faced a few mishaps in the past, but we still stick together."

"Wait a moment. You grew up in the same Children's Home as Mason? I thought, I mean, you are a Warren, aren't you?" Autumn asked. "And, your family has money—a legacy—and you have a dad who loves you."

"It's a long story but I promise to tell you all about it some day. My girls are waiting, and I've had a very busy day. But I didn't feel right not being up front with you. Goodnight," Shannon said as she finished her lemonade. Before she left the room, she turned and added, "If you ever need someone to talk to or help of any kind, we'll do whatever we can to help. But remember, our family's safety comes first."

Autumn was stunned that Shannon included Mason in their Children's Home Family. And from the look in her eyes, Autumn had better not be considering putting Mason in harm's way. Even after a quick shower and escaping into her very feminine and roomy nightgown and the Grampsy blue plaid cotton robe that practically dragged the floor, she still felt uneasy.

For the first time since she had known Mason, she went to bed before he returned from his routine security jaunt of the nine holes closest to the Carriage House. It wouldn't take him long this evening because he told her he would take a cart instead of walking. She was still too upset to talk, thus left him a note and was asleep when he returned.

She was up two or three times during the night but just couldn't get comfortable. The following morning, she was up sitting in the garden room, just as the sun peeked over the horizon, when Mason joined her.

The moment she looked up and saw Mason standing in the doorway, she flew into his arms and began to cry.

"Honey, what's the matter? Are you in pain?" he asked as he held her gently.

"I was uncomfortable all day yesterday. Dr. Ashley said I could have false labor pains, so that's apparently what was happening because I'm not in pain now, but… but…" she said as she struggled through her tears.

Her fear of losing her baby to her foster parents had become more and more frightening as her delivery date came closer and closer. And since Shannon's visit, she felt even more overwhelmed with what she was doing to Mason's life as well.

"What did Shannon say that upset you?"

"How did you know she was here?" Autumn asked.

"I was in the cart shed and the cart mechanic mentioned it. What did she want?"

"Your sister and Shannon know I'm not your Grandpa or even a distant relative. What did you tell Richard?"

"I told him you were like family," Mason replied.

"You told Richard I'm *like* family? Just what does that mean?" she asked softly. She didn't know whether to be encouraged by his statement or dismayed by it.

"It means that I would like us to be a family."

"Is this your way of asking me to marry you?" she exclaimed so loudly that a pair of doves that had made a nest right outside the garden room, scattered in a rush.

"Are you saying you would consider it?"

"Consider it!" she exclaimed. "I've always wanted a family. I've just been afraid to…to…"

"To trust your heart to anyone again?" he suggested.

She couldn't believe he had just said what she had been thinking. "But you're a positive thinking man," she began, "It doesn't appear you have the tiniest fragment or doubt when it comes to trusting God. I would have thought fear would be absent from your vocabulary, as well as your heart."

"Everyone has doubts and fears," he continued softly, now rubbing her back as he continued to hold her. What should have been relaxing was doing crazy things to her insides and she tried to look away but couldn't. The look in his eyes, his gentle touch was making her heart race.

"Is this your way of saying yes, maybe or no?"

She nodded and replied, "I guess."

He reached in his pocket to retrieve a midnight blue jewelry box that had been in his pocket for so long the velvet covering had been worn smooth. He knelt down on one knee and held the open box in front of her and asked, "Autumn, will you marry me?"

He waited in silence, a hopeful and somehow choked expression on his face.

"Yes, I'll marry you," she said softly, struggling because his hands were shaking so hard he almost put the ring on her right hand instead of her left.

She smiled through her tears and said, "But this is all wrong."

He sobered and started to pull away when she added, "I just mean I had this dream of a fancy garden, moonlight, music, dancing, you looking drop-dead gorgeous in a tux and me in a violet blue slinky, shimmering silk dress and heels. But instead, you're dressed spiffy to work in the office today and I'm in a man's robe, my hair needs a salon style and cut and…"

"Now you stop right there. I've fallen in love with you and the child you're carrying, just as you are."

A fluttering sound reached their ears from the bushes outside. Mason shot out of his chair and peered through the garden window. "Probably just that pair of Doves picking at the raspberries again," he said in answer to Autumn's questioning look. He rubbed his stubbly cheek and examined her from head to toe. "I can see that the baby has dropped. Are you still as uncomfortable as you were earlier?"

"No, but I was praying the baby would wait another few weeks."

"A few weeks," he repeated. "Are you talking about

your birthday? What does when you turn eighteen have to do with when our baby is born?"

She didn't miss how he said, 'our baby' but continued, "Because then in the eyes of the law, I'll be an adult. At age eighteen, I will have a better chance of keeping my baby."

Mason gave her one of those warm, slightly goofy grins she loved so much. "But what if we're already married by then?"

Mason had been against telling anyone about Autumn and her baby until after they were married, but they didn't know anyone in the area whom they trusted except Dr. and Mrs. Ashley, Richard, and his sister, Brandi.

Maybe it was time to put their trust in a few more souls. And Shannon had said their family had weathered many storms. Plus, Autumn couldn't help trusting Shannon after she had spoken so plainly about Mason being part of her Children's Home family.

David and Shannon opened the door together as if they had been expecting visitors. Indeed, Shannon looked as though she were worried Mason might be upset for possibly confronting "Gramps" the night before.

Before either of them could speak, Mason said, "May we come in? I hope you don't mind, but I called Brandi too. She said she would meet us here."

"Of course." Shannon ushered them inside and led them to the sitting room. "Do you want something to drink?"

"Not right now, thanks. I pray the two of you will

understand why I have not been very sociable," Autumn began.

"Before we begin," Shannon interjected, "our daughters were out picking berries for breakfast and overheard a lady crying." She turned to Mason. "They also said they heard a marriage proposal."

"So. It was the twins who were outside the garden room? Thank You, God. I was afraid they had found me," Autumn responded with a grateful sigh.

Just then, Brandi burst through the front door, yelling, "Mason! Mason! Are you okay?"

"Hey, Sis. I'm fine. I'm sorry maybe my request may have been a bit abrupt," Mason said, as she raced into the sitting room and grabbed his hand. "But now that everyone is here, we have a story to tell you," Mason said.

"First of all," Autumn began. "Thanks to Mrs. Ashley and Mason, with the help of makeup, a wig, and men's clothes, we created Gramps Davies."

Mason tucked some scatter pillows around her back as she settled as comfortably as she could. Then Autumn took a deep breath and gripped Mason's hand momentarily remembering what they had discussed.

"The disguise was not meant to hide me from any of you, but the grandfather of my baby. We think he hired someone to find me. He was angry because I left the home for unwed mothers where they left me. I was their foster daughter and as such had no rights."

"What about the father?" David asked.

"The father attempted to pay her off in exchange for her silence and then left her for dead in a wrecked car in a freak snow squall," Mason replied, his other hand squeezing one of the pillows as if throttling it. Until that moment, Autumn had not realized how angry he had been.

"But what makes you think the foster grandfather has had you followed?" Shannon asked.

"I read my file at the home," Autumn explained. "My foster parents were paying for my stay, plus my medical bills and there was a bonus in it for me after I signed my baby over to them. I'm still a minor and they are my legal guardians until I turn eighteen."

"I see," Shannon replied. She stood and began pacing from one end of the sitting room to the other.

"But if Autumn and I get married," Mason suggested, "Wouldn't I have a say as to whether our baby has to be given up?"

"We'll call Judge Oglethorpe and ask him," David suggested.

"Could he marry us?" Mason asked softly.

"He's retired, but he is also a Justice of the Peace," Shannon mused. "So he should be able to."

"I hope I haven't done something wrong by inviting you, Brandi. I don't want you to have to do something illegal," Mason added.

"Didn't I tell you, all you had to do was call?" Brandi said.

"Yes, but we want to be married sometime today if that is possible," Mason replied.

"It's about time you decided to trust *someone*," Richard said from the kitchen doorway behind them.

"Richard!" Mason nearly yelled in surprise, leaping

to attention in an unconscious remembrance of his military training, "I'm sorry, sir. I should have been more upfront with you. We'll never be able to repay you for your hospitality."

"No apology necessary. I understand why the two of you felt you had to be so careful. So that was what you meant when you said that you would leave immediately rather than bring any harm to me or my family. I think it's a good idea for the two of you to get married," Richard continued.

"Before our baby decides to make its appearance," Autumn added, as she looked at Mason.

The look the two of them shared was so filled with love that no one in the room doubted their love for each other.

When the doorbell rang, the twins raced to the door. "Aunt Marcie, you arrived just in time for a wedding!" they shouted happily.

"A wedding? Who is getting married?"

Lauri Rose said, "It's a secret."

"And it's a surprise," Lily Anneé added.

Marcie looked around the room and her eyes fell on Brandi. "It's about time!" she said. "Who else have you told? You and Jonothan are going to pull off a real coup here."

"Not me!" Brandi protested. "It's my brother."

"I see," Marcie said, obviously caught off guard. But she recovered herself quickly. "A secret, surprise wedding. Well, unconventional weddings are our specialty!"

***

Thus, when Shannon's brother, Sheldon, arrived, he was asked to help with the camera setup.

Richard's wife, Grandma Eileen had furnished a few things as well and was presently enjoying Marcie and Sheldon's baby daughter, Amber Beth-Eden.

When Marcie was introduced to Brandi's brother, Mason, she couldn't help but be amazed. "I remember you as a scrawny kid. You've not only grown into a very handsome man, but from what I've heard you're a hero as well."

"Thanks. I remember you and your brother, David, but only recently did I find out why Shannon looked so familiar. Her name used to be Sheri. Right?"

"That's right," Brandi replied.

"Hey, Sis," he said more quietly when Marcie moved off, "What was that she said about you and someone named Jonothan? Am I to understand you may be getting married soon as well?"

"Yes," Brandi said curtly. "We're still working on setting a date."

"You two can visit after the wedding," David interrupted, and to the others he announced, "The Judge was in town visiting his granddaughter, Wendy. He said he will be here in about an hour."

"We'll make good use of that time," Shannon said as she turned to Autumn. "Now that I know you're not marrying just because of the baby, we're going to get you ready for a wedding. I can't see the judge marrying you dressed in this getup."

Shannon and Brandi led Autumn to Shannon's art

studio and the walk-in closet overflow from Shannon's bedroom closet. Autumn looked on in astonishment. "You mean I get to dress like a woman for a change?"

"Indeed you do. Sit here and enjoy. We are going to have fun with the transformation," Shannon gushed. "We do love weddings."

From the moment Autumn removed the Gramps wig and loosened her hair, Shannon and Brandi knew there wasn't much they were going to have to do, but have fun styling her hair in an upsweep.

Thirty minutes later, they all looked into the mirrored walls in Shannon's studio where the Shadow Angels practiced their moves, and it was all the three of them could do to contain their tears.

"My brother is one lucky man," Brandi said softly. "I know now isn't the time, but the two of you must have quite a story. I can't wait to hear it."

Autumn smiled and said, "I feel so blessed, so overwhelmed. It's been a very long time since anyone has stood up and fought for me. Except Mason, of course."

"Then there was someone you thought cared?" Shannon asked softly.

Autumn nodded and looked up at the sound of impatient tapping.

"It's the twins," Brandi said.

"Auntie Brandi," they squealed. "We're the flower girls."

"Roses," Autumn said softly.

"Grandma helped us pick them from the rose garden," Lily Anneé added.

"They are lovely," Autumn replied. "Do I hear music?"

"Apparently the men have been busy too," Brandi said proudly. "Should I check on everything downstairs?"

"The Judge is here—" Lauri Rose began before catching sight of Autumn. "Wow, pretty." Then she looked at Autumn's belly and asked, "Can we feel the baby when it moves?"

"Lauri!" Shannon exclaimed.

"Oh, it's okay," Autumn soothed. "Come here, girls." She took each of them by the hand and placed two miniature hands gently on her tummy.

Their response was one of awe as their eyes glistened with excitement. "I think your little girl will be very strong," Lauri Rose pronounced.

"And she will have a gentle heart," Lily Anneé added.

At first Autumn didn't know what to say, but looking into their eyes she knew they had some sort of insight that was rare.

She kissed each on the cheek, smiled and said, "Thank you for blessing my baby girl."

The twins were sent to help Grandma Eileen with Marcie and Sheldon's baby girl while the bride's attendants got to work fitting Autumn into the dress. The crème silk shantung and filigree Italian lace was perfect with her coloring and hair.

"Eileen was right," Shannon said. "We won't have to do many alterations at all. Dad bought her this wedding dress in New York a few years ago."

"This fit Eileen?" Autumn asked.

"She's lost about forty pounds since then," Shannon added.

"We're going to have to do something with the shoulders and droopy neckline," Marcie suggested, as she and Brandi searched through Eileen's sewing baskets.

"How about these shoulder pads?" Brandi asked as she tucked them in the dress and all of them looked in the mirror to see the results.

Removing the bracelet pin cushion, Marcie suggested, "A few tucks here with a swirl of lace. What do you think?" Once again they all looked at Autumn and then in the mirror.

"Can you finish her hair, Shannon?" Brandi asked. "While Marcie and I work on the gown."

In another forty-five minutes flat they had the bride transformed. "All right, let's run through the traditional fours: something old, something new, something borrowed, something blue and a penny for your shoe."

"I believe the old and borrowed are well taken care of," Autumn giggled.

Brandi looked at Shannon and said, "We need something new and blue."

Shannon knew exactly what Brandi meant and went back into her studio and brought out a jewelry box and handed it to Autumn.

When she opened it, she exclaimed, "It's gorgeous, but—" Autumn sputtered and then read the note inside aloud. "This Bluebird of Happiness is a gift meant to chase away all your blues."

"You can wear it as a pin or a necklace," Shannon added. The gift is from all your bridal attendants. "Shall we try putting it in your hair for today?"

Suddenly the door burst open. The twins skidded to a stop and stared. They looked around at everyone and Lily Anneé said, "Mommy, you're not dressed for the wedding."

"Come help me pick something out, girls. Just give us five minutes."

Marcie returned and handed Autumn the bouquet Eileen had arranged. The pastel roses were exquisite in crème, pink blush and buttercup yellow.

In the meantime, Mason had rushed through another quick shower, and with Richard's guidance, Sheldon and David had pressed his uniform and polished his regulation dress shoes. Richard was to be his best man and Brandi the matron of honor.

It was time. Richard's wife, Eileen, and accepted grandma of the twins, handed Amber over to her daddy and started playing the preliminary wedding march. The twins did their part scattering rose petals on the edges of the carpet runner so Autumn wouldn't slip and fall, followed by Marcie, Shannon and Brandi.

The room was filled with the aroma of bouquets of roses from Shannon's rose garden. When it was time for Autumn to walk from the steps of Shannon's studio to the fireplace, Richard joined her and held out his arm.

"Thank you," she said softly.

But when she saw Mason in his Coast Guard Military White uniform, she felt faint and would have stumbled if Richard had not placed his gloved hand over hers. She looked at Mason and smiled through her tears. Mason looked so devastatingly handsome she wondered why she had fought her attraction to him.

After Richard had guided her across the room to Mason, she was in for another surprise. The judge announced, "The groom will now sing to the bride."

Facing each other and holding hands, he swallowed hard and began singing, "I'll Be Loving You Always." His baritone rendition and the look in his eyes as he sang directly to Autumn touched the heart of all in attendance.

From the moment Autumn walked into the rose filled room, Mason saw no one but Autumn and she saw no one but him. The magic of love was so powerful that even Judge Oglethorpe was moved.

Brandi Returns
Turtle Crossing

Brandi drove into Turtle Crossing so full of love and happiness that she could barely wait to share the good news about her brother Mason's wedding, which was the most moving, brief, put-together-at-the-last-minute wedding she had ever attended.

But while driving home from Winthrop, she decided not to tell Jonothan about seeing her brother. Seeing him wasn't the half of it. She was so proud of him she wanted to shout it to the rafters. All these years, the picture she had carried in her mind was of a sad scrawny fourteen-year-old kid. Now he was a 6'3" married young man with his wife's child on the way.

I really messed up by not following up on leads Will sent me. I should have known better than to believe his first letters telling me he finally had a family and was happy. Why didn't

I get the message that he knew the administration read all correspondence? If he was unhappy, would he have had to return to the children's home?

She felt selfish and heartsick for not having been there for him when he didn't have any family to count on. It was time she was there for him even if it meant her job as a Deputy Sheriff.

From the description that Autumn and Mason had given about someone asking questions about them, it was apparent that Will was the one who had been hired to locate Autumn. He had refused to take on helping Bea claiming a "conflict of interest."

That was probably for the best, Brandi admitted to herself. Bea's request to the Shadow Angels probably worked out better anyhow because instead of keeping a low profile while Will investigated, they had turned up the heat throughout the shopping mall, the local florists, and the Longacre Offices. Plus, Bea was seldom alone whether in or out of her office—Jonothan and Jace had become great body guards.

Yet even all of these measures had only sort of worked. The flowers were still coming, with deliveries now from out-of-town florists. All hallways and staircases were lined with hidden cameras, but they still had no usable image of the person or people delivering the flowers.

Brandi still felt she was missing something. *Is whoever has been after Bea just waiting for us or Bea to make a mistake?*

When Brandi finally arrived home, she phoned Marcie just to make certain she had made it home safely. "I had to stop three times for coffee, just to keep awake. See you tomorrow."

Brandi knew she couldn't continue working without sleep, and called the station for an unusual request—a day off.

"Brandi," the Sheriff replied, "You're overdue a weekend off."

She left a message for Jonothan with Opal when she couldn't reach him, shut off her phones, and fell asleep on top of her bed.

That evening, Jonothan let himself in to Brandi's apartment with pizza and root beer on ice. He was surprised to find her still sleeping. *Did she sleep all day?* he wondered. While he laid out plates and glasses for supper, she finally emerged from her bedroom.

"Hey, beautiful! Where were you last night? I tried to reach you all evening."

When she didn't answer right away, he said, "You still don't trust me? Well, that's okay, honey. I know you'll tell me when you're ready."

"It's not that," she said. "You know what, Jonothan Arden Carpenter?" She was still trying to clear the cobwebs out of her half-asleep mind.

"What sweetheart?" Jonothan asked. She looked so sweet and tousled, he was more than ready to help her wake up.

"Why haven't we set a date for our wedding?"

He stared at her in disbelief. "I've been waiting for you."

"Let me get a quick shower first and I'll tell you all about why you couldn't reach me yesterday."

But before she made it into the bathroom, the doorbell rang. Jonothan answered the door. "Marcie, this is a pleasant surprise."

"Brandi forgot to tell you I was stopping by?" Before he could answer, Marcie pushed through the door and heaved a bulging briefcase onto the table. She immediately began removing photos from the day before. "I thought you might want to look at the fun part before we get to the work part."

"Okay. Well," Brandi began, "Jonothan, you wanted to know where I was last night. This is where we were."

"And you couldn't reach me," Jonothan clarified, "Because Miss Bea and I were out all evening on appointments," he said, a bit of remorse in his voice.

"I didn't know what I was going to find when I arrived," she continued. "Mason just called me and said he needed me. And gently reminded me that I had said he was to call me, anytime he needed help. I was so upset I didn't call anyone. I just went. He apologized for scaring me out of a year's growth!"

"And Marcie, you were there because?"

"The twins called. Believe me they can pour on the charm. They especially invited me to come and take pictures of them. And when they call their Auntie Marcie for help, how could I refuse? They were very mysterious at first, and then said, they had finished their school project early and needed pictures taken by a professional, that afternoon."

"Jonothan, you can't tell anyone about these photos or the fact that I've finally found my brother, or we found each other," Brandi added.

Scanning through the photos, Jonothan remarked, "I understand. So why the rush? I can see that your brother has grown up; he favors you a bit, you know. But I have a feeling that there is more to this young woman's pregnancy than meets the eye?" he asked, pointing to the formal photo of Autumn and Mason.

"He's been protecting her."

"And who is this dude in the bib overalls?"

Brandi smiled as she bit into another piece of pizza.

"Tell me, Jonothan. Would you believe this gramps and this bride are one and the same?"

"No way! You're serious?"

"I'm serious."

"Just how much time did it take for this wedding to come about?" Jonothan asked.

"Preparation time was about an hour." Marcie replied.

"An hour!"

"The transformation took an hour," Brandi amended. "But you have to understand, there are complications and deadlines."

"Ladies, even I can see that there is at least one deadline," he pointed out when he held up the side view of Autumn.

"When aren't there?" Brandi replied. She held the photo and studied the look on the faces of the bride and groom, remembering the emotion-filled room when they had held eye contact long enough for everyone to feel the powerful connection between them. A heavy silence filled the room when the Judge had asked, "And do you, Autumn, take this man to be your wedded husband?"

The look of wonder in her eyes when she nodded yes and then the smile between them when she realized she had yet to say I do had been precious. And when the judge pronounced them married, their kiss was hesitant and unpracticed.

The memory filled Brandi with a restlessness she couldn't quite describe. After all, Mason's happiness was no longer unsettled. He and Autumn had made a decision. She and Jonothan should do the same.

"Look if the two of you want to talk or smooch for a while, I can leave," Marcie suggested.

"That's okay," Jonothan and Brandi replied together. However, the look he sent Brandi told her plainly that he was not leaving until they settled a few matters.

"The facts are," Marcie began, "The young lady is a lovely redhead. She and Brandi's brother were just married. The baby's real father is already married. The grandpop is the one who wants the baby which is why they have been on the run."

"Is Mason just being a nice guy or do you think he has really fallen for her?" Jonothan asked.

"There's no doubt in my mind they would have fallen in love regardless, had they had the chance to meet under other circumstances," Brandi replied.

"So, how do they know a private investigator has been hired?"

"That's why I stopped by," Marcie began. "From

Mason's description, we think it might be Will!"

Jonothan now knew why Marcie and Brandi were worried.

"You know Miss Bea tried to hire Will when someone started leaving flowers at her office almost daily and Will teased her about them being from an old beau," Marcie continued. "He graciously declined and said he was already working on an out-of-town case that involved a stolen baby. And with Will and Wendy's due any time, it's understandable why it would strike a nerve with him."

"And," Brandi added, "Autumn mentioned that while they were still at the lighthouse, the local Sheriff and some tall, dark, and handsome gentleman with eyes as dark as midnight had stopped by within days of the accident. She said Mason and a dog named Bo caused a distraction and kept her hidden."

"Surely she's had medical care since then," Jonothan began. "Sorry ladies, but I'm having trouble with the picture of Grandpa Overalls sitting in the doctor's office on baby day."

Marcie and Brandi both smiled and Brandi continued, "They were on their way to Winthrop, but due to a couple of wrong turns and a detour they ended up in Sunrise. They parked in the only available parking space on Main directly in front of a costume shop. The owner's hubby is the only doctor in town."

"I've been in there a few times when I needed a costume for a birthday party when I was doing catering," Marcie added. "So, do you suppose they have been helping Mason and Autumn with this cover-up?"

When Jonothan gave them a look of disbelief, Marcie quickly asked, "What type of help did your brother ask for, Brandi?"

"He is being cautious because he doesn't want to get me in trouble since Autumn is certain that the grandpa of her baby still has legal custody of her until she is eighteen."

"Did Judge Oglethorpe have any questions about her age?"

"No reason to. When the Judge got to the part about 'Who gives this woman,' Richard said, 'As her temporary guardians, my wife and I do.'"

"Are they going to stay in Winthrop?"

"That's the challenge," Brandi replied. "Mason said he didn't want to bring any trouble to the Warrens, so they may leave soon."

"Where will they go?"

"We didn't get that far. But, he said they won't go anywhere without letting me know," Brandi added.

"There is one way to find out who hired Will," Marcie suggested. "Just ask him."

Brandi shook her head. "He'll just say it's confidential. I thought you might be able to check with someone in the area of the lighthouse. Isn't there a question or two that you as a florist could ask another, or perhaps you could talk to the owner of Lady Ashley's Costume Shop? You said you know her and you know Will. He always leaves his business card."

"In the meantime," Jonothan began, "Miss Bea gave me a couple of days off and Brandi has the long weekend off as well. I think it's time we had some together-time."

"Sure thing," Marcie said. "Let me know for certain when you set a date so I can save at least a week to acquire and prepare the flowers for your wedding. Do we have a deal?"

"Of course, but you know why I'm afraid to commit to an actual date," Brandi said so softly, Marcie had to read her lips. "I'm afraid something will go wrong. Or Jonothan will change his mind."

"Hey, when have any of our weddings *not* been a bit unconventional?"

Brandi smiled. "We'll be in touch."

"Don't miss the Angels' Monday night meeting," Marcie said. "They want to study more detail on the film you and Jonothan took and try to match it up with the collection of drawings and a couple of old photos. You look surprised. Didn't Jewel tell you that whatever you observed and discussed would be on film?"

"Nothing was said about any film, but if what you say is true, then I need to see it first. It's imperative! What if someone took film of our Shadow Angels when we were on a case? I'll call Jewel. Besides what we reported when we first returned from the Tunnels, we also put in writing. I'm working on the Sheriff to give me clearance on the photos that I requested."

After Marcie left, Brandi looked at Jonothan and asked, "How long can we be gone?"

"You know what?" Jonothan asked. "Even if there is a film record, I can't imagine it picked up anything useable."

"I agree. It was too dark. But, just in case the people we saw have to be protected."

"I know," Jonothan said slowly. "I know you can't agree or disagree, but apparently my half-brother has really turned over a new leaf."

"Jonothan."

"We'll stop by my place, leave our respective notes, and be on our way. Who is driving?"

"We'll take turns," she called over her shoulder as she headed to the bedroom to pack a little bit of everything. And because she was so upset about the film, for once wasn't worried whether she was forgetting something— she would just buy new.

"What do you say we stop at the Welby on our way out of town," Jonothan suggested. "We still have to decide on the date and place of our wedding."

"That's fine with me," Brandi replied.

Ten minutes later, Jonothan was waiting to pull out onto Turtle Crossing's Main Street and another car flashed past. "Oh, wow, now who would take a chance with other people's lives by driving at least seventy miles per hour in a commercial zone? I've got to call it in."

"Oh no you don't, sweetheart. I know you've already memorized the car's make, model, year, and color. You can call it in from the Welby. Deal?"

"Deal."

The moment they drove up to the picturesque, southern plantation style mansion turned bed and breakfast, they fell in love with the setting and were surprised that Turtle Crossing had such a lovely historic home. It was built well off the main road, high and dry beyond Turtle Lake. The mansion's long front porch was dotted with white wicker rocking chairs and planters overflowing with asparagus ferns.

"You've never been here either?" Brandi asked in disbelief, as she read the sign, *The Welby Mansion Bed & Breakfast.*

"No. When I was a kid, we used to swim in the lake but we never went to this end because we were warned it wasn't safe. It's very deep and there was a crazy story about someone drowning there. I think it was something our parents made up."

He followed the signs around to the parking lot in the back. Fifty yards uphill from the bed and breakfast, a wide waterfall ran in white sheets, shooting rainbow spray into the air. Brandi was amazed.

"You used to swim here? Why didn't you tell me there was a beautiful waterfall here?"

"Honestly, I didn't know about it. We only swam down in the shallow end of the lake, like I said. This was always private property."

Jonothan got out his binoculars and then handed them to Brandi and said, "Does it look to you like there's another access road up near Hillside Road?"

"We were called out to investigate when a young boy was hurt in an accident on that stoned road which had only been used as a logging access," Brandi explained, holding the binoculars to her eyes. "Otherwise, Hillside Road doesn't really go anywhere but winds up to the top and back down. However, the Welby's private drive forks sharply to the right into a wooded area and unless you know where to look for the gated drive, you could easily miss it."

She lowered the binoculars and found Jonothan smiling at her. "I do believe you are as anxious as I am to check out the Welby. We could stay here for the night or the entire weekend."

"I like your way of thinking. No one will know where we're staying and we can still be close by if my new niece or nephew decides to make an early appearance. Why don't we park in one of these carports just in case someone we know just happens to stop in?" Brandi suggested.

Jonothan parked the car and they walked hand-in-hand back along the shaded channel walkway. Peonies were in full bloom. Another couple was seated under a willow that cast soft shadows across the entire front yard and narrow drive leading to a partially hidden marina that was filled with tethered fishing boats and pontoons. An archway overgrown with honeysuckle led to a picnic area that had recently been mowed plus ample parking for over a dozen boat trailers.

"I'm starting to wonder if they'll have any rooms available," Brandi said as they sped up to check in before someone else beat them to it.

"I'm sorry," said a young woman in white gloves when they inquired at the desk about a room, "but the bridal suite is booked through the month. However, the Evening in Paris Suite is available. How long will you be staying?"

"Just the weekend," Jonothan replied.

The woman nodded and made a note in her ledger. "Lunch Buffet is open from noon to 1:30 p.m. Breakfast

Buffet from 7:00 to 9:00 a.m. Snacks, salads, sandwiches and desserts are available in the glass fronted refrigerator on my right. Guests are on their honor to put money in the teapot for their purchases. This evening's meal will be chicken and dumplings, mashed potatoes and gravy, and choice of two vegetables, fresh peach cobbler for dessert. Will you be docking a boat in the marina?"

"Not at this time."

"Do you need help with your luggage?"

"No. We'll take care of it. Thanks." Jonothan replied.

"What is the dress code?" Brandi asked.

The woman smiled. "Dress code is casual. Enjoy your stay."

"Jonothan," Brandi exclaimed as they walked away from the desk. "Now I know why this is one of the best kept secrets in Turtle Crossing. Did you see the price? I can't afford to blow a month's wages for a few nights stay."

"Honey, you weren't supposed to see that."

"Then you knew?"

"Only because Miss Bea stays here once in a while, and I accidentally saw her receipt," Jonothan admitted.

They walked in the back door and took the elevator up two floors. The private quarters of the Bridal Suite was on one side of the hall and the Evening in Paris on the other. When they entered, they were bowled over by the opulent furnishings but more so by the view. Coming in the back, they had not been paying too much attention that the drive went uphill. The suite was three floors up and overlooked the lake.

Their third floor private veranda wrapped around the

back of the building and the front was separated from the Bridal Suite with an elaborate garden and climbing Rambling Red Roses. "Let's forego the big evening meal—pack up some snacks and drinks in our back packs and have a look around the grounds.'

"Good idea," Jonothan replied. "Mom left her bird-watching binoculars in the trunk, so we'll both have our own set; and you have your camera and usual gear. Do you have a spare pocket for one of these walkie-talkies?"

After they had loaded their packs, they excused themselves from the suite and headed back outside.

"Do you suppose that waterfall comes from a natural spring," Brandi asked as they walked across the lawn toward it.

"Could be. From the view of our veranda, the waterfall appears to disappear into the pool at the bottom," he responded, "then runs down this stream and empties into that football-field sized Marina which overflows into the channel which empties into Turtle Lake and overflows into Turtle River, just like on the map where we checked-in."

Brandi stopped suddenly. "Was that my imagination or did I just hear a horse whinny? Don't tell me they have stables here too."

"Let's walk on a little further. Perhaps we could introduce ourselves to the horses.

As they walked on around the Welby grounds, Brandi pulled out her binoculars. "My former mother-in-law had horses and taught me to ride. That's the only positive memory I have of those two years of my life."

"I bet we could get an idea of this place a lot better from the air. We normally avoid flying over here because of the higher elevation."

Brandi fiddled with something in her pockets. "There's a man up on that ridge with a rifle," she whispered.

Jonothan pretended to stretch and used the movement to shift his line of sight up toward the ridge. "It isn't hunting season for a few months yet," he replied.

"He's looking down here," she said. Her camera had materialized in her hand and she was snapping shots from the hip.

"Well, then, we should let him know we're not a threat. The best defense is a smart offense, so what do you say we start out with a few passionate kisses and head back."

"Ooh, Jonothan, I like the way you think. I hope one of these photos turns out."

"Don't even attempt to take anymore, okay?" he warned just before he kissed her. But she didn't take her eyes off the person on the ridge until he disappeared in a stand of trees. Jonothan pulled back. "I didn't have your full attention did I?"

"Not really, but I'm enjoying the practice." Brandi replied as they joined hands and headed back toward their suite.

When Ariel Ern, owner and manager of the Welby, returned early and saw who her new boarders were and the note her assistant had written, she wondered why they were really here. *I pray those two didn't see me that morning when I scooted out of Sadie's kitchen into her pantry. Hopefully they are just planning to book their wedding reception here.*

She called Miss Bea immediately. "Did your group, those Shadow Angels, send a cop and your newest employee out here to spy on me?" Ariel burst out.

"No, of course not. He has a well deserved weekend off and from what I've heard they are working on setting a wedding date."

"Bea, my regulars come here for the peace and quiet. The locals know who they are. It doesn't look good—those two not being married yet and all. I will lose my clientele and my chef."

"First of all, they are upstanding members of this community. But since you're questioning their reason for being there, why don't you ask them? Find out what their plans are?"

"You're certain they don't know who I am?"

"The only way they will find out who you are is if you tell them. You're my client, and as such—"

"Okay. I remember all about that client privacy stuff. You're probably right. They'll really get suspicious if I don't talk to them," Ariel concluded.

Newlyweds
Winthrop

The day after the ceremony, Autumn and Mason were treated to a fabulous wedding breakfast in the garden room at the Carriage House. The entire Warren Family was in attendance.

"Why don't you take the day off," Richard suggested.

"I appreciate the offer," Mason replied, "But you have an all-day shotgun-start corporate golf outing today. And we might need a few days off when the baby comes. Plus, Autumn and I talked about it last night and we thought it best if no one knows we're married until after the baby comes. I understand that the *Winthrop News* only prints marriage announcements once a month so hopefully by the time the next monthly report is released, the baby will be here. But just in case, I requested that it not be printed in the paper."

"And," Autumn shyly suggested, "We want to have a party and invite all your employees and their families."

Tugging on Autumn's sleeve, Lily Anneé asked, "After the party, then we can tell people about our new family?"

"Just family," Shannon suggested. "You know all about family stuff, right, girls?"

They both nodded. "Are you really Auntie Brandi's brother?" Lily Anneé asked.

When Mason nodded, Lauri Rose looked at him directly and asked, "Then that means you're our Uncle Mason, right?"

"That's right."

Satisfied, she smiled and curled up on the couch beside Autumn. Then placing her hand on her tummy asked, "Why do bad people want to steal your baby?"

As astute as these girls were, Mason nudged Autumn because he didn't know what to say short of being untruthful, and he just didn't have it in him to be dishonest. Autumn in turn looked to Shannon and David for their approval before answering.

Shannon and Autumn had discussed this earlier; however Autumn mistakenly had hoped she would have a little time to come up with something that would pacify the twins until her baby was born.

"I—We," she clarified, "Mason and I know this is asking a lot, but because you girls are so smart and see things other people miss, if you can help keep our secret for a few more weeks, we would be honored if you would help us name our baby."

Mason added, "You see we have several picked out,

but we need a middle name. We need a name that would go with Andrew if it is a boy and Angel if it is a girl. "Then when everything settles down and Autumn is feeling stronger, we would like to take you to the zoo in the fall. Of course, if you would like to do something else, within my budget of course, just say the word."

The twins disappeared for a few moments and quickly returned. "We've decided," they said in unison. "Storm."

"You rescued them from a storm, Uncle Mason," Lily Anneé explained.

"And Daddy said you came here in a storm," Lauri Rose concluded.

Mason laughed. "It's hard to argue with your logic. Thank you, girls, that's a beautiful name. And thank you, Shannon, for bringing breakfast."

Tears stung Autumn's eyes, as she battled with her feelings for this family who had unconditionally accepted her into their circle of love. In the past only one or maybe two people had ever given her anything without expecting something in return.

A soft breeze circled through the garden room after everyone left. The twins had wanted to stay but Shannon suggested they stay with Grandma Eileen today because Mommy and Daddy had to go to the office.

Autumn was feeling overwhelmed after such a lovely wedding day and wedding night. Okay, so the real wedding night would have to wait, but Mason had held her in his arms and kissed her and let her know that he would be a patient, impatient groom.

But she had no doubt that Mason loved her. How

could she when her mind kept going back to their wedding? If Richard hadn't been gripping her elbow when they commenced walking from the bottom of Shannon's studio stairs towards Mason, she was certain she wouldn't have been able to walk across the Warren's formal living room on her own.

She couldn't recall any other time when time literally seemed to stand still. Mason looked so handsome and proud in his Coast Guard dress uniform. The look in his eyes when he'd sung to her had stolen her breath away. Even now, she thought her hormones must have really been topsy-turvy. Staring into Mason's eyes when Richard had laid her hand in Mason's had almost been her undoing. She had felt faint even though she had never fainted in her entire life.

Now, a day afterward, she couldn't remember a word she had said. When the Judge had said "Repeat after me," she knew she had followed his directions. Other than that, she didn't recall what had been said because when Mason held her face gently in his hands, her mind had gone blank.

Then when he kissed her with several months of pent-up passion, she felt the coldness in her heart melt, leading her to believe that he really could love her. Maybe he wasn't just being a nice man who rescued ladies in distress, willing to help her through this traumatic situation in her life, but meant every word. She wanted the kiss to go on and on. However he had the common sense to pull away and then he kissed her gently on each cheek and whispered in her ear, "I love you."

She was certain if she lived to be a hundred, she would cherish this moment forever. Mason had changed his entire life just for her. It was time for her to do something for him. The answer came as she was straightening the living room.

When she reached across his chair to stack the local newspapers, she caught her toe on something solid and tumbled into his chair head first. In her rush to collect the papers, she had forgotten to watch where she was going. She hadn't been able to look straight down and see her feet for at least two months.

She grabbed the back of the chair to steady her balance and checked out the floor to see what she had tripped over. It was Mason's Bible.

That was it! Surely she could set aside her past feelings about church and attend with him. But then she questioned whether they would be less noticeable if they stopped in for a Sunday morning or evening service? Whatever he decided would be fine. Hopefully the congregation would assume they were just travelers passing through.

In the meantime, there was also the baby to think about. Autumn had spent weeks constructing different-sized baby gowns, diaper sets and receiving blankets and embroidered baby ducks, bears, and kittens here and there on the clothes and crib quilt. She crocheted a white, blue and pink sweater set as well. Today, after cutting out a hooded soft yellow terry cloth bath towel, she took time to relax with a tall glass of lemonade.

I could get used to married life, she thought.

Shannon stopped by one afternoon and helped Autumn pack her suitcase for the hospital. Shannon was astonished when she saw Autumn's talents revealed in the extra baby items she had made. "Your baby will never be able to wear all of these."

"I know," she replied.

"David's sister, Marcie sectioned off a corner boutique in an alcove of her florist show room. I have no doubt these would be bestsellers in Turtle Crossing."

"Turtle Crossing?" Autumn exclaimed jumping out of her chair.

"Yes," Shannon said, surprised at her reaction.

"I can't go there. It's far—far away anyhow!"

"Autumn, please sit down. You're white as that sweater you are holding in your hands. Has your labor started?"

"No! No, I just got caught up in the past, that's all."

"Well, no matter what you say, I'm calling Mason."

"That won't be necessary. He'll be here in about thirty minutes. We have a doctor's appointment in Sunrise later today."

Shannon left, but instead of leaving to go to her office she stopped by her dad's office. "Daddy, where's Mason?"

"He's in his office, Honey. Why are you so upset?"

"It's Autumn."

Mason had been in the hall when he saw Shannon rush into Richard's office without knocking, which wasn't like her. He tapped on the door she had left ajar which was followed by, "Come in."

Mason!" Shannon gasped.

"What's wrong?" Mason asked.

"Autumn said she has a doctor's appointment in Sunrise today."

"Yes. We're going to make an afternoon of it."

"Hasn't Dr. Ashley told her both Sunshine and Turtle Crossing have excellent hospitals?"

"No. That's on today's agenda," Mason replied.

"Be forewarned," Shannon continued, "She went pale when I mentioned Turtle Crossing. She doesn't seem to know how close it is to Winthrop. She's frightened of something or someone there."

Mason didn't want to upset her, but was glad that Shannon had told him about their strange conversation. He returned to the Carriage House for a snack and to check on Autumn. Putting on his cheerful face the minute he walked in the door he began, "Autumn, um, Mrs. Davies, would you do me the honor of accompanying me for dinner at the fanciest restaurant in Sunrise this evening?"

"Mrs. Davies? Do I know anyone by that name?"

"You better," he replied and chuckled as he hugged her and got kicked by the baby for his efforts. Her surprise and smile was what he had been hoping for. The baby reminded him he would do whatever he had to do to keep both of them happy and safe.

"I can't wait until I can wear a dress and high heels again," she grumbled. "But, I'm not complaining, honest," she added as she twirled her hair up in a bun and put on her wig. "It's a good thing my due date isn't far off, because I would have had to buy a larger pair of bib overhauls."

"What's the suitcase for?" Mason asked.

"I want Lady and Dr. Ashley's opinion on what I've packed for the hospital when I have our baby; you know, just in case I've forgotten something."

Mason parked behind the best steakhouse in Sunrise. As they were walking in the door, a young man was coming out and stared at Mason so long, that Mason began to feel uncomfortable and finally asked, "Do we know each other?"

He immediately replied. "No, I don't think so. Perhaps you just remind me of someone."

Mason held his breath until after the young man had walked away. He didn't think there were any wanted posters out for their arrest, but he felt much better knowing that he was the one the young man had been staring at, not Autumn.

"Isn't this restaurant rather fancy?" Autumn asked when she noted the linen table cloths and crystal glasses. When Mason didn't answer and proceeded to remain mostly silent through the course of the meal, she finally said, "Mason, you've been distracted ever since we arrived. Are you troubled about something? Are you concerned about the young man who looked at you like he knew you?"

"No. Well, maybe a little bit, but don't let it concern you, honey. What would you like for dessert?"

"You're changing the subject." Autumn teased.

"That I am. Ladies are not the only ones who can change their mind."

"True, kind sir, but the young man who rushed out

the door and stared at you reminds me of Brandi's beau in that photo the twins have hanging in their room."

"You mean Jonothan?"

"Yes. That's his name, but this man didn't have the gentleness in his eyes that Jonothan has. Wouldn't that be something if Jonothan has family in Sunrise?"

Brandi Falls
Turtle Crossing

Jonothan and Brandi finally met the owner of the Welby Mansion Bed & Breakfast of Turtle Crossing after their first night's stay. She had introduced herself as Ms. Ariel. No last name. Just "Ariel." She was dressed in an antebellum pre-Civil-War reproduction gown. It was apparent that her gown and wig were part of the setting, which included the furnishings and the wording of the menu.

Brandi knew that sometimes pretense could be a form of protection. The former Carpenter Aunts' Card Club—now The Shadow Angels—had used pretense, their own creativity and savvy to solve numerous issues, a half-step ahead of and sometimes in cooperation with the local police.

Brandi had not only seen the good the Shadow Angels were capable of, but had been a part of it. It was the liars who hurt the innocent that they could not condone. And this woman seemed uncommonly uncomfortable and nervous for a seasoned hostess. Either something illegal was going on here or the owner, Ariel, was scared of someone or something.

Scared enough to be concealing a knife in her hand-tooled leather riding boots. Brandi saw the hilt for the briefest instant when the woman lifted her skirts to give a practiced curtsy.

However, Brandi could not get herself too worked up about Ariel's eccentricities. Carrying a knife was not a crime, after all, and she and Jonothan had other matters to deal with during their stay. Plus they wanted some together time without crazy distractions.

But that time would have to wait. The evening of their second day, they sat together in a stand of trees, watching Hillside Road. Brandi carried her usual camera while Jonothan had binoculars with another built-in camera, Brandi jotting down the make, model and license number of any car that passed by for later reference.

They watched a nondescript 1953 Chevy pickup when it appeared up on Hillside Road in near sunset shadows, loaded with bales of alfalfa grass hay for the black stallion they had seen circling inside the paddock behind the barn. Either whoever had driven the truck was still in the barn, or the person who drove a green Jeep out of the attached shed was one and the same.

"The person driving that Jeep doesn't appear to be in a hurry," Jonothan commented.

"Maybe they don't want to kick up a big cloud of dust.

It hasn't rained for weeks and that stretch of road is basically hardpan."

He nodded. "Point taken. That might draw unwanted attention. Speaking of attention," Jonothan reiterated, when he saw who was coming towards them. It was two of the men he and Brandi had seen down in the tunnels. "We need to move. Now!" He picked her up and spun her around behind the trunk of a willow tree.

He didn't give her time to get her breath before he was kissing her. Brandi had her camera set to take a photo of the area where she expected the Jeep to appear. The thought that he had ruined her shot drifted to the back of her mind when he kissed her, but then she felt his tension and knew at least part of it was for show.

"Can you get a shot of them?" she murmured.

She felt one of his hands leave her back and lift his camera to snap a few photos of the two men walking toward them. Not only were they the same men from the tunnels, their build was similar to the men who had rushed out of Sadie's Diner on his first day as a snoop. He'd only seen their backs that day, but he'd bet all of the fancy technology in Jewel's basement that they were the same men.

"How long," the shorter, pudgier man began, "Does he want us to wait around? I'm getting tired of this one-horse-town. That little gal isn't going to show up here."

"You don't know that!" the taller one grumbled. "He's certain of the date that baby is due. All I want is my money!"

"Hush! We'll talk later."

Brandi was certain one of the men quit walking while the other one continued walking, so she initiated a kiss this time. She didn't see the man turn around, but was aware of being watched. Thus all he saw in that moment between sunset and the rising of a half moon was a couple in a heated embrace, the woman's camera dangling from her wrist.

As she started to pull away, Jonothan moved his hands gently up her back to her neck and whispered in her ear, "I got a half dozen shots. How many did you get?"

"Only one or two because you distracted me," she whispered back. "Who knows what I got with the camera set on automatic."

"Great. But we'd better stay here awhile just in case they come back."

Brandi smiled. "I guess we'd better."

They waited a full ten minutes before pulling apart and took their time walking back to the Welby Mansion so it was fully dark by the time they returned. Before going inside, they swept the mulch off their shoes in the wet grass.

"Do I look okay to go into the lobby?"

"Brandi," his voice husky with emotion, "you look beautiful."

"Blame it on the moon and the atmosphere," she added, trying to be melodramatic.

Above them, Ariel was standing silently on the verandah outside her personal quarters that doubled for her office after hours. She saw what they wanted her to see—a couple very much in love. But what they didn't know was that she knew who they were.

The lobby was carefully lit with tall and short lamps plus wall sconces discretely positioned. Jonothan stopped by the reception desk to pick up a brochure and said, "I see you have overnight film service."

The desk clerk said, "Yes. The Turtle Crossing Pharmacy offers this service for our guests. They pick up at 8:00 this evening and deliver by 9:00 in the morning."

Brandi looked out the hillside window and felt a foreboding chill. *Perhaps it's time the Sheriff's Department did a few spot checks on the surrounding area,* she thought.

Jonothan joined her and asked, "What do you think about getting our film developed overnight?"

The Sheriff's Department had its own film laboratory, of course, but she wasn't technically on the job. "The sooner the better," she replied having filled out the envelope from the pharmacy, placing their film inside, sealing it shut and placing it in the special bin marked *Film Pickup*.

They returned to their suite, and the moment Jonothan closed the door, Brandi said, "I've just thought of something. Shannon's twins said my brother and his wife are going to have a little girl. What if she is the woman those men were talking about?"

"Now, honey, don't go jumping to conclusions," Jonothan soothed.

"How can I not? I need to have a talk with Mason as soon as possible."

"We'll go for a walk tomorrow," he said as he pulled a leaf of paper from the desk, "and find out where those guys are hiding. Let's draw up a map."

He began to sketch the area in detail, while Brandi added little things he had not noticed, like an imported birdbath that had perpetually running water that dripped down onto a rocky outcropping. The area was surrounded by shaded benches.

"Let's put this in its place as well," she suggested, taking the pencil and lightly sketching in the Jeep that had been driven in under the owner's second floor verandah and parked behind a latticed enclosure.

"You're very good with details," he said.

"My boss doesn't like it. He says my descriptions muddy up the facts. Will has always complimented my attention to detail on more than one occasion." She sketched in the stand of trees where they had hidden to take pictures earlier in the day. "You know, if each of our fact-finding missions end like this one did today, I'll be tempted to break my oath of celibacy."

"I know. You're driving me nuts too," he replied calmly. "But if we keep our heads, we can do this."

"How many fingers do you have crossed?" she teased.

"As many as possible," he agreed. "Now, go take your shower! I'll wait."

When she came out of her shower, he knew there was no way he could spend one more minute in the same room with her without touching her and that could lead to somewhere they had promised each other they would not go. "Brandi, pick a date for our wedding soon or I'm going to fly you away, marry you, and we'll spend the next month on a private island. Your choice. See you in the morning."

Brandi was surprised. Had he just suggested they elope? She had always thought she and Jonothan would be married in a little church with all their friends and family to celebrate with them. She was reminded of other weddings and she wanted hers to be special, different, and memorable. Ever since their weekend at the Trails End Island Cottage in Canada the previous summer, she had been keeping notes in her Bridal Journal. Then again, hadn't her brother's wedding just proven how nice a small and hasty wedding could be?

She blinked rapidly, realizing she had been standing in the middle of the room in her robe, daydreaming about various possible weddings and elopements for several minutes. She opened the door to her room but something didn't feel right. The room was dark. She was certain they had left a light on. It took her eyes a moment to adjust to the change in lighting. Her suitcase had been turned inside out and her verandah doors were open, the sheers billowing in the light evening breeze.

Very slowly she backed out of the room, gently closed the door, turned and literally ran into Jonothan as he came out of the shower. "Whoa, what's the rush?"

"Someone was in my room and ransacked my luggage! The verandah door was still open. I could still smell their cologne when I opened the door! It looks like we're going to have to involve the department sooner than I thought."

"Hey, now come on. Calm down." It had been awhile since he had seen her this angry.

"Let's check your room," she suggested. As soon as

they opened the door, they saw that his luggage had also been ripped apart. "Are you still thinking that I should calm down?"

"I have just one thing to say. This mausoleum had better install security as soon as possible or I'll trash the owner's credibility to smithereens!"

"Thank heavens we had all our identities with us today," she said as she jerked open the closet door in their suite shared sitting room. "Everything is here." She breathed a sigh of relief and turned into his arms and wept like a baby.

He held her until she was weak with the effort of her tears. "Honey," he began, "I have to lock up and make a phone call. Sit here and don't move."

"This is supposed to be my job."

"Not this time," Jonothan replied as he dialed. "Will, do you know where the Welby Mansion Bed & Breakfast is located?"

"Sure," Will's voice came on the line at once, sounding surprised.

"Brandi and I are at the Welby. What we thought would be a relaxing weekend just boomeranged. We've become someone's targets.

"Are the two of you okay?" Will demanded.

"Physically, we're fine. Someone broke into our rooms and ransacked our luggage. Literally ripped out the lining. Brandi is so angry, that she broke down and cried."

"That's a first!" Will exclaimed. "I'll be there on the double. I have seven of my men with me."

"We haven't touched a thing. I'll dial the owner and

tell her that Brandi needs to see her personal physician. We don't want to alert or upset anyone unnecessarily, so, 'Doctor' Will, just pretend that Brandi forgot her medication."

"For what?"

"Blood pressure?" Jonothan suggested on a whim.

"Fine. Let her know that you have friends who will be on site until we get to the bottom of this. I'll call Marcie and fill her in. If the owner doesn't want the entire Sheriff's Department breathing down her neck, she will have no choice but to cooperate."

Jonothan telephoned the owner as Will had suggested.

As the owner, Ariel was aghast with remorse. "I have never had anything like this happen here, ever. I just don't understand."

"Well, ma'am, we're not very happy about it either. All we wanted was to spend a quiet weekend away from our jobs and I had heard this was the ideal place. But, lady, you're security stinks. You can tell anyone who asks that our friend Will is a doctor. Did you get that?" Jonothan ordered. He was surprised how his anger still simmered beneath the surface.

"Yes. I'm sorry. What can I do to help? Anything that was damaged will be replaced immediately. At no cost, of course."

"Well, look at it this way. Either you get this place up to snuff, security-wise, or you'll be out of business very shortly. Is that understood?"

"Jonothan, don't be too harsh," Brandi coaxed.

"You were put at risk," he fired back.

"I'm a Deputy Sheriff for heavens sake."

"And you've been working too many hours, between the Shadow Angels and the force."

"All of this caught me off guard. The Sheriff would be very disappointed in me. Why don't we pick up Pepper?"

"Honey, I know you miss your Canine Corp Partner, but let's wait and see what Will's take is on this, okay?"

They took turns pacing and sitting and throwing impatient glances out the window and at the road below for the next half hour until a timid knock on the door distracted them and Jonothan checked and opened the door.

"Your doctor is here, Miss," Ariel announced. "I would also like to see the rooms, please."

"In a moment," Will replied, forcing her to wait in the hall and fume. He closed the door, gently embraced Brandi, and asked, "Were you hurt?"

"No! I'm infuriated!" she snarled.

He stepped out onto the verandah and signaled down to one of his men.

The young man signaled back that everything was secure on his end.

"Brandi, how far inside the room did you go before you sensed something was wrong?"

"About three steps. I didn't even turn on the light."

"And the verandah doors were open like they are now?"

"Yes."

Ariel knocked again and Will took his time getting to the door. And because she wasn't one to stand by and let someone else take charge, she marched into the suite sitting room towards Brandi's room.

"You can be here, but don't touch anything," Will demanded as he slipped on a pair of gloves.

Ariel was taken aback by his tone of voice, but did as she was told.

Brandi had answered similar calls, however this time it was she who felt violated and sick to her stomach. Her clothes and the inside of her suitcase were in shreds but nothing else was disturbed.

Will checked out the room and signaled to one of his nephews who had used an extension ladder to gain access to the verandah. "Anything out there?"

"No forced entry. Whoever did this had a key to both rooms."

Will turned to Ariel. "Ma'am? If you intend to stay in business, you need to have up to date security installed and the sooner the better!"

"I always felt I couldn't afford it, but now I see that keeping my boarders safe has to take priority," Ariel replied.

"I'll look over your property and give you a quote within twenty-four hours." Will suggested. "If any of your guests question why my equipment is up on Hillside Road, you can say we're a university group on location for a photography class. We'll only be parked here for a few days. Now if you don't mind, I have to speak with Jonothan and Brandi in private."

Ariel was again taken aback not only by his angry tone of voice but by the look in his eyes. She understood Jonothan's anger—he was in love with this red-headed Deputy Sheriff who had a reputation for being relentless when it came to the law. Even Henry Carpenter who was still in prison had kept his distance from her, and she had just been a rookie then. But this 6'4" tall giant they called Will had held Brandi like a treasure and looked at her, Ariel—not some desk clerk, but the *owner* of the Welby—like she was the reason the suite had been trashed.

She retreated to her office and called Sadie.

"Ariel," Sadie ordered. "You do whatever Will says. You hear me? No doubt those two pieces of riff-raff you've got staying there are the problem."

She had just hung up the phone when she heard someone pounding on the bell at the registration counter. The two men Sadie had called "riff-raff" were standing together at the counter. One was skinny and almost as tall as Will, the other was shorter and more rotund. They had registered for their rooms as brothers, John and James Smith, though now that Ariel thought about it, she realized any fool could see these two men were not related.

"Hey, Missy," the tall skinny guy demanded.

"What can I do for you gentlemen?" Ariel asked politely.

"Well," heavy one began, "We thought this was a quiet little place but we're not sticking around now. Two guys in blue coveralls, came to our door, real quiet-like you know? They were wearing hats that read *Exterminator* with an upside-down bug on it. Why would you need exterminators?"

Then, the skinny guy had to almost shove the chubby guy out of the way to be heard. "They even came into our room and asked us if we'd had any trouble with a break-in."

"Did you?" Ariel asked.

"Nah, but all the same, this place just doesn't feel safe anymore, you know?" the short one said, leering at her.

"So, you're checking out now?" Ariel was so thrilled to be getting rid of these two that it was all she could do to keep from doing cheers behind the counter, but she kept her calm, professional smile in place. Especially when she read a note propped on her phone, *visited the Smith Brothers only.* It was signed with a smiley face and *The Exterminator* business card.

"That's right, lady, and make that on the double."

"Give me a moment please while I tally up your bill." The paperwork was simple, but she quickly typed up another statement. "I would like you to sign this as well."

The tall one signed it without hesitation while he eyed the exit door. It was apparent he couldn't wait to leave; but his partner was more cautious.

"What's this for?" he asked, not at all happy to sign his name to yet another paper that looked to have been written by an attorney.

"You said your room wasn't broken into. I just need your signature stating that you don't plan to sue me for lost property later on."

He signed it and paid in cash.

The moment these two men rushed out the door, she followed them just to make certain they weren't packing an antique or two from their room in the trunk of their car. She watched until they had cleared her drive and then returned to her office to call Sadie again. By the time she hung up and made her way back to the front desk, two of Will's men had already finished dusting her pristine clean counter for finger prints.

Will started firing questions at Brandi and Jonothan the moment Ariel left. "Where is your ID? Your cameras? Your gun?"

"My cameras are in my photographer's supply case," she said as she removed the items in question from their padded pockets in the bottom of the specially designed backpack Opal had made for her. She unzipped the bottom to show Will that everything was right where it was supposed to be.

"When did you put our cameras away?" Jonothan asked.

"When you were out on the verandah."

"So, one of you has been in this room since you returned?" Will asked.

"Yes," Brandi said. "This lounge area was never left completely unoccupied after we came back from our walk, but I turned on a bedside lamp and slid my suitcase into the closet before we left for our walk, but when I opened the door that bedside lamp was off. My suitcase and my clothes were spread all over the bed. I was afraid someone might have still been in my room and backed out and closed the door. Will, you've taught me to trust my instincts, remember? The moment I turned the door knob, all the hair on the back of my neck stood on end. The whole situation felt creepy and wrong."

Will nodded. "As I told you on the phone, I notified Marcie. She is bringing extra clothes for the two of you. In fact, she should be here any minute. The Shadow Angels are on alert, and—"

The telephone ringing was like a gunshot to Jonothan's nerves, but Brandi calmly picked it up on the first ring and just listened. She replaced the phone on its stand and calmly reported, "That was Sadie."

"From the diner?" Will asked

"Yes. She asked that we not run a background check on the owner. However, the owner has agreed to speak with Will."

When Marcie knocked, Will answered. She had barely cleared the door when Brandi wrapped her in such a hug that Marcie barely held onto the garment bag she was carrying.

"Come on, Brandi," Marcie coaxed. "You'll feel better once you're dressed."

"What about me?" Jonothan asked.

"Your clothes are here in the bag."

When the women went into the bathroom, Will said, "Get used to this woman thing, Jonothan. And by the way, when do the two of you plan to get married?

"Soon," Jonothan murmured.

"Look, I know you've been working on a case together, and you're bound to secrecy. But Brandi knows, as do Marcie and I, that what happened here tonight was deliberate. They were looking for something. Probably the photos you took today."

"You can rest easy about that. The film was picked

up by an overnight photo service the Welby has for their guests."

Will nodded, a distant, puzzled look on his face. "I'll wait here while you get dressed. It won't take Brandi long."

When Jonothan returned from his room, newly dressed, he found the others waiting quietly. He poured a cup of coffee. It was midnight. Brandi was too quiet.

"I'll give you the rundown on what's happening," Will began. "We're running a background check on the two men you met on the garden walk earlier this evening from their fingerprints and security cameras we had installed minutes after our arrival. They checked out shortly after I arrived and checked in at the Lucky Arms Hotel across town.

"But," Will continued, "what do the two of you plan to do? You can go back home, or you can stay in the owner's private quarters. She has a guest room and has offered it *gratis* for as long as you like. For the time being, she plans to sleep in the back of her office."

Jonothan looked at Brandi and an understanding passed between them. Even if the men who had rifled through their belongings were gone, there was still something odd happening in or around the Welby.

Jonothan answered Will's question for both of them, "We'll be fine at the owner's private quarters."

"Okay," Will replied, "I need to call my wife and let her know that I will not be coming home tonight, and I need to talk to the owner, so don't go anywhere or make any plans without talking to me. You all know my men can be relentless when they are on duty, especially when it involves family. For your information, the Blue Foxes travel in our own bus which includes a fully stocked semi-trailer. It is parked just off of Hillside Road near a stand of trees."

The telephone rang and this time Jonothan picked it up. She refused to hang up until Jonothan and Brandi had both assured her several times that they were unharmed and making plans with Will for their continued safety.

After the call, Brandi looked between Will, Marcie and Jonothan. "I would like to get some sleep. We'll have an early morning," she added as she slipped on her photo vest.

"Before that," Will asked, "Marcie and Jonothan, I'd like a word with Brandi alone please." The others excused themselves into the adjoining room, and Will said, "Since no one else was involved, can we keep this private and not involve the Sheriff's Department?"

"For the time being," Brandi replied. "Both of us were supposed to be taking a few days off. Orders from our bosses."

"Good. We'll try to clean up your luggage once we've checked it over. Sleep well. We've got a busy day tomorrow. Are the Shadow Angels going to be involved?"

"Opal called and she knows we're both okay right now."

"They know you're here and that I have a unit here?" Will asked.

"Yes, but I'm honor-bound to keep them appraised of whatever is happening; and they will notify one of us if they feel the need to intervene."

"And just so *you* know, we're back in town because our out-of-town job was cancelled," Will said, his demeanor solemn.

"Cancelled? Does that mean you found the stolen baby?" She had to struggle to catch her breath like she had just run the mile in competition.

"No. The person who ordered the search cancelled it. He already has twin grandbabies, and this other child can disappear for all he cares."

All that ran through her mind was that she hoped the person who had dismissed Will had also dismissed whoever else he had hired to abduct Autumn's baby. But she had a gut feeling that the two men who had torn through her suite were still planning to get paid for kidnapping her future niece or nephew.

Autumn's Visit

Winthrop & Sunshine

Mason and Autumn arrived an hour before her doctor's appointment, so they went window shopping and stopped to browse through a gift shop.

Autumn spotted the miniature lighthouse the moment they stepped in the door. When she read that the light had several settings she had to see the price. No matter what happened in the future, she wanted this for her and her child. It represented so much about their lives.

"You just can't seem to get your fill of lighthouses, can you?" he teased.

"I just thought it would make a great nightlight for the baby's room," Autumn said as her eyes sparkled with unshed tears.

"Then how about I buy it as my first official present to the baby?"

They crossed the street to rest on a shaded park bench. It was quiet and peaceful at the city park, when Mason stopped so suddenly she thought something had upset him. "Mason, what's wrong?"

"We haven't even planned a nursery!" Mason exploded. "That's what's wrong!"

"Not yet. But with our temporary situation, the travel bed is suitable."

"A travel bed? But that is for vacations and visiting family and friends. No child of mine is sleeping in makeshift rooms. A child needs somewhere to call home. Some place where they know they are safe and can build loving memories."

Autumn could only stare in amazement. "It doesn't have to be a castle. Look at the Carriage House. It is small but it has been the first real home I remember that gave me such a feeling of peace and joy; and the Warren's support and encouragement has given me hope. With you beside me, anything is possible."

"Sorry, I guess I got carried away for a moment. Things aren't really that bleak. It's just that I'm not used to sharing my hopes and dreams, you know; but you've just helped me make a decision."

"Really," Autumn replied, pleased to hear the excitement in his voice.

"Yes. Richard and I have been working on a project." Remembering Brandi's warning about Autumn being frightened at the mere mention of Turtle Crossing, he deliberately left out the location. "There is some low land that floods out every year which is near…a small town that has expanded their industry base, resulting in the construction of several housing developments."

"Land?" Autumn repeated, nonplussed.

"Fifteen-hundred acres of water and about that much in good, useable land."

"Then you and Richard are planning to invest in this property?"

"Richard already owns it. He has asked me if I would like to be a part owner too. We've been waiting for the green light approval to move forward with construction. Our plans include a full fledged marina and building sites. We'll need fully licensed people who…"

"People who could save lives like you did when that man fell in the pond behind us on the golf course. Right?"

"That too," Mason agreed.

"But I thought the blueprints Richard had spread out on his drawing board were for a golf course."

"You apparently didn't see the second set of blueprints, did you?"

"I didn't want to appear nosy," she replied.

"Richard thinks several things have to come together to make it more appealing to the area residents and we need to be prepared to rule out and handle the opposition."

"But sometimes growth and change are good," she said softly. "The only thing I worried about when I was growing up was where my mom and I were going to sleep at night and if there would be anything to eat that day or the next."

Neither one spoke for several minutes. From the bench, they watched families and commuters passing through the park, enjoying the perfect day.

"My dad beat my mom often," Autumn said. "And hurt her so bad *that* night, that she was afraid for me; and told me to go to grandma's house. But I didn't know my way. I lived by myself on the street all that summer and into fall. I was supposed to be in school, and someone found me sleeping in a shed in back of the church. I was told this later. I don't remember being taken. Social Services told me my mom had died."

"That's awful," said Mason softly, a look of horror on his face. "I'm so sorry, I didn't know."

Autumn gave him a smile that made her look much older than she was. "We both have skeletons in our closet. But we have an entire lifetime to clean them out together."

The temperature was in the 70's with a light breeze and just enough shade to set the peaceful scene—at least until two women who had been sitting on another bench around the bend from them started arguing.

"I can't hire *you*," one of them screeched, her voice sounding thunderous in the quiet of the day. She had long blonde hair tinged with red.

"But I like your town," the other woman whined.

"Sorry," the blonde said as they parted.

Mason was jerked back in time. The whiney woman's voice sounded so much like his mom that he watched her as she crossed the street and turned East towards the main street of Sunrise.

He shook his head and chalked that flash of memory to his melancholy frame of mind.

Autumn rose from the bench as well and started towards the strawberry blonde who had already left the park. A car door slammed. Tires squealed. The smell of hot rubber filled the air as she sped west out of Sunrise.

"Autumn," he said softly. "Honey, you're trembling."

"Sunrise must have put a spell on both of us then, because if I didn't know better I would say that woman who just drove away could have been my mom. Wishful thinking. I didn't get a good look at her face, but something about her stirred my memory. Maybe it was her walk—the set of her shoulders and her profile."

"Really?" Mason asked. "For a second I was sure the other woman was *my* mother." He gave himself a little shake. "Well, it has been a few years since we've seen our mothers. But my mom lived in the northern part of Ohio."

"And I think my mom grew up in Turtle Crossing," Autumn said.

They arrived home earlier than Mason had expected. But by his estimate, the surprise birthday party Shannon had planned for Autumn should just about be ready. Mason hoped the party wouldn't be too much stress on her, but Shannon had insisted, not only because it was Autumn's eighteenth birthday but also because of what it meant to her, the baby, and to Mason.

"Autumn, do you feel like taking another short walk? Perhaps deliver the bracelets you bought for the twins," Mason suggested.

"You don't miss much do you?"

"Something tells me that you are going to spoil this baby rotten, Mrs. Davies."

"And you are going to help me, right, Mr. Davies?"

"Indeed I will," he replied.

They walked leisurely to the Warrens' main house, and when they knocked on the front door, Shannon welcomed them, grinning broadly. "There you are! We didn't want to make a big issue about your birthday but wanted you to know we were thinking of you."

She put her arm around Autumn's shoulders—hugging her from the front was nearly impossible at this point—and directed her inside. A pile of wrapped gifts lay on the coffee table, where the rest of the family was impatiently waiting for them. David gave Autumn a swift peck on the cheek and wished her a happy birthday, while the twins practically danced with excitement. Autumn handled the fuss admirably, exclaiming over the gifts and thanking everyone over and over.

When she had opened every gift on the table, Autumn retrieved the bag Mason had carried inside. "We have something to show all of you too. We had some spare time and went window shopping. Look what we found."

She handed each of the girls a small box. They opened them at the same time and put the charm bracelets on.

"Thank you Auntie and Uncle Mason," they cried.

"We also picked up something for the baby's room," Mason said, lifting the box containing the lighthouse out of the bag.

"Yes. We would like your approval," Autumn added.

As soon as he removed the wrapping, the girls were enchanted.

"Oh, mommy, plug it in," Lily Anneé cheered, when

she saw the electric cord hanging from the bottom of the lighthouse.

"We want to see it with the lights on," Lauri Rose added.

David dimmed the lights and suggested, smiling and nodding his approval, "Autumn, you were right. This will be a very special nightlight for the baby."

Autumn looked at Mason with tears in her eyes. She would cherish the memories of their first few weeks together at the Marblehead Lighthouse. He had completely changed his life around for her and her baby.

Shannon carried the birthday cake blazing with eighteen candles while they sang "Happy Birthday."

"Make a wish," the twins squealed.

Autumn closed her eyes, made her wish, and blew out the candles. Her baby kicked so hard her smock fluttered. Mason gently caressed the area and the baby calmed immediately.

"Thank you. I'm not used to anyone remembering," she said softly. "Not since I was a little girl."

"We'll help you a'member cause mommy has it on her birthday calendar. Right, Mommy?" Shannon nodded.

"We've had a long day," Autumn sighed and added, "Thank you for the birthday party and sandwiches and especially the cake."

"We enjoyed every minute of it. But you didn't eat much cake, so take a couple of pieces home," David added as he helped Mason put her gifts in a shopping bag.

As they left to return to the Carriage House, Autumn

asked, Mason, "How long have you known they planned to give me a party?"

"Just a few hours. Shannon called and left me a message at the doctor's office."

Autumn nodded contentedly. The party had been enjoyable, but that was only part of the reason she felt so happy right now. She had prayed she would turn eighteen before her baby was born, and her prayer had been answered.

Maybe there is something to be said for prayer, she thought as she clutched Mason's arm. "The birthday party and our wedding were already unexpected special gifts."

"The Judge doesn't think there will be an issue with custody unless the birth father decides to make a claim to our child," Mason added.

"He won't. I don't know why he would want to pay child support, especially if his wife doesn't know anything about me. That's why he gave me money that day. It was his way of telling me goodbye."

"What did you do with the money?"

"Nothing. I just left it in the bottom of my duffel bag."

"All this time?" Mason exclaimed.

"I planned to give it back to him after our baby is born. I can't chance it before."

"We could forward it by mail to his office and then you wouldn't have to worry about it anymore."

"I hadn't considered that. But what if the wrong person opens it?"

"We could send it by registered mail and have Shannon drop it in the mail on her next flight out of town."

"Let's do that," Autumn said.

When they arrived home, Autumn made directly for the closet and dug out her old duffel bag. Inside, she found the wad of money that Autumn had described plus a green leather bank deposit envelope. When Mason unzipped it they found several thousand dollars with a bank deposit slip dated the day he had found Autumn in a wrecked rental car.

"This is a sizable amount. I have no doubt that this caused quite a stir at the bank if he is still working there. Perhaps Shannon knows a local courier."

Autumn immediately dialed her number. "Shannon, I have something of a delicate nature to attend to. Do you have a courier service you trust?"

"I most certainly do. I would trust any of Will's detectives. And they are very discreet. If it is of a sensitive nature, I would send along a personal delivery letter that they have to sign."

"That's a great idea, but I don't know him personally."

"Just leave it at the office in the morning and I'll take care of it," Shannon said.

After Mason and Autumn left the house, Richard asked Shannon and David to look over his blueprints.

"Are you really going to do this, Dad?" Shannon asked.

"I just received the call. The Township Trustees have agreed to all of our plans and also approved Mason's request. However, the County Commissioners and Town Council haven't given their final approval yet. I just have one major concern. What if we have to do some blasting?"

"Is that a must?" Shannon asked. After what she had seen at the last Shadow Angels meeting, she wondered if blasting might do irreparable damage to the tunnels that apparently snaked around under the town of Turtle Crossing. Rather than leave all this to chance, she telephoned Opal.

"I know some people who work in this field," Opal replied. "Personally I don't think it would be a wise decision. Ask them if they have made alternative plans. Better yet, Shannon, put Richard on the phone."

Shannon passed the receiver to him.

"Evening, Opal," he said.

Opal's voice carried strongly enough over the line that her voice was still audible to Shannon in the quiet room. "Do you have a way to connect that low area where they finished digging last fall and Turtle Crossing Lake without blasting?"

"These are Mr. Welby's original plans and nowhere does it mention blasting."

"Thanks for giving us a heads up on this, Richard. I'll ask Jonothan to make some calls and we'll get back to you."

Not a Honeymoon

Turtle Crossing

From the moment, Brandi and Jonothan unlocked the door of Ariel's apartment; they felt propelled back in time. Some of the furniture was over 100 years old, yet it had a dignity and grace that was timeless. Jonothan recognized a pair of Windsor chairs, a Chippendale Tea Table and a Shaker Washstand.

"Well, we know one thing about the owner, she has an eclectic collection," Jonothan commented as they stood in the doorway of the formal foyer. "The hodge-podge, regal and homespun furnishings definitely makes a statement."

"I agree," Brandi added. "I love the idea of a rocking chair in the kitchen."

Jonothan liked this side of Brandi and couldn't recall her acting so much at home anyplace else except his mom's and Granny Oates's homes, but she had never mentioned what she wanted in her own home.

He walked ahead of her as they continued their tour, which led them down a narrow hall. He pushed open a door and said, "Two bedrooms and a bath. All the comforts of home."

"And this is probably the linen closet," Brandi began. "Wow! This Ariel lady can't be all bad. Not with such a romantic flair."

"I'm not sleeping in here," Jonothan said adamantly when Brandi turned on the light and stepped inside fingering the lace doilies on the mirrored vanity. But what she saw reflected in the mirror took her breath away. She moved over to a grand four-poster bed draped in pearl, crème, and ecru fine lace.

She pulled back a corner of the pearl satin quilted bedspread, and then brushed her fingertips across the matching satin sheets. She had sketched a similar bed in her bridal journal.

She was so nervous she started laughing and crying at the same time. When she looked up, Jonothan was standing still as a statue in the doorway.

I can do this; she kept repeating as she turned out the light, and gently closed the door. Then in a nervous rush, she turned too quickly and nearly fell into his arms.

"It's okay, honey. I keep complaining to you about taking cold showers, but I wasn't real certain until this moment, how much *you* wanted *me*," he said softly as he caressed her back, brushed his hands gently through her hair and tipped her face up to his.

"I'll give you two weeks!" he said softly. "The only thing our invitations need is the date and place, right?"

"How did you—?"

"Will said Wendy has them set up ready to print. She even has the envelopes addressed. Why haven't you said anything to me about this?"

"I didn't want to bother you," she said lamely. "I know when you're not out showing property, you are busy in the office, talking to clients or helping the Shadow Angels in the evenings."

At the same moment, by nearly telepathic consent, they drew apart. They each saw the same rueful expression on the other's face.

Jonothan cleared his throat. "Honey, Will and I thought you might like a very special visitor. Granny is bringing Pepper here. We *wanted* it to be a surprise."

"Pepper is coming here? You are wonderful, you know that."

"Thanks," he said softly. "She called earlier and said that Pepper was homesick for you. She didn't want to leave him with anyone else while she and Doc are away on a weekend trip."

"If you want my opinion, she and Doc just wanted to check out this place. She has been anxious to meet the new owner. Granny and her first husband were close friends with the Welby's years ago."

As if summoned by his words, a knock echoed through the apartment from the front door, followed with a well-known whimper.

Brandi threw her arms around Jonothan and kissed

him soundly, then kissed him on both cheeks. Her eyes were sparkling. She couldn't wait to see Pepper, but she still took the time to peer out the front window of Ariel's apartment before opening the door. Granny and Doc stood out side the door with Pepper on a leash. Granny unhooked Pepper's leash when Brandi opened the door, but Pepper, ever the police dog, didn't move until Brandi motioned him forward.

She was on one knee with her arms around him, rubbing down his flank and his neck, telling him what a good boy he was and how much she loved him. Then she practiced talking to him in German. He lifted his head and licked her face and her hands until she offered a small treat she had in her pocket.

Only after this reunion did she hug Granny and Doc.

"He's been shut up in the back of Doc's station wagon the entire trip, except for one quick run and potty stop," Granny offered.

"We'll not be long," Brandi replied as she and Pepper went out for a run. She wanted Pepper to become acquainted with the grounds around the Welby House.

"We brought food," Doc added to Jonothan. "You know how Granny is. She thinks the two of you might starve without a basketful of goodies."

"And he thinks everyone who is on their honeymoon is going to be having so much fun, they will forget to eat," Granny added.

"Come on, you two," Jonothan said.

"But this is the honeymoon suite isn't it?" Granny asked.

"No. This is the owner's apartment. Were the two of you hinting that we might need chaperones to keep us accountable?"

"I apologize," Doc said, amused. "I'm the one who doubted, not Granny. Don't forget I was young once too."

Brandi and Pepper returned and she couldn't help but overhear the tail end of his confession. She knew Granny and Doc had spent more than one night together on out-of-town trips before making their commitment legal, but she had never mentioned it to Jonothan, or anyone for that matter. For all she knew their nights could have been as innocent as hers and Jonothan's.

Pepper greeted Jonothan and then snuffled through the entire apartment before finding a place to lie down where he could keep Brandi in sight.

"Jonothan, you're more of a man than most," Doc admitted.

"To what are you referring?"

"I've been a veterinarian most of my life, but that dog is almost human at times. Pepper and Brandi interact and understand each other like twin people. Some men would be jealous or intimidated by that kind of relationship."

"In the beginning I prayed that someday she would trust me as much as she does him, and…"

"And I do," Brandi replied as she set a pot of coffee and a plate of Granny's nutritious goodies on the table.

"Hey, Doc, how's your heart?" Brandi teased.

"My heart is fine. Why do you ask?"

"Oh, no reason, but since The Welby is booked up

the rest of the weekend, I thought you two might want to spend the night in the honeymoon suite."

"We don't need anything like that," he chuckled, raising his eyebrows at Granny.

"Oh, I don't know. It might be fun!" Granny added. "May I see it?"

When Brandi opened the door and turned on the light, Granny sighed. "Wow! And I understand the new owner is single? Well someone has certainly added a few more frills since the Welbys were alive. I love the rose-colored lace draped over the lampshades. Nice touch."

"And you have your own private bathroom facilities," Brandi added.

"Speaking of facilities," Granny asked, "just what the devil is going on here? I recognized Will's trucks parked up on Hillside Road, but of course he wouldn't tell me a thing."

"I'll tell you what I know in a moment. Thanks for bringing Pepper, but how did you know we were here and where were you planning to spend the night?"

"Will called. He said he and Jonothan talked. We were going to park up at Will's encampment and sleep on the mattress in the back of the station wagon," Granny said. "It wouldn't be the first time."

They returned to the kitchen to find that Jonothan and Doc had left.

"They probably went out to collect your luggage and park the car," Brandi suggested.

The two women moved around in the tiny kitchen

with easy familiarity as Brandi shared what had happened since their arrival.

They had the table set, carried matching chairs from the bedrooms, and were ready to sit down when the men returned. They set the luggage in the foyer and joined the ladies in the kitchen.

"Did you find a place to park?"

"Will drove it up to their encampment," Jonothan said.

"Why? Doesn't he want anyone to know we have guests?" Brandi asked.

"I think," Jonothan replied, "Will wanted a chance to drive Doc's souped-up station wagon. That engine shakes the ground like a herd of elephants on the run. Brandi, have you seen it since he had it painted black?"

"I have. Did he tell you what he has under the hood? Granny? Can I tell Jonothan?"

"Of course, but most men think we women aren't supposed to know about mechanics."

"It has a Ford 29 Super Cobra Jet with dual mufflers," Brandi said.

"And the ride is so much more comfortable since he customized the interior in white leather and bucket seats in the front," Granny added, a glint of mischief in her eyes.

"But you only drive it for fun and not on vet calls any more, right?" Brandi chuckled.

"Granny told you about the fully outfitted pickup truck she bought me, right?" Doc replied.

"It was my way of paying my lifetime neighbor for free veterinarian service," Granny clarified.

"So," Doc began, "what do you have planned for tomorrow?"

"We're going hiking," Jonothan said. "At dawn."

"Just make certain you check in with Will," Doc admonished.

"We'll keep that in mind," Brandi agreed. "You two go on to bed. We have to take Pepper out again and finish up the few dishes. We'll see you in the morning."

They strolled out towards the parking lot and circled back around the bird bath. The trees along the path to the entrance to their apartment were strung with colored lights. Pepper was busy checking out the air around them.

Once inside, Brandi asked, "Did you notice the owner's Jeep was not in its usual parking place?"

"Yes. But not to worry—Will probably has someone tailing her."

They had returned to the kitchen and were doing the last few dishes that were in the sink, when Brandi asked, "Did you see what I just saw from the kitchen window?"

"You mean the waterfall with the moonlight on it?"

"Yes. What else?"

"Come and look. It looks like lights behind the falls. I doubt it can be seen from any other angle."

"Now what do you make of that?" Jonothan questioned.

"Remember the day after we had been in the tunnels, you said it reminded you about being separated from your mom in the tunnels when you were in the third grade?"

"Sure. Are you referring to the part where I heard a

waterfall? But this couldn't be the same one. We're too far from town."

"I thought the same thing, before I saw this," she said as she led him back to the pantry. "Look at the Welby property on this wall map and the true distance as it curves around towards town. See, when you look at Turtle Lake, it sweeps around away from the hillside and Turtle Crossing, but when you drive back towards the hills and the falls, the Welby is closer to town than the lake."

"How did you happen to notice this map shut away back here in the pantry?" Jonothan asked.

"I was looking for a broom to clean up the coffee I spilled on the floor."

"This is an aerial view. So, where does Hillside Road end? The Welby brochure only mentions hiking on Hillside Road. It doesn't list a cave or tunnel."

"Maybe we can check that out tomorrow. Do you want to make plans for tomorrow?"

"Yes, we'll set out well prepared. And just in case we need backup, I'll leave a note for Will and one for Granny."

The two of them were up by 5:00am, quickly showered with non-scented soap and slipped on their hooded sweatshirts that made them look like they had shopped at the Hunter's Paradise section for outdoor enthusiasts. They noticed that the owner's Jeep was parked in its usual spot behind the latticed enclosure with a tarp tossed over the back. However, it was apparent the motor was still warm because a warm mist hovered over the hood of the vehicle.

Rather than press their luck, they jogged in the open and walked under the cover of trees. In the distance they could hear the purr of a couple of fishing boats traversing through the channel to Turtle Lake—fishermen getting an early start.

Jonothan and Brandi stopped while the boats passed by and took the time to drink half of their juice and shared a huge blueberry muffin before taking their last jaunt to the waterfalls.

They slipped on their hooded rain gear and covered Pepper. They advanced a bit further before he stopped. He had smelled something or someone. They immediately went down on one knee on either side of Pepper. Using their flashlights they checked the area around their feet and then checked ahead of where Pepper stood.

"Sensors," Brandi whispered.

Jonothan waited while Brandi and Pepper investigated the area around the waterfall. The sound was deafening. Then she spotted tracks in the dew that wound back and around the entrance, aimed towards Turtle Crossing and away from Hillside Road.

She sent Pepper to fetch Jonothan. She knew the barn was only about 150 yards from the waterfall. They had to get out of sight before the sun peeked over the horizon and Will's men would be able to see them. For the moment Brandi wanted to keep their party small—less chance of being discovered that way.

A few minutes later the tracks appeared to stop. Jonothan felt cautiously around through a thicket of thorn bushes near the spot but found nothing. Meanwhile

Brandi took a chance and switched on her larger deputy issue flashlight.

Pepper tugged on her shirtsleeve and Jonothan ducked down at the same time. They waited. A few seconds later, one of Will's men walked right past them. They waited another five minutes before Brandi whispered, "I found a power box with a tricky side door inside a fake birdhouse. Two buttons are marked lights and the rest are blank. However, the third button has an oily fingerprint on it."

"Let's do it."

She pressed the button and a door wide enough for a Jeep to drive through rumbled open. The area behind the falls was like a theatre. The twenty-foot ceilings appeared to go on forever. The falls weren't as loud inside as they were outside.

However an area behind the falls had been walled off, apparently to discourage unexpected guests. The Welbys had gone to great lengths to insure their privacy. Because the wall didn't reach the ceiling, fresh air circulated into the tunnels. Brandi found another door that opened into the tunnels cave area behind the falls, but didn't open it for fear it also had a sensor.

As the sun came up, light entered through the falls, illuminating the first several hundred feet of the tunnel. They had walked about a half a mile when Pepper heard something again, coming from somewhere ahead of them. They stopped and backed against a wall, waited and listened.

Evidently the tunnels had at least one more entrance, and Jonothan wondered how many more they were going to find. As there was nowhere to hide if they were discovered here, they trudged carefully back to the door near the falls. Once outside again, Jonothan pressed the button to close the door and waited until they were satisfied they had not been spotted. Then immediately slipped off their night gear and shoes, and stashed them in their backpacks.

The sun was up and blistering hot. But they climbed up Hillside Road despite the heat in the hopes of getting a good view of the surrounding land. They were not disappointed. Even before they reached the top, in one direction they could see the entire layout of the Welby Mansion Bed & Breakfast, and in another direction, the town of Turtle Crossing was laid out below them.

Jonothan was quiet as he drew out his binoculars and scanned the town. He motioned for Brandi to look where he was looking, at the street behind the church and the Johnson Auto Sales.

"What would unmarked trucks be doing in that alley?" he asked

"I don't know. We need to inform Will about this. Someone could…"

"Someone could what, Brandi?" Will asked, his head cresting the hill behind them. "We found your note, and have combed this area for over an hour. Jonothan, your mother would like to see you two as soon as possible."

"Why?" Jonothan asked at once.

"She didn't say. She wants to meet at Johnson's Truck and Auto Garage in Walnut Alley."

Jonothan and Brandi exchanged a glance and headed back down the hill immediately. Less than an hour later, they found Opal waiting for them outside the garage, in the auto sales parking area.

"I'm so glad the two of you could get away," she said. "I dropped my car off this morning for an oil change and saw something intriguing," Opal began as they walked towards the auto showroom, where a series of paintings hung on the wall, portraying several prominent buildings in downtown Turtle Crossing. "Turn around and tell me what you see."

Jonothan looked left and right and then said, "What am I looking for, Mom?"

In the meantime, Brandi had been looking at a packet of carefully dated photos of Wendy's that seemed to correspond to the buildings in the paintings. "Jonothan, look at these photos."

The photos showed six different businesses in Turtle Crossing taken over a period of years, almost like before and after photos. The odd part was, not many people would notice why the businesses looked different. The changes were subtle, like a bank of newly installed windows on one side of the old three-story warehouse.

"This is a very clever painting," Jonothan commented., standing before the artwork that depicted the warehouse. "The windows look so real. So, when we were trying to determine if some of the businesses in town may have made have had ulterior motives, in reality they were just updating the exterior."

"Yes," Opal agreed as she led him to another painting on the other side of the room. "Does this bring back memories?"

"It's the Longacre Grocery!" Jonothan whispered, certain he was dreaming. "Has Bea seen this? Who is the artist?"

"Jonothan," Brandi suggested. "Catch your breath. This is why the maps couldn't tell us a thing—because all the changes were cosmetic. And I believe the trucks we saw parked near the warehouse and auto sales earlier were there for repair or reconditioning."

Puzzled, he asked, "When did you make that connection?"

"Looking at these pictures reminded me that I had seen those trucks before. They belong to a sign and advertising company. I believe they did Marcie's Florist and Party van."

"Mom," Jonothan said suddenly, as if just remembering something himself. "I have another question, about the entrance to the tunnels. The day that tornado hovered over Turtle Crossing, how did we get into the tunnels?"

She had prayed that was one question she would never have to answer. "We raced through Johnson's Garage."

"But, wasn't Dad there working on his truck? I waited up until after midnight and he never came home."

Opal took a deep breath and replied, "Yes, Jonothan, your dad was there. For years a segment of the garage built inside the Tunnels was used to store their racecars. The public entrance was through the truck garage door."

Jonothan nodded. An elusive part of his memory of that day was similar to a partially opened curtain which opened so slowly he thought it was a figment of his imagination. His Dad had been standing right here the day of the tornado, and a little boy who looked a lot like him, Jonothan, was standing beside his dad's truck with a blonde woman. And someone else too…

It was so long ago, yet the reality hit him in increments. His words came out in a whisper. "Mom, you've known about Dad and Pearl and their son, Jace all these years?"

Opal struggled to make eye contact with him. "I'm sorry. I was hoping you would never remember that day."

Jonothan took her in his arms. "I know, mom. And I love you for trying to protect me. But why was Uncle Henry there?"

Opal took another shaky breath, as if answering was costing her a great deal of effort. "Henry knew about Pearl and Jace too. He said that if your father didn't make his payments on time, he would expose him as a bigamist."

The Next Move
Winthrop

Autumn felt she owed Richard a debt of gratitude for the job he had offered her immediately after she and Mason had arrived in Winthrop. She was almost certain she had grown an inch taller the day she handed the cashier her own earnings to purchase the material and notions to make her baby's clothes.

She wanted to be prepared for when her baby arrived. She had frozen several meals ahead for when she returned home from the hospital, and had pressed and refolded stacks of baby clothes. She had also laundered and ironed all of Mason's shirts and trousers. Short of washing down the walls, she had run out of nesting related things to do.

Mason's idea to return a business envelope filled with the cash that her charlatan of a husband had left her was like closing the door on a nightmare and opening a door to her new life with Mason.

However, hearing the voice of that woman who had raced out of Sunrise like she couldn't get out of town soon enough kept haunting her. Maybe it was because she was just about to become a mom herself. And maybe it was because she had been envious of the pregnant women who could sit in the doctor's office accompanied by their mothers or husbands, until very recently she had had neither.

Someone was pounding on her door and calling her name, "Auntie A, Auntie A."

She opened the door to the sweetest little girls she had ever had the pleasure of knowing, tugging on their little wagon filled with grocery bags. "What project are the two of you working on today?"

"Auntie A, can you help us bake mommy some cupcakes?" Lauri Rose began.

"Of course, but since when am I Auntie A?"

"We're learning our alphabet."

"And Auntie Brandi is Auntie B," Lily Anneé replied.

"This is a great way to learn. Should we put the alphabet on the cupcakes?"

"That sounds like great fun," Lily Anneé replied.

"White, chocolate, spice, brownies or lemon drops," Autumn suggested.

"Lemon drops?" Lauri laughed. "Lemon drops are candy, not cup cakes."

"Mommy's favorite is carrot cake. But we couldn't find a repice."

"It's a *re-sip-pee*," Lily Anneé corrected.

"I have a recipe," Autumn said. "But, I don't have any carrots."

"We don't have any either, but Grandma Eileen does," Lauri Rose said. "We'll call her. Maybe she would like to help too."

So they called Eileen, who agreed that the twins' project sounded like fun and arrived less than ten minutes later with carrots and a few other items Autumn did not have on hand.

The measuring cups were out on the counter, the mixer was ready, and everyone was giggling. Lauri Rose had flour on her nose, because in her rush to see how everything worked, she had gotten too close when flour drifted out of the bottom of the sifter. Lily Anneé was busy trying to fish out the pieces of egg shell that had fallen into the glass mixing bowl. Eileen had finished grating the carrots and Autumn had just finished chopping and measuring the pecans.

Mason arrived in the midst of the soundtrack of *The Sound of Music* blasting from the stereo, with Lily Anneé singing the loudest.

"Give us just a few minutes and we'll have the cupcakes ready to go in the oven," Autumn announced.

"I need to talk to you in private," Mason said, hating to interrupt what appeared to be a fun production.

"That will give the girls and me time to walk over to my house," Eileen said as she set the oven timer. "We still need cream cheese for the icing. Come along, girls."

"What's wrong?" Autumn asked, puzzled that he

would take the time off work to come by so early in the day.

"I just talked to my sister. Brandi just heard about the real estate plans that Richard and I have been working on, and she said it is imperative that we make a personal appearance in Turtle Crossing to set the story straight. We'll have to be there for a little while. Maybe weeks."

"After all your work and the money you have spent to purchase the property—are you saying she is against your plans?"

"No. Not Brandi, but there could be some glitches," Mason continued. But I don't want to go without you."

"Wait, did you say Turtle Crossing?" she exclaimed.

"Yes," he replied, taking both her hands in his. "Autumn, you act as through you've seen a ghost. Talk to me, honey. What is it about Turtle Crossing that frightens you?"

"Oh, Mason, I was born there. My mom died there. And I was placed in several foster homes as a result."

He waited a moment and added, "But you're an adult now and you're married. I promise I won't let anyone take you away," he added, hugging her close. The baby kicked reminding them who else had a vote in their decision.

Her eyes glistening, Autumn squeezed Mason's hand and smiled. "But what if our baby decides to make an early appearance?"

"It won't be a problem. Dr. Ashley splits his appointments between Sunrise and Turtle Crossing. Shannon said they each have excellent hospitals."

Mason couldn't tell what she was thinking, but hoped

she would be willing to go with him. Especially because if this plan worked out, they would be living long term in Turtle Crossing instead of the Warren Estate.

"Can you give us a half hour to frost our cupcakes?" Autumn asked as she removed the cupcakes from the pan and placed them on cooling racks. "I'll go wherever you need to go," she added and prayed no one would remember her. She would be well protected with Brandi as a Deputy Sheriff. Right?

Mason saw the twins skipping along with Eileen and knew how much they were going to miss this family. "See you later, ladies," Mason said as he held the screen door open for them.

"Thank you, Uncle M."

"You're quite welcome," he said as he bowed. The girls giggled as they set the cream cheese, margarine and powdered sugar on the table.

"We could smell the cupcakes all the way from Grandma's house," Lauri Rose said.

"Really?"

Later as they were piling fluffy white icing on each cupcake, Lauri Rose asked, "Do you think mom is going to like our surprise?"

"She is going to love your surprise" Eileen said as Lily Anneé sprinkled colored sugar on top of the icing. "This is yours Auntie A," Lily Anneé said proudly. Autumn smiled when she saw the squiggly A in red sprinkles.

They packed up the cupcakes into sealed containers and carried them across the lawns to David and Shannon's house. In the kitchen, Autumn put water on for tea.

"Your mom is coming home early today, isn't she?"

"How did you know?"

"Because Grandma Eileen invited her, and because I need to see her as well," Autumn replied.

"Did I hear my name mentioned?" Shannon announced as she came in the door.

"Mommy, it's a surprise tea. And we made your favorite cupcakes."

"We're saving a few for Daddy, Grandpa and Uncle Mason."

"We made lots and lots," Lily Anneé said.

"Yeah. We'd all get tummy aches if we ate all of them," Lauri Rose added, as she giggled and took a big bite out of her cupcake, then tried to lick icing off her nose.

When Richard, Mason, and Shannon's husband, David, came in the back door, Autumn knew this would be one of those fun moments she would look back on and remember the rest of her life.

"Alright, ladies," Richard said as he aimed the camera their way. "Say cupcakes!"

They followed his direction. After their tea party of peanut butter with lettuce sandwiches and egg salad sandwiches, plus several pots of tea, they boxed up the leftover cupcakes plus a few graham cracker doubles they had made with the leftover icing. Shannon told her daughters, "Tell Autumn thank you and so long for now, okay? She and Uncle Mason are leaving for a little while."

"Do you really have to go, Auntie A?"

"Yes, girls, we do. But we'll be back."

"But where will you live?"

"We'll be living with Jonothan's mom, Aunt Opal," Mason said.

"Are you going to need help packing?" Shannon asked.

"We don't have much to pack," Autumn said. "But I won't have time to clean the Carriage House before we leave."

"We have maid service for that," Eileen said as she hugged Autumn.

After all the hugs and tears, Autumn was suddenly feeling very tired. They packed and loaded the car, but once they were on the road, she started getting jittery and prayed they would be safe in Turtle Crossing.

"Autumn," Mason suggested, "I hope I'm not asking too much of you, moving us to Turtle Crossing when the baby is coming so soon. I had no idea you had such strong feelings about that place."

"The first eight years of my life were spent in some grungy parts of several towns. My mom and dad could always find a job, but he spent most of their money on alcohol and looking for a big break that never came. He hit my mom a lot. The worst times were when he came after me and she interceded. She was hurt really bad the last time I saw her. Then she was gone. I didn't get to tell her goodbye."

"I'm sorry," Mason said.

They passed a posted sign, *Turtle Crossing—10 miles*. She hadn't realized she had been this close to Turtle Crossing these past few months.

"Have *you* ever been in Turtle Crossing?" she asked softly. "Before you started this deal, I mean."

"No. At first, Richard asked me to ride along with him to look over the acreage he had purchased about three years ago. David, Sheldon and Shannon were busy with Warren Enterprises, and he said he needed an uninvolved person to keep him in a professional mode."

"I take it he is so excited about this that he can't think straight," she commented.

"Oh, you bet," Mason replied. "I know you saw the blueprints last evening, but I want you to see the area before you tell us how foolish you think we are."

"You have that much regard for what I think?"

"Honey, why do you think Richard asked you to continue working in the office as long as you felt good enough? I treasure you, and you have to admit Richard wouldn't have paid you what he did unless he thought you had earned it. You've seen how scrupulous he is about keeping tabs on the pennies let alone the dollars."

"So, when did you decide to partner up with him?"

"We were sharing ideas and visions of what we wanted to do in the future and part of that included our backgrounds. Richard is more into the development of the golf course with plans to allow for affordable homes or condos. Whereas with my experience and background in the Coast Guard, he thought we would make an excellent team. However, there may be a problem with the person who just happens to own a big chunk of land on Turtle Lake. She runs the Welby Mansion Bed and Breakfast of Turtle Crossing."

"I remember hearing something about the Welbys.

Weren't they the richest family in Turtle Crossing?" Autumn inquired.

"I don't know the history of the area. We'll be there soon. Maybe you could read through some newspaper clippings later on this evening."

When they passed the Turtle Crossing Corporation sign, Autumn began frantically looking right and left, picking out what she remembered and what had changed.

She held herself together until Mason asked, "If you're hungry, Richard and I ate at a place called Sadie's Diner when we were here on our first visit together. Brandi said it has the best milkshakes in the county and I know how you love milkshakes."

"Did you say Sadie's?" Autumn whispered. Memories of a lady called Sadie who had put food out in the alley for her for weeks became as real to her as her baby kicking up a storm. *I'm sorry, little one,* she soothed as she brushed her hand gently over her abdomen. *I didn't plan to upset you.*

"Do you have a problem with eating there?"

"No. A milkshake sounds wonderful."

Mason parked behind the diner. He helped Autumn out of the car and took that moment to kiss her.

"Ah, Mason," she blushed, and smiled. "We're in a public place. What if someone was watching?"

"What if they were? We're married. It isn't against the law," he replied as he locked the car and took her by her elbow as they maneuvered around parking barriers and curbs.

What they didn't know was—someone had spotted them, but they were looking for a nasty redheaded teenager who was expecting a baby, not a beauty like this one who had a husband.

It was cool and dark inside the diner and it took them a moment to adjust to the change in atmosphere and lighting. But it wasn't long before they were assaulted with mouthwatering smells emanating from the kitchen. Brandi had spotted them when they entered and had motioned him to join her which eliminated being put on a waiting list. The diner was packed.

When they were seated, Sadie's daughter brought coffee for Mason and a small strawberry milkshake for Autumn. The waitress said, "Brandi ordered these. I'll give you time to look over the menu," she added as she moved from table to table to refill water glasses, iced tea and hot coffee for the patrons.

"I hope you aren't feeling too tired, because we have a little dinner party scheduled for this evening. Here are Opal's house keys," Brandi continued as she handed them to Mason. "She has your room ready and said to make yourselves right at home."

Autumn didn't have to look at the menu; she ordered her childhood favorite, Sadie's memorable pot roast with potatoes and carrots.

"That sounds good to me too," Mason replied. "After we eat, I think Autumn will need to rest for awhile, and then we want to take a drive."

"Actually we have a little party planned for you two this evening," Brandi said. "But even if we didn't, I think it would be better if you wait until tomorrow. There have been some 'what if' rumors in the editorial segment of the newspaper about out-of-towners coming in and taking advantage of the locals. So lay low and don't discuss it with anyone until this evening. The party consists of a very select group of our friends and family."

"I'm going to need a part-time job while we wait for some of the contractors' bids," Mason added.

"Don't worry about that. You may be offered a couple of opportunities this evening, so the two of you just relax and enjoy this time together, because I am going to need your wife's expertise in helping me with the organization of my wedding. We have two weeks."

"Two weeks?" Autumn squealed.

"Hey, we pulled yours together in less than two hours."

The Falls

Turtle Crossing

Brandi and Jonothan bid Will adieu and stopped by the barn to greet the black stallion. It took Pepper and Night Whistle mere moments to decide they were friends. First, Night Whistle tossed his head and pranced around the paddock, showing off. Pepper barked as if applauding the horse's efforts until Ariel called the stallion back inside.

"Going by the dust on your boots," she said, "I would say you two were up scouting out the hillside."

When they weren't forthcoming with a reply, she prayed they hadn't gone near the falls. Protecting them was getting harder and harder, especially since Will had decided her place needed security. She had a feeling of unrest as though her world was about to crumble and there wasn't even anyone she could tell.

"You know, Ariel," Jonothan began, "I do believe you are keeping the best secret in Turtle Crossing."

Startled, Ariel gripped the paddock gate. They couldn't know who she was, could they? No, the sheriff would never tell anyone, not even his best deputy.

"The Welby is almost like a hidden resort up here," Jonothan continued, making a sweeping gesture that encompassed the entire grounds.

"I—Thank you," said Ariel, recovering herself.

But Brandi had seen Pepper go into alert mode with his attention focused on Ariel, and said, "Jonothan, honey, I would like to cool off with a shower and a tall frosty lemonade. Let's head back to our room."

"What's the rush?" Jonothan asked once they were out of earshot, passing by the marina. "I thought we were going to try to get to know her better."

"That was the idea, but Pepper felt something. The fur on his back was standing at attention. "I'm very interested in what Ariel is going to do after we talked with her."

"Sure enough, there she goes," Jonothan replied, craning his neck to watch Ariel's Jeep speed up Hillside Road behind them. "But why go up there?"

Ariel was beside herself. She retrieved her car and made for the falls. She hit the garage door opener, switching the Jeep over to its electric motor as the door opened, drove inside and closed the door in a matter of seconds. This was the first time she had entered the tunnels without checking the inside first, but today she was in a hurry.

There wouldn't even be time to visit Sadie. It was too late in the day.

She backed into an alcove, switched off the Jeep, and slipped out and around Bend #8 just in time to hear the sheriff say, "We're going to have to make some quick decisions before this bunch gets a real toehold on Turtle Crossing. Someone is in town, causing a stir which has thrown a monkey wrench into their immediate plans, which may be good. I don't think either side knows exactly who the others are or why they are here."

"When is your next meeting with the men who plan to expand Turtle Crossing Lake?" the city council president asked.

"Tomorrow," the sheriff replied.

"Great. Get back with us immediately afterward."

"I'll call you. The sooner we open this up to the public, especially the Historical Society, the sooner we will be rid of the illegal drug running."

Shortly after the men dispersed, Ariel was certain she heard echoes from beyond Tunnel #6, though the council president had left by a completely different route.

She knew she was taking a chance when she signaled the sheriff, but he was discreet as he slipped into a recess in the wall while the others departed through Tunnel #7. As soon as he joined Ariel, she had trouble containing her frustration and anger, and hissed, "Someone broke into the suite where your favorite deputy and her fiancée were staying. And now Will Fox and a whole team of detectives are camped out on Hillside Road."

Without giving the Sheriff a chance to respond, she fished in her purse. "Here is the tape of the two men who were at my place for over three weeks. When Will showed up, they couldn't wait to check out. However, Will's men had already installed a camera. I thought you might need this before you hold a town meeting."

The Sheriff accepted the tape in startled silence. He had rarely seen Ariel so discomposed.

"No matter what, I think you should tell the townspeople what is going on. Show the slides and the future plans. Let them decide if they want the tunnels to be a drug distribution center or a historical center—something unique they can take pride in. We need to take charge before it's too late."

"Ariel," he said, "isn't it about time you took off the mask and took the next step?"

"I'll think about it. I need to get back."

Jonothan was peering out their apartment window, binoculars pressed to his eyes, when he said, "Our disappearing hostess just arrived. No wonder we couldn't hear her when she returned the last time. That car has an electric motor. Makes sense," he reflected. "It not only is quieter, but the exhaust in parts of the tunnel would be like running a gasoline engine in a closed garage.

"Hey," Brandi said distractedly, "instead of worrying about what kind of motor she has, come over here and help me decide where we're going to get married."

"You mean you've more than one place in mind?" he teased.

"Actually, I have three."

"I would marry you today, right here, right now. But, I know that's not what you want."

"No. The first time I married, I felt rushed and I had no say in anything—from where we would get married, to which dress I would wear, to who was invited. You agreed with your mom on the colors for the attendants and we agreed to let Marcie take care of the flowers. Wendy has our invitations ready. She just needs the place and time," Brandi concluded.

"And the honeymoon?" he asked softly as he gathered her in his arms for a kiss.

"Oh well, I thought that was already decided."

"That will depend on the date. It may already be reserved."

"Oh not again," she groaned when someone knocked on their door.

When Jonothan opened the door, they were both surprised to see the sheriff and Ariel. "To what do we owe this pleasure?" Jonothan asked.

"We need to talk," the sheriff said as he guided Ariel in the room ahead of him. Ariel on the other hand, seemed uncertain, and Brandi felt the woman would have rushed right back out of the room, except that the sheriff kept his hand on her elbow as though she were a ship he had to control.

"Brandi, are you aware that your brother is expected to visit Turtle Crossing in a couple of days?"

"No. Why?"

Jonothan was suspiciously quiet. When he said

nothing, Brandi asked, "Did you know anything about this visit?"

"Yes, but Richard and I wanted his real estate plans kept quiet for awhile. You know how rumors run as rampant as an unguided missile in this town. I've heard everything from a downtown factory to a racetrack down Main Street."

"You've got to be kidding. So, what will he be doing in Turtle Crossing? He and his wife are expecting a baby in a few weeks. Should she be traveling?" Brandi asked.

"Her doctor gave his approval. For the time being they will be staying at my mom's place."

"Jonothan!" Brandi cried in outrage. "How long have you known?"

"About that last part? Only a few hours. Your brother wanted to surprise you."

"Oh, I'll act surprised, but what does his visit have to do with us?"

"We want you to have your wedding reception here at the Welby and your wedding at the Falls," Ariel suggested softly.

But as she spoke, Will pushed through the door behind the sheriff and Ariel, and blew his stack. "You are not going to make a mockery of their wedding. I will not allow it."

"Will? What's happening here?" Brandi demanded, and thought, *This can't be happening again…Will won't allow it? Jonothan and I will decide!*

"Sheriff, why are you and Ariel here?" Jonothan asked as he moved forward and put his arm around Brandi, more to calm her down than control her.

The sheriff answered, "The City Council needs a big event to appeal to the voters to pass a levy to develop a section of the tunnels into a historical venue. There have always been family stories that the tunnels were once a part of the Underground Railroad. Many of these areas were kept so quiet in the past that the information was not all handed down. And sadly some of these locations have since disappeared."

"Tell her the rest of it," Will insisted.

The sheriff had heard of Will and thanked his lucky stars he had never had to cross him until now. "Brandi, there is something you need to know before we go any further."

He handed her a sheaf of papers which she accepted and quickly scanned. The sheriff, it seemed, understood a great deal more about her life outside the police force than she ever would have suspected.

"So you knew I had another meeting this evening?" Brandi asked

"Yes, and I enthusiastically approve. I would like you to be the emissary between the department and the Shadow Angels."

"Jonothan? Did you know about this too?"

This time he shook his head. "It's the first I've heard about their plans. Sheriff, Brandi and I are not getting married for other people's amusement."

"Jonothan!" the Sheriff yelled. "No one wants to see your wedding become a three-ring circus, but if it helps convince the townspeople what is best for this community, then I think that you both will see the need for it."

"But where does a wedding even fit into all this?" Brandi asked. "What's the bottom line?"

"The bottom line is that a group of outsiders have been attempting to use our tunnels as a headquarters for the distribution of drugs, and if we can generate enough goodwill in town to renovate the tunnels as a tourist attraction, the drug traffickers will have no choice but to pull up stakes and find another sewer in which to do their dirty business."

"Well, Sheriff, you don't pull any punches, do you?"

"You know I don't," he replied.

"Do you have proof that drugs are their true agenda? Brandi asked, her eyes on the sheriff.

He finally broke eye contact, but not before she saw indecision in his eyes. She looked at Will and knew he had seen it too. Will already knew that the men who had hurriedly checked out of the Welby the night Brandi and Jonothan arrived had their own agenda, which was why he had men watching them.

If Brandi had learned anything about relationships, it was not making decisions without discussing them first. "Jonothan?" she said, turning to her fiancée. "What do *you* think?"

"Honey, at least we'll have a good crowd," he chuckled. "I'm not going to be looking at anyone but you that day, and if it helps your brother, we have to do it."

This was the last answer Brandi expected. "What does my brother, Mason, have to do with any of this?"

"Richard and Mason have extensive plans for the expansion and fulfillment of Mr. Welby's lifetime dream, which included cleaning up that bottomland playground for mosquitoes. Until Ariel opened this complex to the public, there wasn't this level of waterway open for swimming, boating and fishing. The sheriff is right; Turtle Crossing needs this development."

"Ariel," Brandi asked, "What do you have to say about all this?"

"I have mixed feelings but nothing gets accomplished when you sit on the fence either. I know that from hard experience."

"Do you have the capability to have lights installed in the Tunnels?" Brandi asked.

"Yes," Ariel replied. "I know lights were used in the past; so installing new ones shouldn't be a problem.

"Remember, I told you when I was little," Jonothan added, "I dreamt about the tornado and remembered the lights. When the lights went out, the only place that wasn't pitch black was around the entrance where the rain blew in. I thought some of the lights were turned back on, but it must have been the sun shining after the storm had passed. I never gave it another thought until recently. Imagine those old tunnels cleaned up and strung with lights and garlands of flowers," he said softly.

Ariel looked pleased for the first time since she had entered their apartment. "Your wedding will be one of the most beautiful weddings that Turtle Crossing has ever witnessed, and I can't wait to meet your brother and his wife," she added.

Revelations

Turtle Crossing

Autumn and Mason left Sadie's Diner and went directly to Opal's house. "Sorry about the change in plans," Mason said. "The meeting this evening was as much a surprise to me as it was to you."

"I gathered that," she said, staring through the car's windows as Mason took his time driving to Opal's. The buildings looked different, yet...*Graham Real Estate—Bea's Place*, she read. "I remember a Miss Bea. She had a gentle loving heart and there was magic in her voice when she read stories to us children. Turtle Crossing dreams and memories sometimes get mixed up for me, but I think I curled up on her lap—just once, mind you, and I felt loved and protected."

However, a couple more blocks down on a side street she read, *Children's Services*. A chill went up her spine and she protectively put both of her hands over her abdomen. "Are you in pain?" Mason asked. When she shook her head no, he asked, "You're sure you're okay?"

"I'm fine. I just had a not so happy memory."

"Tell me about it," Mason asked, still concerned about whether bringing her here was the best idea.

But she only shook her head. "There's Opal's house," she said, pointing out towards the windshield. "It is so lovely and inviting. My mom always wanted an asparagus fern growing on her front porch some day. She had a lot of someday-dreams. I have a few too. I can picture our house with a porch just like this one, rocking my baby on warm summer days, watching fireflies on summer nights, listening to a soft breeze sighing through the trees—and you beside us. And we'll need you to sing the lullabies because I can't carry a tune. I'll just hum along."

Mason smiled, thinking, *I've been afraid to dream of a home of my own...but why not? I have a wife with a child on the way. I never thought I could love a child that wasn't biologically mine, but I do. Perhaps it's because a couple chose me to adopt. And after I felt they just might love me, they found out they were going to have a child of their own and couldn't keep me. First my mom didn't want me, then another family didn't either. If Autumn wants a house like Opal's, I'll move mountains to see that happen. And not just for her—but for our children and for us.*

He swung his Jeep into Opal's driveway and pulled into the garage, which had been left open. He didn't want to tell Autumn that Brandi had instructed him to park in the garage closest to the house and not linger outside.

"Honey, after tonight we'll know whether that dream is near or far, but for now you had better lie down and take a nap. We had a long drive today and I don't know what to expect this evening."

She had been considering taking her usual evening walk but now thought better of it. She wasn't certain whether she was ready to walk any of the streets of Turtle Crossing just yet anyhow. When they had crossed the alley behind Sadie's Diner, Autumn had wanted to run and hide. But the Tumble In Bar that had once been behind and across the alley from Sadie's was gone. The space had become a parking lot, where the sun could chase away the shadows, but not the memories. She prayed the memories she had buried for so long could stay buried forever, but they kept racing through her mind until she finally fell asleep.

Mason was keyed up. There was so much riding on their visit here in the town where Autumn's memories were anything but pleasant. And Richard was counting on him to smooth the ruffled feathers of a handful of people who were against change.

Mason had carried his and Autumn's suitcases and boxes into Opal's house but he was still restless. Then realizing that pacing back and forth was fruitless, he sat down at Opal's kitchen table with several back issues of Turtle Crossing's weekly newspapers. Editorials were about 50% for and 50% against growth in Turtle Crossing.

A couple of hours later, with notes in hand, he heard Opal's key in the door and rose to greet her.

"Welcome, Mason," Opal greeted when she walked in the door. "Sorry I wasn't home when you arrived, but I had a few little odds and ends to take care of at school. Is our little mama-to-be still resting?"

"Yes," Mason replied. "And before she joins us, I need to know how much people here know about us. Did you know that the grandfather of Autumn's baby had made plans to take her baby and raise it, which is why she ran away from the Home for Unexpected Births?"

"And you have been protecting her ever since," Opal added. "I had no idea that things had gone that far. But what is it you're not saying?" Opal asked.

"Yes. I'd like to know the answer to that too," Autumn said from the doorway.

Mason spun around to face her. "Nothing I want you to worry about, Honey," he said after a moment.

"Don't you understand? The more I know, the better."

"All right!" Mason exploded. "We've been tailed ever since we arrived and I felt someone was watching me when I unloaded the car."

Autumn was surprised to hear him raise his voice. She knew he was frustrated, but never had she seen him this angry. "And you still want to stay in this town?" She couldn't even think Turtle Crossing without feeling nauseous.

Opal wasted no time dialing Brandi. "Did you put a tail on your brother?"

"Yes."

"I'm surprised you didn't tell them."

"I didn't want them getting any surprises."

"Then I'm afraid your plan didn't work very well," Opal said dryly. "Does that mean someone is watching the house right now?"

"Yes."

"I thought as much. Are we driving my car or Mason's this evening? And what time are we leaving?"

"Neither. Plans have changed. I'll be driving into your carport around five and will pick up all three of you."

"That was Brandi," Opal began. "She said she did have someone tailing you, but only since you left Sadie's Diner.

"I heard," Mason said, glowering. "And she is picking us up in about an hour."

"Why all the intrigue, Opal?" Autumn asked. "There must be some reason why Brandi is being so cautious?"

"Yes, Honey," Mason added. "She doesn't want us out talking to people in town until after the dinner party this evening. Apparently all will be discussed then. How are you feeling?"

"Rested. Opal, can you tell us a little about the people who will be at this dinner party?"

"Suffice it to say that the Shadow Angels and the Blue Fox Detective and Security Agency will have representatives there. Understand that who you see and what is discussed is to be kept in the strictest confidence."

"If they have a plan to protect Mason, my baby and me, I can be a clam when it comes to keeping secrets. I grew up on them," she grumbled. Then she added, "But there is no guarantee how well kept a secret remains. When others are involved, the secrecy alone cannot always protect you. The last words I remember hearing my dad yell at my mom was, 'You bitch. You didn't hear a thing, right? You keep your mouth shut! You tell no one, right?' That night he hit her so hard she fell into the closet right beside where I was hiding. I heard a door slam and my mom's eyes were all swollen and red. Her throat was red and her voice was raspy when she—when she—" Autumn stammered, "when she whispered, 'Go! Now! You crawl out the bedroom window and go to Grandma's house. Hurry! Go Now! Go! Now!' I never saw her again."

She hesitated a moment and Mason and Opal sat staring at her as she stared out into a past that broke their hearts.

"I kissed her on the cheek and when I touched her neck her ear ring fell off and slipped onto my pinky finger. I laid my hand on her neck. Her heart was still beating in rhythm to mine. I hid behind the shrubs in our backyard for several nights, but the house was always dark. Mom's radio was silent. The carport was empty. I knew they were gone. The moon was full two more times before I ate a daytime meal. I don't know why the welfare lady told me my mom had died or why she was so angry with *me*."

"But where were your grandparents?"

"I couldn't find them. I didn't know their real names. I think Mom used to tell me stories about them, but I thought they were imaginary. You know something she wanted me to believe in so I wouldn't feel so lonely."

Not wanting to hurt her further, Opal said, "If you'll excuse me a few moments, I need to shower and change.

Just relax. There is mint sun tea and lemonade in the fridge. Glasses are in the pansy stained glass cupboard."

"Thanks," Autumn replied. "Your kitchen is a work of art. Whoever did your stained glass has the touch of a master."

Opal waved and said, "Thanks. I've never been called a master of anything, except my degree in education. But stained glass is one of my passions."

Autumn relaxed as she studied not only Opal's cupboard doors, but a cabinet, several lamps, a couple of windows and partitions that framed her front door. The setting sun angled through jeweled prisms and brought a smile to Autumn's face. Her profile was regal.

Mason wondered whether her mother really had died. If so, where was she buried, and who were Autumn's grandparents?

While Opal's shower cooled her body, her thoughts were with the troubled young woman in her kitchen. Given Autumn's story, there were only three families in town that she and her mother could have come from. As Opal dressed after her shower, she decided to look through old school annuals she had started collecting for the Genealogical section of the town library.

Brandi pulled into the carport at 5:00 as promised. "Where's your vehicle, sis?" Mason asked as he assisted Autumn into the front passenger seat and folded his height into the back.

"Living on a corner has its advantages. I parked my car in Opal's old garage around back. This is her car."

"Will your fiancée be joining us this evening?" Autumn asked.

"Yes. Jonothan and Opal will be following us."

"I wouldn't be surprised if he had an appointment on his wedding day." Mason teased.

"Just so he gets to the church on time," Brandi added, enjoying the fun banter.

When they arrived at Aunt Willi's house, they were instantly intrigued with her home. It had been built of local stone and oak and appeared to have grown out of a hillside amidst trees and rocks. The well lit flagstone path wound down and around a walled off section which opened into an outdoor garden just a few yards from a creek that curved around the garden and disappeared into the darkness.

Lights from the interior beckoned and Autumn suddenly stopped midstride. "Mason, what's the rush? I don't know whether I'm ready to tell a bunch of strangers what a mess I've made of my life—and yours."

"Oh, don't disappoint them," Jonothan coaxed as he slipped up behind them. "You and Mason are the honored guests this evening. We'll let you lead the way, Mom. Brandi and I will follow."

But Autumn didn't move. "Brandi," she said, her smile fading. "We haven't done anything against the law."

Brandi looked surprised. "I know that."

"Then why do you have so many men watching us?" she asked, sweeping her arm to indicate all of the supposedly hidden guards from Will Fox's team. "Surely we don't need this much protection."

Brandi and Jonothan exchanged a quick glance. "Better safe than sorry, right?" she said at last. "Everything should become clear at the meeting."

They entered Willi's home in a line with Autumn in front and Brandi at the rear. Mason and Autumn were escorted immediately to the meeting room.

"Jonothan," Brandi said quietly, "I'm going to ask Jewel if she knows if any tunnel library entrances have been changed recently."

"Alright," he muttered back. "I need to talk to mom." Something about seeing Autumn in her blonde wig had tickled a memory. Who did she remind him of?

But Opal had seen Bea and she had her own questions to ask. "I've started looking through old Turtle Crossing High School Annuals. There weren't too many Turtle Crossing graduates—right out of high school who had a daughter."

"Who are you looking for?" Bea asked.

"That's the problem. I'm not certain yet." But something about Bea's appearance distracted Opal. "Say Bea, is your necklace new?"

"No. I found it a while back, but was nervous about wearing it until I found the perfect chain. I didn't want to lose it again."

"Didn't your hubby, Abe buy an exact replica of that very nugget as a wedding present for you?"

"Yes. He had it engraved—*Abe loves Bea*. He told me someone stole it on our wedding day and because it was one-of-a-kind design, he assumed it would never be found."

"I understand," Opal assured her. "You only had eyes for Abe."

"Didn't they blame the theft on the organist, Homer Thomas?"

"What ever happened to Homer T?" Bea asked.

"He bought your grandparents' old place right after you and Abe married."

"Really?" Bea replied. "His name isn't on the title. Some corporation supposedly bought it."

"Willi," Opal asked, catching the hostess as she walked past. "Is your magnifying glass in its usual place?"

"Sure. Help yourself."

When Opal and Bea headed for Willi's private office, Jonothan followed. Opal extracted Willi's huge magnifying glass from the desk and said, "Bea may I see your necklace?"

The three of them crowded around and peered down at the reverse side of the medallion. The words were slightly dulled by time but easily legible, *Abe loves Bea.*

When they read the faint initials, Bea's heart was filled with nostalgia, remembering her astonishment when she had felt the indentions, and wanted to believe it was real.

"You're right Bea," Opal said. "Abe was so excited he showed it to me before your wedding. And now you want to find the jerk that stole it, right?"

Bea's nostalgic tears turned to anger. "You don't suppose? No! Homer T wouldn't do that to me."

"Wouldn't do what, Miss Bea?" Jonothan asked.

"He wouldn't do anything to frighten me, or steal a gift that Abe had designed just for me."

"Maybe not," Jonothan said, "But his son would. He's always looking for easy money."

Bea's eyes widened. "Remember, I said this guy who ran through the alley that day was slight of build like Homer T when he was younger?"

"And that's where you found this heart-shaped medallion?" Jonothan asked softly.

When she nodded, he replied, "I'll look into it. I mean, Brandi and I will."

Opal hugged her son. Bea dried her eyes and added, "It can wait until after the wedding. And in the meantime, I will file a report with the Sheriff's office."

The Meeting
Turtle Crossing

While Jonothan and Opal hurried off to discuss something with Bea, Brandi led Mason and Autumn into the main room for introductions. The sound of birdsong—muted, but cheerful filled the room. Autumn was looking around to see if someone had left a window or door open somewhere.

"You won't find any wild canaries in here," Brandi whispered to Autumn. "Willi likes to record her backyard friends and then uses it for background sound while we shuffle around and fill our plates."

"Oh. I was certain that a goldfinch was sitting on my shoulder warbling a personal message," Autumn said as she turned around and smiled at Mason.

"She has a vivid imagination," Mason commented as

Willi entered and announced the people could start filling their plates at the buffet.

What a nice surprise, Brandi thought. *I immediately loved Autumn like a sister. So is this what has been missing in my life? Between Jonothan, Mason and now Autumn; I'm beginning to feel as though being a part of a family is a real possibility.*

"Are you nervous about talking at the meeting?" she asked aloud. When Autumn nodded, Brandi continued, "That's understandable, but you'll be fine. The hardest part of the evening will probably be deciding what to choose from all this delicious food."

Autumn smiled and tried a sample of the cooling strawberry Jell-O swirled with pieces of angel food cake and whipped cream, plus a glass of ice water with a slice of lemon. Mason pulled out her chair before sitting down beside her.

At this point Willi called for attention. "If everyone will find a seat, we still have a couple of things to cover this evening. As usual, if you have questions, please jot them down and if it takes us until midnight we will either answer your questions, take your suggestions under advisement or refer you to the appropriate person to help you work it out. We'll start with old business first. Will, do you have Wendy's report on the series of stories she plans to run in the Turtle Crossing *Weekly News?*"

"Yes," he replied as he stood up and read Wendy's notes, "The headlines on the front page will read, 'Coming Soon: A Pictorial History of Turtle Crossing, The Turtle Crossing Library,' and 'The Welby Mansion Hosts the Wedding of the Decade.'" He sat down and said, "Brandi?"

Brandi nodded her head. "There are several reasons why we are waiting to release this information to the public until the day before our wedding day."

It was the first time she had publicly announced her marriage plans, and she flushed bright red when the room broke into applause accompanied by a few whistles. A few seats away, Judge Oglethorpe half-rose to shake hands with Jonothan.

Composing herself, she continued, "Our wedding flyer will launch full coverage of the interesting and conflicting emotions involving the tunnels.

"On another topic, Will has been assisting us with the research of two men who have been hanging around town for several weeks. Their likenesses appeared on the tunnel tapes and we think they were the culprits who broke into Jonothan's room and my room at the Welby just a few days ago."

Brandi heard her brother's gasp, patted his hand and explained further. "We were out for a walk when this happened. They didn't trash our rooms, just our luggage. And nothing was compromised," she added for the regulars. "So far, these two have been ruled out as having drug trafficking connections; however when Will and his crew showed up, these two were in a huge rush to check out. So much in fact, they almost forgot their luggage."

"They are under surveillance," Will clarified. "The same rule regarding interactions with these men is still in place." Everyone nodded to show their understanding.

They had all been handed a photo and profile on both men, but were not to attempt to detain them unless someone's life was at risk.

"The front cover of *The Winthrop Weekly News* insert will be an open invitation to our friends in Turtle Crossing to attend our wedding which is scheduled to be at the Welby Falls. However, only those here this evening and the owner of the Welby know that the ceremony will be held in the Welby Chapel."

"I don't mean to interrupt," Miss Bea said, "but do you mean the chapel behind the falls? Didn't the Welbys also choose to be married there?"

The room fell quiet and Jonothan asked, "How do you know about this? Do you have any physical records?"

"I most certainly do. I have a lovely photo of the double wedding of the Welbys and my mom and dad," Bea added proudly.

"Would you consider allowing this photo to be featured on the front cover of this insert?" Jonothan asked.

"If they were here, Mom and Dad would love it. They were lifetime friends with the Welbys," Bea replied. "They would be thrilled to be a part of our plans to not only protect the people of this town but to put those who break the law behind bars."

"Where was the photo taken?" Brandi asked softly, so excited about this revelation she could barely contain her feelings.

"It was taken in front of the falls. I've heard it would have been rather dark in the chapel even for a flash photograph," Bea added.

Bea was distracted momentarily when the young bride of Brandi's brother turned her head a certain way. Bea had mistakenly identified more than a few young women as the little girl she had tried to adopt—often enough that she finally quit looking for the little girl she had wanted to adopt and raise as her own.

But when Mason's wife smiled, Bea was pretty certain she knew her. She would remember that smile anywhere, whether the girl's hair was blonde, blue, or bright pink. If Autumn wasn't that little girl whom she had loved so much, she had to be related to her.

"How do you know how light or dark it was in the Chapel?" Brandi asked.

"Um. I'm sorry," Bea replied. "I was distracted momentarily. Your question was how do I know it was a bit on the dark side? Because Judge Oglethorpe's dad performed the ceremony and talked about all the lanterns they needed. He said it was one of those times when a good memory and a flashlight came in handy otherwise he wouldn't have been able to get through the vows properly."

"Alright, moving right along," Willi announced, "It is time to give the floor to our guests of the evening."

Autumn stood and began, "Good evening. My name is Mrs. Autumn Davies. I was born in Turtle Crossing but coming back here hasn't been easy. Moments I thought had been erased from my memory have been surprising me at every turn. However, I can't let that interfere with the safety of our baby. We're concerned that someone may still be planning to steal my—*our* baby," she amended with a smile at Mason, "when it is born, even though I am over eighteen and married. The grandparents of my baby placed me in a home for unwed mothers and paid the bill with the understanding that my baby would be theirs. I never signed any papers to that effect. My foster father wanted the family name to continue, but without me."

Autumn hesitated.

Mason stood, took her hand, and whispered, "Do you want me to finish?"

She shook her head, gripped his hand, took a deep breath, and continued, "I telephoned my baby's father insisting that I needed his help. He came immediately, on the condition that in exchange for his help, I would allow him to forget that I or his child had ever existed. Because he and his wife were expecting a baby, he gave me money to do whatever with *my* baby. I gave him papers to sign my release while the administrator was away. What he signed also released him of his rights to my child. However I'm not certain how legal that paper was because I wasn't of age when he signed it."

Looking at Brandi, she continued, "After leaving that home together, we drove into a snow squall off Lake Erie. It was like driving blind. The car went into a spin and he lost control. When I came to, I was alone in the car. Mason rescued me; saving my life and the life of our baby. He has been looking after us ever since. It was Mason's idea for me to masquerade as a guy. And Lady Ashley of Sunrise taught me how to use makeup, a wig and hat, pretending to be Mason's Grandpa Andy," she added, lowering her voice.

Mason smiled and squeezed her hand and she continued. "Thanks go to Opal for this maternity dress. It's so much less confining and cooler than the bib overalls." *And feminine,* she thought.

Bea stood, cautiously, her insides shaking, her eyes locked on Autumn. "You grew up in Turtle Crossing?" Heart pounding, afraid to be disappointed once again but needing to be certain of the identity of this young woman, Bea's voice came out in a whisper. "Are you still wearing a wig now? Is your hair really red?"

"I feel safer, keeping up part of the pretense," Autumn replied, thinking something about the woman was familiar.

"Its okay," Mason encouraged.

She nodded and he helped her slip off the blonde wig and pair of thick glasses she didn't really need.

Have my prayers really been answered? Bea wondered, then blurted out, "Are you Autumn, my little red-haired girl?" She couldn't bear to be wrong again.

Autumn stared at her for several seconds. "Miss Bea?" she said, her voice barely a whisper.

Bea couldn't move fast enough as she rounded the table and rushed over to Autumn—both of them in tears.

Shocked silence greeted this reunion. Willi recovered herself first. "We're due a coffee break," she announced loudly. Let's take ten."

"Oh, bless you, dear child," Bea said holding Autumn tight.

"Is it really you?" Autumn asked. "I never forgot how nice you were to me, and have wondered if I would ever see you again."

Bea couldn't take her hands or eyes off Autumn, as she brushed her hair with gentle hands, then took her hands in hers and dried her eyes. "I never stopped looking for you," Bea said softly.

"I've missed you too," Autumn replied. "You and Mason are the only people who truly loved me, besides my mom of course."

"I feel honored to be in such good company," Bea said.

While everyone else was enjoying the heartwarming reunion, Will left the room to make a very important call. Marcie saw him leave and followed. By the time she caught up with him he had already dialed the telephone in Willi's office. She closed the door when she heard his angry outburst. "You told me you were pulling the search, so what are a couple of your hired goons still doing in Turtle Crossing?"

He listened for the reply, his knuckles white on the receiver. Marcie had never seen him so unhinged.

"Well, if the public image of your family is so important to you, then perhaps you should keep something else in mind. If you or the goons you hired so much as make an attempt to do anything to this baby or its family, your beloved son may find himself looking at jail time for statutory rape!" he screamed into the phone, and slammed it down.

"Will?" Marcie asked. "What is going on?"

He spun around, breathing hard. "I don't like being used or lied to!"

"Is this the case you took all those months ago? Didn't you do any research before you took the assignment?"

"Of course," he snapped.

Marcie and Will had been and continued to be friends. She knew him well. And knew she was one of the few people he trusted enough to allow his temper to show.

"But you knew you were supposed to take a baby from its mother?"

The question and his respect for her forced him to make eye contact. "Yes. I could only imagine how I would feel if a little gold-digger was holding my child for ransom." He closed his eyes, calming himself. "I've taken care of it."

With that, he brushed past Marcie into the hallway and back toward the meeting room. She followed him a moment later.

"Please be seated," Aunt Willi announced. "Our other guest has a brief presentation and would like feedback. Mason?"

"Good Evening. I'm Mason Davies, brother of Brandi. Three years ago Richard Warren came to Turtle Crossing looking for the right color brick to repair and expand one of the Warren properties which had been damaged by a nasty tornado. On his return trip, he saw this property with a For Sale sign in the field and stopped. The owner took him for a drive and told him about his dreams, but admitted he had run out of time to fulfill them.

"Using some of this man's vision, Richard has been working on a plan ever since. He purchased the property, drew up the blueprints and acquired the permits, as well as your township trustees' approval. What he has not shared with the public is that someone else has been falsely claiming they own the property, and have been promising real jobs. And, that they know more what this town needs than some group from out of town.

"What sort of plans does Mr. Warren have?" Willi asked.

"Let me show you," Mason suggested as he spread the blueprints on the central table where everyone could gather round. Pointing out locations he began, "Richard asked me to design a marina where we could give water safety lessons on boating and the use of proper gear, as well as rescue."

Willi looked closer and exclaimed, "Some of these were drawn up by Daniel Welby himself. His ancestors platted the town of Turtle Crossing. His great grandfather was this town's first mayor. This should put a stop to those who are trying to undermine your plans for a golf course and opening up the expansion of Turtle Lake to the public, so they don't have to go somewhere else for this type of relaxation."

Will nodded at Willi, stood, and, glancing at Brandi and Jonothan, announced, "It also looks like your wedding will be one that Turtle Crossing will long remember."

Others echoed him, but deep down Will wasn't happy with using his friends' wedding as a means to an end. Which was why he still planed to question the two men that trashed Brandi and Jonothan's luggage at the Welby.

Ariel's Decision
Turtle Crossing

Jonothan and Brandi had been relaxing at Ariel's apartment and were feeling a little restless, wrestling with the possibility that their very public wedding above Turtle Crossing could turn into a fiasco.

"At least there aren't any questions about your dress," Jonothan commented.

"But how do your Mom and Autumn know what I want?"

"You said that you accidentally left your wedding journal at Shannon's last week. Well, apparently your brother's wife is a whiz at design. She is eager to show you samples of fabric and her designs. She combined the choices you had marked on several magazine cutouts and stuffed in an envelope. When it fell out of your journal, the cutouts scattered all over the floor. Then she combined her dream wedding gown with yours. She needs your approval today."

"Today?"

"Yes, as in an hour from now," Jonothan added. Will's group will be taking charge of security and parking and the Shadow Angels have committed to taking charge of the buffet and inside security. What else do we need to check off our list?"

"The all important date and time," Brandi added.

They were interrupted by a knock on their door. This time Ariel was alone. "I would like to take you to the falls," she suggested.

However before the door closed, Will joined them and said, "Not without me!"

"Fine," Ariel replied. "Please come in and close the door," she said to Will.

Her tone of voice had much more impact than if she had yelled. Her body emanated courage, her eyes filled with resolve and sadness.

"Please, may we sit down?" she requested, as she removed a letter from her apron pocket. She carefully unfolded the fragile letter that was yellowed with age. "This is a letter that my aunt left in the safe of The Welby. However, I hadn't read it until this morning. It says, *Never reveal what you know about the tunnels. Whoever does will most assuredly meet with pain and suffering.*"

She carefully folded the letter again. "But now I disagree. Sometimes secrets can cause suffering too. The people of Turtle Crossing deserve to know more about the history of not only Turtle Crossing but how their ancestors stood up for what they believed in and in the process saved many lives."

"Are you referring to the local stories that the tunnels may have been a part of the Underground Railroad?" Jonothan asked.

"Yes. And by bringing light back to the tunnels, your wedding will encourage positive discussions. It is my hope that this will put a stop to the rumors that are flying all over town, and give them a chance to see that the tunnels are not something they need to fear but to be joyful about and support our growth plans for Turtle Crossing."

What she failed to reveal was that she would be putting herself and her family in danger. But time had taught her that she couldn't look back—or continue to expect others to put together the broken pieces of her life. She had made the choice to marry a man who had his dark and lazy side and she would probably always pay for that. It was time to take action and pray she wouldn't have to leave town again.

"Brandi, ever since you told me about seeing the lights behind the falls, I knew then I had run out of time," Ariel said.

"Time for what?"

"Time that I wasted, doing nothing and hoping someone else would make the necessary decisions and I could just watch from the sidelines."

"And now?" Will asked. "I have a feeling that you are not telling us everything, but there comes a time in life when you have to start trusting someone."

"Can you understand that for three years, my life has been peaceful and uneventful," Ariel said.

"But were you really living, or just existing?"

Ariel spun around and looked at Will as though she were afraid he knew something she didn't want him to know. It was apparent she was afraid of someone, and everyone in the room knew how that felt.

"You've turned my entire life topsy-turvy!" Ariel yelled. She calmed herself before explaining more. "Before all these recent happenings no one knew or cared what was going on here at the Welby—or to me for that matter. But ever since the three of you arrived, I feel like I've been propelled into the eye of a hurricane. Even the Sheriff's Department has become involved."

"Then why do you want us to get married at the Welby Falls?" Jonothan asked. "That will just draw more attention to you."

"Because I have an idea, but I need your help to pull it off. But before that, there is a very good reason why I want you to visit the falls before nightfall. Are you ready? Bring your flashlights. I have everything else we'll need loaded in my Jeepster."

"If you don't mind," Will replied. "I will drive up to our site and then ride with you from there."

"Not at all," Ariel replied. Her nerves were strung tight as a drum, and her shoulders and neck ached as though she had pulled double guard duty.

Pepper had been quiet all during the time that Ariel was in the room, but when she led everyone out, he followed, unseen by Brandi or anyone else. And surprisingly, instead of going with Brandi, he jumped in the truck with Will. "Pepper, nice of you to join me but why are you with me instead of your partner?"

Pepper just stared straight ahead and didn't so much as wag his tail, but his antennae ears were on alert. *No wonder Brandi said he is as much human as he is dog,* Will thought.

Will drove up to the Blue Fox home base and notified his crew where he could be reached and quickly joined Ariel, Jonothan and Brandi. Pepper had been with him the entire time, but as he looked around, Pepper was nowhere to be found. He decided not to mention this to Brandi. The dog could take care of itself.

Once Will was in the Jeep with the others, Brandi turned to Ariel and said, "Now what did you want to show us?"

"You'll see in a moment," Ariel said. They drove the last few minutes to the hidden entrance to the falls in silence.

Jonothan squeezed Brandi's hand when Ariel approached the same entrance they had found the day before. Ariel hopped out, pushed the button, the door opened, she drove inside, pushed another button and the door closed.

Her guest's brief glance of the Welby Chapel lit by waning daylight disappeared in the blink of an eye as they struggled to acclimate their vision to the near absence of light. It was dark as a near moonless night, with a sliver of light creeping high up through the backside of the Falls. The Welby Chapel was the size of a four car garage, but with a vaulted ceiling.

They had just adjusted to the sounds of nothing but the falls when Ariel turned on her floodlight and said, "Each of you slip a pair of these knee-high rubber boots over your shoes. Watch your step when you get out of my vehicle. The floor here is like trying to walk in freshly plowed soil after a rain."

Using her huge floodlight, she aimed it at the wall just ten feet from the falls. The wall looked dingy and unappealing. The walls were coated with a heavy layer of squishy, slimy substance. However, as she moved her light closer and closer to where the walls were wet from the splashing of water from the falls, the substance had been washed away to reveal something much more beautiful.

"I want you to see what is beneath this black muck."

"Bat droppings," Will said, squinting—unhappy about disturbing their habitat as he scanned his light up into the gloom.

"The bats left about ten years ago," Ariel continued. "I don't know why. Brandi, shine your light over here."

Ariel picked up a bucket, dipped a sponge in the soapy solution and swiped it across the rough wall. The results were astonishing.

"It looks like gold," Jonothan said softly. "Fool's Gold. It's Pyrite. The red, yellow, gold and brown are forms of the iron sulfide in the rock which can be found in some limestone quarries. Some calcite materials can be found in sandstone caves," he said, as if reciting an old lesson.

"Sounds like some of your momma's teaching," Ariel said, her beautiful, teasing smile taking everyone by surprise. "But, yes. I was thinking that clean wall of pure Pyrite would make a lovely backdrop for a wedding."

"Lovely," Brandi agreed, though something was puzzling her. She had seen someone else with that smile. But who? Shaking her head, she said, "We can't just wash this stuff into Turtle Lake. It's pure fertilizer."

"That's the dilemma. Any ideas?"

"I know someone who cleans out septic tanks, but the hose wouldn't be long enough to suction the runoff from outside the tunnels," Jonothan suggested.

"The soap I'm using would be safe enough to spray on my roses," Ariel added.

Jonothan and Will looked at each other and Will said, "We'll find a way."

"Fine," Brandi said looking at Ariel, "but I'm curious about something?"

"What's that?" Ariel asked.

"Can we block off the tunnels from the chapel so we don't have to worry about someone venturing off and getting lost?"

"That won't be a problem," Ariel added. "The Welbys had a very natural looking wall built and installed to keep people from ever finding the chapel. Though there were always rumors about it."

"That's it, then," Brandi began. "Our wedding invitations will read, *to be held at The Welby Chapel*. Now that ought to be enough incentive to get the whole town here in attendance. How many people can we seat here?"

"May I make a suggestion?" Ariel quickly replied. "Don't mention the chapel to anyone beforehand. The

Welby Mansion should be enough information. Then no one will—"

But she broke off and pointed back to the waterfall. "Brandi, look at the falls."

Brandi turned as instructed and let out a gasp. The chapel was transformed completely, like they were standing inside a prism. The sunlight angled through the falls, reflecting off the chipped stone, which looked like real gold.

"Is this why you wanted us here before sunset? Oh, how beautiful."

"Before the sun sets completely, we need to think about lighting and a portable floor or stage," Will suggested and then broke off as thunder echoed through the chapel, audible even over the waterfall.

Ariel threw one more glance through the sparkling waterfall before moving back toward her vehicle. "I wouldn't have thought such a beautiful sunset would bring on rain, but the sky has been unsettled all day. I think it's time to leave."

They all piled into Ariel's Jeep and headed towards the barn and Will's encampment. She parked beside the door to the stable. "Night Whistle hates lightning," she said. "I can't believe he isn't raising a ruckus."

"I can tell you why? Look who is in his stall," Jonothan said, sliding out of the vehicle and motioning towards Night Whistle.

"Pepper? I thought you stayed at our apartment," Brandi questioned.

"Well, I must say, there is something special about

that dog," Ariel said. "Night Whistle has barely tolerated dogs ever since he had to fight off a mongrel that thought he ruled the universe. It left a physical scar as well as an emotional one."

"Pepper?" Brandi said softly and motioned him to come. "Why did you stay with Night Whistle? Will, maybe you had better call your men in this evening. If Pepper felt the need to stay with Night Whistle, there must be a reason. He's restless. Something doesn't feel right. Do you feel it?"

If anyone else had asked him that question, he would have ignored their request, but he was beginning to believe that more than one woman in his life had instincts that belied putting a name to.

Jonothan and Brandi took an hour to wash up and relax before dinner, and on their way, they stopped by registration desk, hoping to ask Ariel a few more questions, but the young woman on duty informed them that Miss Ariel had retired to her suite for the evening and had left strict orders not to be disturbed.

Brandi addressed the woman by her nametag, "Shorty, does the Welby have a lending library for its guests? We're looking for something on local history of the area."

"You might find a journal written by Mrs. Welby herself interesting," Shorty suggested as she took them into an alcove that Brandi had thought was part of the office. She handed them three books and a map and the journal plus a new monthly brochure about festivals and craft places in the area.

When they returned to their apartment, Pepper was waiting on the porch. Brandi placed the journal on top of the books Jonothan was carrying and knelt down on one knee to have a talk with Pepper.

"You've been getting your exercise. Since when do you take off without me?" she asked gently as she rubbed his flank and neck and then tipped his face up to look into his eyes. "Do we need to go for another walk or are you ready to go inside?"

Jonothan held the door open and Pepper waited for Brandi before entering. After he locked the door he said, "The Jeep is gone again. No wonder Ariel can't be disturbed—she isn't even here."

Brandi motioned Pepper to come and proceeded to brush him. His muscles were so tight one would have thought he had run a marathon. "I don't know why you stayed with the Stallion while we were in the Tunnels but I trust your instincts," she added as she offered him a treat, set out his food and fresh water before joining Jonothan.

The two of them had kicked off their shoes and were both intently skimming through the books when Brandi gasped as she reread an entry aloud.

"Listen to this—*my son slipped through the crevice just south of the falls. He is only four years old. He was missing most of the day. When we found him he was covered in black muck.*

"And here's another entry that she has underlined in red: *The tunnels are not beautiful anymore. They are dark and evil and filled with spirits of the freedom people and children.*" She looked up. "Jonothan, remember the anteroom off your office—the bookcase that revolved into the old file room where one wall was covered with newspaper headlines like 'World War II Veterans Return Home,' with a list of names and photos. There was also one titled, 'The Tunnels.'"

Jonothon was already standing. "Say no more. Do you want to head in to my office at Bea's and follow up from there?"

"Only if everything here is under control, and it might be best to check all this out with your Mom."

"And your brother," Jonothan added.

"Yes, Mason too."

The Attack
Turtle Crossing

Though they had set their wedding date themselves, Brandi and Jonothan were thrown into a tizzy with wedding plans crunched into less than two weeks. They were always bumping into each other, but they still couldn't find a quiet corner for more than a hello/goodbye kiss because there was always someone rushing them hither and yon.

Opal's home had become wedding dress central. Autumn and Mason were staying in the master bedroom where Autumn could work on Brandi's dress and nap whenever necessary.

When Jonothan stopped by for lunch while Brandi was in for a fitting, Autumn chased him out. "Sorry Jonothan, but you'll have to eat out on the porch. You can't see the bride in her gown before the wedding."

"I know you've worked very hard, Autumn, but you're not doing too much, are you?" Jonothan asked, concern in his eyes as he gathered his lunch on a tray.

"I've never been happier," she replied. "And if your tuxedo needs any adjustments, you let me know. Have you seen Mason today?"

"Yes. He's a very smart man. And just think, we'll soon be related," Jonothan added as he closed the back door.

"Brandi, your prospective bridegroom left," Autumn called. "You can come out now."

"I actually feel beautiful in this dress," Brandi said. "You have a real talent, Autumn."

"Thanks. You're really not used to thinking of yourself as beautiful are you?"

"No," Brandi replied, as she stepped up on the riser borrowed from a temporary window display from Jewel's Emporium.

"Stand still for just a few more minutes, okay?" Autumn suggested. "Now, if this little soccer player of mine would settle down, we'll have this finished yet tonight."

"The entire hem and the veil?"

"Yes. Opal and Jewel want to help with the hem, and your mom and half-sister are putting the finishing touches on the veil. They wanted to surprise you, but I didn't want you to worry."

"What?" Brandi demanded. "I don't think I'm ready for my mom or my half-sister. Not now."

"Oh, yes you are," Autumn admonished as she checked a piece of lace she needed to finish after she nipped in the waist another 1/16th of an inch. "I just wish my mom could have been at my wedding. I know she would have been a wonderful grandma. Just try. I don't think your mom expects—" She broke off, eyes wide. "Your mom! Oh, my heavens! That means she is Mason's mom too. He tried for years to find her and then gave up. I can't believe I didn't make the connection earlier. All these family links are so new to me."

"Oh, Autumn, how am I ever going to tell him?" Brandi began desperately. "He and I aren't really brother and sister. His mom and mine, Pearl Carpentier, were sisters. Her story is that my dad took off when she told him she was expecting me. So when I was born, Pearl gave me to her sister to raise as her own. Years later, Pearl married Jonothan's dad while he was still married to Opal. Together they had Jace and Samantha, which makes Samantha my half-sister. And to muck this up just a bit more, my half-brother, Jace is also Jonothan's half-brother. They live in Sunrise."

"Wow! It sounds like Jonothan's dad was a very busy man."

Pearl and Samantha arrived in a flurry as was Brandi's mom's way. Samantha stepped into the room and squealed, "Brandi, I take back everything nasty thing I ever said about you. Will you let me do your hair for the wedding? Please? I can't wait to see the veil on you."

"Well, bring it in, Pearl," Autumn invited. "Perhaps the two of you had better handle this. With Brandi in heels and on the riser, I don't think I can manage it properly."

They didn't hesitate to circle around the bridal train to place the veil just so.

Opal stuck her head into the room. "Brandi, would you like to see what we're seeing?" She motioned Samantha to help her bring the full length mirror into the living room.

"I can't believe this is really me," Brandi said as she stared into the mirror. "Thank you so much Autumn, everyone. Do you think Jonothan will think I look beautiful too?"

"Are you kidding, big sister, you'll blow his socks off. And frustrate the poor man to near insanity. Did you count the buttons this dress has in the back?"

"Now behave," Pearl said. "This is a one of a kind veil, honey. Opal and Autumn helped us with some of the embroidery and designs. Thank you all for including us in the plans."

"Alright," Autumn said, "Bridal preview over. "Let's help her get out of the dress and put everything in Opal's room.

Outside, Jonothan had just sat down on his mom's front porch with a tray of food when Will joined him. "I was talking with Mason earlier. He still isn't sure whether those two men are here to steal Autumn's child or foul up Richard Warren's real estate plans. Personally, I think once we bring everything out in the open, the people of Turtle Crossing will embrace the curiosity and historical value of the tunnels and those two goons will clear out of town."

"You're right about that," Jace Carpentier added as he and the Sheriff ambled up the front walk and settled on the front steps.

"Gentlemen," the Sheriff said, as he joined them. "May

I introduce you to Deputy Jace Carpentier, Brandi's half-brother? He has been working undercover for our department, on loan from Sunrise."

"A deputy now?" Jonothan asked.

"That's right," Jace said brusquely. "We've learned that Autumn's foster father has been working with a couple of developers to force the owner of the Welby to sell out. They think they can then use blackmail to acquire the Welby annex as well."

"Are you certain they are not aware of the tunnels?" Jonothan asked.

"Not to my knowledge."

Ariel was caught in the middle. In just a few days the Chapel was sparkling. She wanted to believe she could continue being who she was, but not for long. She would just have to disappear. Again.

But for the moment, she had a wedding to host. "Brandi, what do you think of the Chapel?" she asked.

"It's like a castle! Jonothan, Will and Mason concur that we are going to have to share this with the people of Turtle Crossing. Once the expansion of Turtle Lake and the golf course become a reality and people build homes, the tunnels could become a shortcut from here in to Turtle Crossing with all sorts of possibilities."

Ariel was excited and feeling let down at the same time. The grounds were looking better than they had since the Welbys' early days. The phone rang and she was prepared to tell the caller that the Welby was sold out for the next two weeks.

However, the caller wasn't someone looking for a vacancy. It was her sister, the real Ariel, the person she had been pretending to be. "Hey, little sister. How is Night Whistle?"

The owner of the Welby stood frozen, her hand clutched tight around the telephone. A shocked buzz seeemed to be filling her mind. "Night Whistle?" she repeated. "The last I heard, you skipped town with my husband while I was lying in a hospital, and you call me after all this time to ask about a horse?"

"They're after me to sell him again," her sister said indignantly. "But he's mine, you know. I love him too much. Keep an eye on him for me, okay?"

"Are you in trouble?"

"Nah. Just the usual, you know. I'm sorry about your hubby dying when he hit that train. He really did try to stop. I know he married you, but he was mine first and I miss him every day. But I still love you and mom and dad. Tell them for me, will you, little sister? Bye for now."

Ariel placed the phone on its cradle and thought, *The only time you told me you loved me, was in the hospital when you thought I was dying.*

With everything in order at the Welby, she headed out the door to tell her mom and dad about Ariel's telephone call. It was her usual night to stop by and see them anyhow. But when she went out to start up the Jeepster, the engine wouldn't crank. Then she saw that the headlamps had been switched on, though she had not done it herself. She had charging cables, but it would take too long to recharge.

She heard a screen door open and close and waited in the shadows. Something tugged on her sleeve and she bent down to find herself looking into Pepper's eyes.

"What's wrong, boy?" she whispered. He tugged and she knew he wanted her to follow him. She couldn't drive the Jeepster, so she lifted her bicycle off a rack under the porch and followed him.

She wasn't even winded when Pepper lifted the latch on the side door in the barn. She got the message. Pepper was worried about Night Whistle. "What's wrong, boy?" Ariel whispered again. She thought Night Whistle might be sick because he was so lethargic. Then when she looked in his eyes, she knew. Someone had drugged him, to keep him calm.

She had to get him some help. She urged Night Whistle forward and Pepper followed them. Together they sneaked right past Will's men. While she opened the entrance into the Tunnels, Pepper led Night Whistle through the door and they waited while she closed it.

She didn't sneak as well as she thought. Will recognized the three and was pretty certain they had entered the Tunnels.

But why? He wondered.

However the why became less important when he heard an explosion. The barn, the corral, and whatever had been inside lit up the sky like huge fireworks. Will notified the fire department and the Sheriff's Department from his communication panel truck that was marked, *Trash*.

Ariel, in the meantime, heard nothing as she and Pepper led Night Whistle through the tunnels with nothing more than a flashlight. Now she knew what Brandi had meant about Pepper. His night vision was the most extraordinary thing she had seen in an animal, and Night Whistle was doing pretty well too, despite the tranquilzers that must still be in his system.

When she arrived at her parents' Tunnel entrance, they met her at the door. "You're early. Did Ariel call you too?"

"Yes."

"We're so glad to see you, and not only surprised to see who you have with you, but that this stallion would even enter the Tunnels."

"He's been drugged. Dad, Mom, meet Pepper."

"Hello, Pepper. We've seen him with Deputy Davies a time or two," her mom said.

"How can I keep Night Whistle safe?"

"Well, we've already heard a radio report saying the stallion died in the barn fire," her dad replied, "so no one should be looking for him. Even so, let me make a couple of phone calls."

"Okay." Ariel stood in the tunnel doorway, splitting her time between rubbing Night Whistle's flank and scratching Pepper's ears, taking comfort from the animals' warm, sturdy presence.

"A vet I have known for years," her dad said, returning from the kitchen, "suggests you watch for an ordinary covered car hauler. You know like race cars are hauled in. No one will notice it because Sunrise is just breaking camp from its annual race car festival. He will back into Walnut Alley behind Johnson's Truck and Auto Sales and Garage, which is the second tunnel exit past Sadie's."

Ariel nodded to show she understood.

"You be careful."

With that very brief visit, Ariel led Night Whistle on through the tunnels towards the proper exit. Pepper stayed right beside them. When the truck backed in, Doc signaled her from the side view mirror. She dropped the lead while she unlocked the back doors and lowered the loading ramp. Pepper picked up the lead and Night Whistle followed him right into the truck and into a special built stall. Ariel slid the window open between the cab and the trailer.

"Doc, I don't know if my dad told you, but Night Whistle's been drugged. He seems okay. I think they just wanted to keep him quiet while they set the explosives in the barn."

"I'll take care of him, don't worry. Granny will be in touch."

She whispered a few more comforts to the stallion and she and Pepper exited the trailer. Quickly throwing the lock; Ariel watched as Doc drove off.

Ariel knew the tunnels like the back of her hand. She knew every rise and fall, every nook and cranny, which increased their speed. Pepper sensed it and acclimated his movements to hers.

However, when they arrived at the chapel, she didn't just open the door and rush out. She could see through the falls in places and didn't like all the commotion close to the door she usually used. Thus she led Pepper through the south entrance which led down and back towards the marina. The two of them clambered into one of the canoes and slipped on through the flora that had been planted along both sides of the channel. It continued around the lawn edge of Turtle Lake and into a seldom used cove. This area was too shallow for boats with motors, but ideal for maneuvering around the lily pads in a canoe. She tied off the canoe and the two of them walked right up the main walk. No one paid any attention to them as they went in the cellar entrance and took the stairs into her apartment pantry.

Brandi took one look at them and said, "Into the shower, the both of you. Ariel, we've told everyone you passed out from the smoke, so lay low. No more adventures outside tonight."

Ariel was too tired to argue. "Have someone return the canoe that is tied up at the cove. Will will understand."

The next morning, anyone who could walk was busy helping clean up the mess from the fire. And no one was allowed to speak to Ariel because she was in mourning after the death of her beloved stallion.

That same day, the real Ariel, the sister of the woman who was partitioned off in her suite at the Welby, received a letter with no signature or return address. It said simply, *You were warned what would happen if you didn't let us have the horse. Now we're even.*

Going to the Chapel

Turtle Crossing

Five short and rather hectic days after the destruction of Ariel's barn, it was time for the wedding of the century in Turtle Crossing. The newspaper insert brought people from miles around. Hillside Road had to be closed for parking.

Ariel had kept Mrs. Welby's organ in the parlor for looks and also because she had always dreamed of playing a piano or organ someday. At daybreak, the Turtle Crossing Music Store owner and his sons carefully loaded the organ in a truck and hauled it up to the Falls, through the single car garage door opening and onto a solid wood platform at the back of the chapel.

Guests wanted their daughters to be married in the Welby Chapel even though the Falls made so much noise, that Rev. C. W. Warren had to use a microphone to be heard. When the seating filled up, new arrivals didn't seem to mind standing. A white carpeted runner filled the aisle, followed by a moment of anticipation.

The mellow sounds of the Welby organ set the tone as the groom and his attendants joined the minister, with their back to the Falls. Shannon and David's twins, Laurie Rose and Lily Anneé, led the procession, followed by the bride's attendants. The sheriff escorted Brandi in from the side door. She was exquisite in a dress she had helped design. The delicate iridescent overlay displayed rice pearls in swirls, roses and orchids bordered by Swarovski crystal beads which reflected their own rainbows. The overlay had been removed from her mother's wedding dress and fastened to the detachable train the day before in a combined effort by Pearl, Samantha, Granny, Opal, Autumn and Mrs. Ern.

After Brandi and Jonothan repeated their vows and sealed them with a kiss, they were surrounded by family and friends. But because they knew there was another reason for their wedding in this storybook setting, Jonothan took the minister's microphone and, with his arm around Brandi, announced, "Thank you all for coming this evening, Rev. C.W. has an announcement. Please give him your undivided attention."

The Reverend took center stage once more. "The Welby Chapel is one of the entrances to a series of old tunnels connecting various parts of Turtle Crossing. Some of you may know about them already, but if not, there is a map of the tunnels in the white tent. It is actually possible to walk from here to Turtle Crossing through the tunnels, though they will need to be washed clean and paved like the Chapel has been. If you have any questions or suggestions for the tunnels, please write them on the provided cards and put them in the gold box."

This proclamation was followed by a great deal of surprised looks and muttering that was audible even over the roar of the falls.

"But this is also a wedding, and we're here to celebrate!" the Reverend continued, smiling. "After you've enjoyed the buffet, we'll start up the music and you are welcome to dance in the Chapel. I'm also told that anyone who stays to see the sunset will be in for a real treat."

As the crowd gravitated toward the food tables, Autumn found herself staring at the woman named Ariel, who had been introduced as the owner of the Welby. When the woman brushed past her, she felt a jolt similar to when she had heard that voice in the park in Sunrise who had sounded so much like her mother. What was happening? Social Services had told her that her mom had died. Not only that, Ariel scarcely resembled Autumn's memory of her mother. Yet she felt a connection to this woman like the pull of a deep sea current.

Mason felt her hand tremble in his and she stumbled in the grassy area near the falls. "Honey, is it the baby?"

"I want to dance one very slow dance with you, and then I think we had better go to the hospital," Autumn suggested softly.

"Autumn," Mason replied, alarmed, "if you're going into labor, I don't think it's a good idea to—"

"We never got to dance at our wedding, so we can at least dance this once, at your sister's."

Ariel caught most of this conversation from her place in the buffet line behind them, and when she heard the tall handsome man address the lovely young woman as Autumn, she almost fainted. After all these years, could this Autumn really be her daughter?

Which led to another, even more shocking idea: was she, Ariel, about to become a grandmother? She recognized labor pains when she saw them, and the young woman named Autumn looked ready to deliver within the hour.

But at the same time, Ariel knew that if she really was Autumn's mom, and that information got out, her cover would be blown and she would have to leave town for her family's safety.

My daughter, Ariel thought. Her heart pounded and she broke out in a sweat.

The plastic surgeon who had reshaped Ariel's face after Jamie busted her jaw had said that even her mother wouldn't recognize her—which had turned out to be true. She had passed her parents on the street several times when she first returned to Turtle Crossing, accidentally of course. And they had not given her a second look until she began visiting them through the tunnels. But Ariel had never considered that her daughter would not recognize her either, if they should ever meet again.

She watched Autumn and Mason revolve slowly together on the dance floor for a minute before she excused herself from the line, pausing only to congratulate the bride and groom as she passed them.

"Do you think our wedding will be memorable?" Brandi asked Jonothan.

"I won't forget it anytime soon. And by the look of this crowd, Ariel could hold dances every weekend. But this is our night, sweetheart. I think we've waited long enough, don't you?"

"Absolutely!

They had lost track of all the people who had attended their wedding. The majority of the well-wishers were not only astounded with the opening of the Welby and the Chapel, but were also anxious to get things moving to clean up the rest of the tunnels.

And seeing the plans with Daniel Welby's name on the corner of some of the blueprints was the deciding factor for Richard and Mason's expansion plans. The Mayor even approached them and said, "I think I could get a majority show of hands tonight that could have your dirt movers in the fields tomorrow."

"If the council is all here, I'm all for that," Richard replied as he and the Mayor left the dance floor and their wives with a smiling apology.

"Come along. We'll see what we can do."

"Mrs. Warren," the Mayor's wife said, "the next time you're in town, we'll have a lady's tea in your honor. It appears your husband will be spending a lot of time here."

"Thank you, that would be nice. You have a good evening," Eileen graciously replied as she continued side-stepping in and around several dancing couples until she found Marcie.

"Marcie, have you seen Sheldon?" she asked.

"Not in the last five minutes," Marcie replied. "Why?"

"I was just wondering. Do you know where we're staying tonight?"

"I believe here at The Welby. Brandi and Jonothan talked the owner into bringing in a dozen or so roll-away beds so we wouldn't have to travel far tonight."

"Well, you know these men. They get to talking business and they will be all night."

"Think again, ladies," Sheldon said, putting his arms around Marcie. Richard appeared a moment later, grinning.

"Richard?" Eileen asked a little puzzled by his reaction as well. "Does that goofy smile mean what I think it does?"

Before he could answer, David and Shannon joined them, each holding hands with one of the twins they had been dancing with. Granny Oates came next, followed by the wedding couple themselves.

"Did you all forget you're at a party?" Jonothan asked.

"Richard was about to tell us something," Eileen said.

He nodded, looking as delighted as ever. "The city council just voted in a special five-minute session their approval of the Warren-Welby-Davies Expansion. They also picked a committee to continue on with the plans to clean up and open the tunnels to the public."

"Did you hear that?" Jonothan asked as he stole a kiss from his bride.

"Does Mason know?" Brandi asked.

But it became quickly apparent that Mason had other matters to worry about when he cut through the crowd toward them, pale and excited and breathless. "It's time."

There was a pause and then the group exploded into activity. Mason had prepared an escape plan ahead of time with the Sheriff's Department in case Autumn went into labor, and despite the unexpectedly high volume of cars parked on Hillside Road, Autumn was moved without too much trouble to the limousine that had been meant for the wedding couple's departure.

Wedding night or not, Brandi was determined to accompany her brother and sister-in-law to the hospital. Opal unbuttoned the detachable train from Brandi's wedding dress just before Brandi jumped into the Sheriff's car waiting in front of the limousine and hit the lights.

Will drove the limo with Granny and Ariel in the jump seat facing Autumn and Mason. Will's men followed in an unmarked midnight blue Lincoln.

"I knew we should have waited to dance another time," Mason fretted. "At least Dr. Ashley will be there waiting for you. Now, don't you dare have our baby in this limo. Granny, you talk to her. Tell her!"

"What is that infernal noise?" Autumn asked.

"I believe someone tied tin cans to the back of the limo."

"Oh, no. But where are Brandi and Jonothan?"

"In the Sheriff's car up ahead."

"Not with flashing lights and a siren?"

"That's the one," Mason confirmed. "My sis leaves nothing to chance."

Doing her best to think about something else, Autumn looked at Mason and said, "Honey, Brandi is your cousin, not your sister. Brandi's mother, Pearl, left Brandi with her aunt—your mother—shortly after she was born. Pearl returned home to Sunrise and—" Autumn broke off during a much longer contraction. "It's okay, though," she assured him when she could speak again. "You're going to be a daddy, and you also have an aunt and some cousins too."

Mason looked stunned, but he shook his head, seeming to collect his thoughts. "We can worry about aunts and cousins later. The most important parts of my family are in this car right now, and one of them is ready to see the world for the first time."

"Try not to push, Autumn darlin'," Granny said. "We're pulling in to the emergency right now. Mason, you were right. It looks like Dr. Ashley is waiting at the door with a gurney. It doesn't look like he trusts your timing all that much, either, dear."

Throughout the drive, Ariel remained silent. The way Granny had propelled her into the limo had left her speechless. Granny's excuse that her midwife services might be needed was pure foolishness. But Ariel would be forever grateful and soak up the pure joy of being included in this momentous happening in her daughter's life.

A Surprising Turn of Events
Turtle Crossing

At first Granny Oates had been surprised at the tight security at Turtle Crossing Memorial Hospital, but considering all the problems the Warren family had had with Henry Carpenter in the past—plus Autumn's meddlesome foster father, the baby's grandfather—and it was no wonder Turtle Crossing's finest were here.

Granny couldn't wait to congratulate and thank her nephew, Dr. Ashley, for taking such good care of Autumn and her new daughter, Allison. And Bea hadn't been this excited since she had filed adoption papers for Autumn all those years ago, even though she had eventually been denied custody. Was it any wonder Bea was already boasting that she had been chosen to be one of this child's Godmothers?

Checking the clock on the wall, Granny thought she saw something through the window below the clock, a shadow crouching in the outdoor garden. But when she looked more carefully, she questioned whether she had seen anything at all. Yet the window-mirrored image of someone making a quick exit was enough motivation for her to practice some of the self defense techniques she had learned since the Shadow Angels had adopted her and Bea as associates.

Thus, when one of the two unsavory men who had been at the Welby came running out into the lobby, followed by a hospital orderly in scrubs, yelling, "Stop that man!" Granny dropped and rolled between two chairs. Her extended cane tripped a blur of blue. The first man went down on one knee, then popped to his feet and limped out a side exit, straight into the arms of one of Will's men and a Deputy Sheriff.

When Granny rolled back she spotted a second man dressed in surgical scrubs, but this one was wearing muddy work boots. He was also carrying a bundle of blankets.

Granny didn't dare trip him in case he was carrying an infant, so she kicked one of the heavy lobby chairs, which slid like a guided missile across the polished marble floor and hit him right behind the knees. He had no more than plopped in the chair when he was surrounded by security.

Granny struggled to her feet while a dozen hospital workers, security men and police officers surrounded the man. But when one of the nurses relieved the man of the bundle of blankets and carefully unwrapped it, a peculiar expression crossed his face.

On film it would have been a comedy. The infant he held clutched in his arms was not real but a one of the dolls the hospital used for training which he had nabbed by mistake.

Mason had been sitting in the nursery holding Autumn's new daughter, Allison, when he noticed a nurse hovering over another newborn sleeping peacefully in a bassinette that had been moved down the line to make room for two more babies that had been born that morning.

The patients and their families were unaware that the hospital was having one of their random security drills. Mason had not moved from the corner rocking chair since the curious, furtive nurse had entered the nursery. He assumed the person who had slipped into the nursery must have been part of an in-residence surgical team because he was wearing gloves, a mask and caplet.

A chill rippled up his spine. *What if the baby's birth father tries to nab Allison? I should have been more attentive. Something about this entire situation doesn't feel right.*

The intruder picked up a bundle out of the bassinette closest to the door, read the name tag and rushed out. The door closed silently. Suddenly the nursery doors locked from the outside. Red lights flashed and dimmed in the nursery. Mason fought the urge to rush the baby into Autumn's hospital room and whisk them both away to safety.

He banked his anger rather than wake this precious child—his daughter. She had quit crying the moment he picked her up and said her name. Then, when he wiped the tears trickling down her cheeks, she gripped his finger, and opened her eyes. "Hi, sweetheart. I'm your daddy," Mason said softly.

He didn't think anyone had been paying attention to his presence until a nurse tapped him on the shoulder and said, "Sir? Don't worry. This has just been a routine security drill."

But when she saw the look on his face, she knew there was only one place he wanted to be. "Shall I ask Deputy Davies to accompany you and your daughter to your wife's room? She can stay with you until everything is back to normal."

The nurse excused herself and returned moments later with Brandi. As she escorted Mason towards Autumn's room, Brandi stated, "It's a circus out there. Dr. Ashley left me with strict orders. I am to stay with both of you, and it might be better if Autumn is kept in the dark as to what just happened."

He nodded his head and said, "The nurse said it was just a drill, which I doubt."

"There *was* a surprise safety drill in action which was inadvertently interrupted an attempted abduction. Nice to know that their previous training paid off, wouldn't you agree?"

As soon as Brandi entered Autumn's room, her demeanor changed. "You have a beautiful daughter," she said as Mason placed the baby into Autumn's arms. Then Brandi grabbed Mason in a hug that he felt straight to his toes. "Congratulations, little brother. Have I told you lately how much I love you? If you need to get some shut-eye, you're welcome to make use of the other bed here. They should be wheeling your daughter's isolette in shortly."

Brandi noticed the look of puzzlement on Autumn's face and knew there was no sense in pretending nothing had happened. "Don't be alarmed. You are all safe."

Autumn's arms closed more securely around her daughter. "Someone tried to take her, didn't they?"

"Yes. There was a kidnapping attempt. We have the same two men in custody that trashed my luggage at the Welby a few weeks ago."

"One was dressed like a surgeon," Mason added. "He picked up one of the hospital's practice dolls by mistake."

"You were there when this happened? But where was our baby?" Autumn asked, holding her newborn gently, protectively.

"I was rocking her in a quietly dimmed corner of the nursery," he repeated. "She was asleep on my shoulder." He wondered if she realized that she had referred to her daughter as "our baby."

"Mason," Autumn asked softly, "what was the name on the nursery isolette that contained the practice doll?"

"Mason Davies, Boy."

Autumn looked at Mason and said, "Thank you. You promised you would move heaven and earth to protect us."

"That's true, however I'm not alone. Have you looked outside?" They all gathered at Autumn's hospital room window.

There weren't any sirens. However, the city and county police plus the fire department's flashing lights lit up the hospital parking lot like a Christmas delivery from Santa Claus.

The following day Granny's favorite veterinarian, Doc, backed his best friend's hearse up to the hospital exit without any fanfare. With the back doors open, it was impossible to see anything but what was expected. But underneath the dark sheet, Autumn lay as still as possible, her tiny new baby daughter tucked in her arm, sound asleep.

Mason had donned hospital intern garb and very quickly sat down on the stool that had been provided for him. Brandi was dressed in off-duty black joined by Granny who was dressed in somber black as well.

They drove directly to the funeral home and once inside the garage, they swapped the hearse for Granny's black Lincoln. She pulled up to the side door and picked up what appeared to be a grieving family all dressed in black. The baby was curled up in a baby carrier sling in the crook of Mason's arm. Brandi helped Autumn into the seat beside Mason and then climbed in the front with Granny.

"Don't you feel like we have just stepped inside the pages of some cloak and dagger mystery?" Mason murmured to Autumn.

"I'm sorry little brother," Brandi began, "but although it may seem overkill to both of you, we feel that we can't be too cautious, especially since someone tried to kidnap your baby. Some strange things have been happening in Turtle Crossing and I feel the top is going to blow off this case very shortly. We're hoping that once we get you settled in at Granny's and the two of you have had some rest, perhaps you can help."

A squawk erupted from Brandi's radio with such force that everyone jumped. "Deputy Davies," she responded.

"Finally!" Jonothan's voice crackled. Where have you been?"

"Jonothan? Where is the Sheriff?"

"Oh, he's here. He thought you might answer if it was me."

"I'm going to answer, but not like you might expect." She wanted to tell him more, but after the last fiasco, she was a bit more cautious. "Remember what we talked about when we were out in the boat in Canada? Now, put the Sheriff on and you'll know soon enough, okay?"

"Hey, Froggy Two," the sheriff replied as Granny turned in her drive and into her recently built attached garage. "Status?"

"We're right on target," Brandi replied, and signed off.

"Well now, I don't believe I've ever heard Jonothan so upset."

"He'll calm down once the Sheriff explains everything to him."

"He's going to show up here, one way or the other." Granny commented.

Mason handed baby Allison to Brandi. "Hey, Auntie, we need your help here. Allow me," he added to Autumn as he scooped her up in his arms, carried her into

Granny's huge old fashioned farm kitchen and settled her into one of Granny's special chairs. Then Granny wheeled a white wicker bassinette from the guest bedroom into the kitchen. Brandi gently laid Allison inside.

"Granny," Autumn asked. "Since Allison is still sleeping, how about you finally introduce the lady who just removed some scrumptious smelling casseroles from the oven?"

"Of course," Granny quickly replied. "This is Ariel, the current owner of the Welby."

"Ariel?" Autumn asked.

"Please start thinking of me as Alexandria," she replied.

Autumn frowned. Her mother's name had been Alex, but that had to be a coincidence, right?

Granny was smiling now. "Would you like to explain?" she asked, addressing Ariel/Alexandria.

"Yes. Please. I grew up right here in Turtle Crossing. My sister, Ariel was the eldest and the prettiest and the most popular girl in school. I was the book worm. She changed boy friends like other people change shoes. Then one guy, Jamie Johnson, stuck around longer than any of the rest."

Autumn stirred at the man's name, looking shocked, but Granny laid a hand on her wrist to soothe her.

"I was a senior when Jamie asked Ariel to marry him," Alexandria continued. "He had even bought her a ring. But she laughed at him and told him no. Then he started flirting with me to make Ariel jealous. I think Jamie and I were both surprised at how well we got along. The brief story is that we eventually married. Ariel left town after that. Jamie had a factory job and our life was fine until I got pregnant. Then, when he went on the late shift, we saw less and less of each other. My little girl and I lived in one world and he lived in another.

"One day he came home from work early because he had been laid off." She hesitated a moment and softly added, "I woke up several days later in a motel far from home. My only memory of that last night in Turtle Crossing was sending my daughter to her grandparents. The only good thing after that was he couldn't hurt my little girl anymore."

Autumn was weeping freely at this point, but she did not try to interrupt.

"He found another job and things went along okay until one afternoon when I came home from the grocery early; I found him in bed with a woman he'd met from the topless saloon after work one night. It was Ariel, my sister. Jamie hit me so hard that I had to have my jaw restructured which changed my appearance. Before I was released from the hospital, he misjudged the speed of a train and was killed. My sister was a passenger in the car with him, but she survived and left before help arrived.

"My nice big sister visited me one night at the hospital and said she had told our parents that I was a loose woman and was making money living off the street. How could I go home and embarrass them and especially my little girl? At least my parents were raising her, or so I thought. Believing she was safe was the other reason I didn't return home. Meanwhile, they assumed my daughter was still with me."

At this revelation, Autumn buried her face in her hands. Mason held her tightly in a one armed hug.

"Several years later, I was managing a restaurant when one evening a customer left a copy of a recent Turtle Crossing Newspaper on the table. That's when I read that the Welby place was for sale. I called my Mom and Dad's attorney and took all the money that Jamie had left in a suitcase, which I had invested wisely, as well as the majority of my weekly checks. I took a bus to Turtle Crossing and bought the Welby outright the day I arrived."

She leaned forward to pick up her coffee that had long since cooled. When she did, her necklace swung out of her blouse like a pendulum.

The sight of the necklace finally moved Autumn to speech once more. "Where did you get that necklace?" she demanded.

"Oh, this is to remind me what can happen when one trusts a bit too much. When I came to after we left Turtle Crossing, one of my earrings was missing. Jamie was angry that I had lost one of the diamond earrings he had bought for me as a wedding present. So I bent the stem around and made it into a necklace. I've worn it ever since."

When Autumn held out the matching diamond necklace she had made from the other earring so long ago, the pieces fell into place. Everyone in the room knew that they were mother and daughter.

"Granny?" Autumn asked, "You knew? That's why she was at the hospital."

"I had a suspicion, yes, my dear."

"So, Alexandria, why are you here now?" Mason asked.

"Because it's finally safe for me to acknowledge who I am. My family has suffered enough because I made some very poor choices. Especially where you are concerned, Autumn. But I was too ashamed, too cowardly, too certain that I could not provide you with the life you deserved."

"But you've been at the Welby for three years and haven't even talked to your Mom and Dad?"

"Not in public."

"You used the tunnels?" Mason guessed.

"It was the only way. We didn't know who to trust."

"We've been there, haven't we sweetheart?" Mason suggested.

"Yes. Yes, we do understand. But why now? Has something happened?"

"Yes. The real Ariel, in a drunken stupor, drove off a cliff this morning. The real owner, Alexandria—that's me—will be changing places with Ariel, and taking over at the Welby," she added, as she removed the uncomfortable wig she had been wearing until she could become herself. "It's time to reclaim my life and my identity."

Everyone turned as two more people entered the kitchen. It was Alexandria's parents. She stood, shocked. "You heard?"

When they nodded, tears in their eyes, her mom said, "Tell them the rest of it."

Alexandria sat slowly. "The Welby deed is in my name, Alexandria Lyndsey Ern Welby. Mrs. Welby and my mom were sisters."

The last few days of Autumn's life had been filled with changes at every turn. She had a baby daughter, a mom she had been told was dead, and grandparents she vaguely remembered, but was anxious to get to know. When she looked up Mason was watching her.

Odd, she thought, *how he just seems to understand when I need his support. Just his smile and a nod of his head is such a comfort. But then, Mason also has an aunt and cousins he hadn't known existed until just a few days ago.*

Allison started crying, and Autumn nodded her approval when Alexandria moved to pick her up. Allison stopped crying the moment her grandma started singing a lullaby that Autumn suddenly remembered.

"Mason, will you help me with a prayer?" Autumn asked softly.

"Of course, honey."

They bowed their heads, and, following Mason's guidance to just say what was in her heart, Autumn began, "Dear Lord Jesus, thank you for guiding all those who were instrumental in bringing our family together after all these years. Doing what's right for others is their main goal in life. Pray keep them all safe. In your blessed name. Amen."

Brandi hated interrupting, but it was getting late. "Mason, Jonothan will be here around seven and we will be leaving for our honeymoon. Are you okay with the Shadow Angels coming here to help with security? Will is pretty busy right now. He and Wendy had a little boy just about an hour ago."

"I'm okay with it Sis. I want to see you as happy as we are. Look at my wife. She and I have been so lost and alone for so long. Now we're a family."

"And you have learned to trust. The two of you found each other. Don't forget that. I know she loves you. Just keep telling each other that the rest of your lives. Nothing else really matters."

They hugged. Brushing away the welcome tears, Brandi added, "I'll always be your big sis. Don't you forget that."

"I know." They stood side by side, arm in arm, neither quite ready to say goodbye so soon. "When do you and Jonothan leave for your honeymoon?"

"We were going to fly to our favorite getaway in Ontario, but in light of our recent discoveries, we'll be returning to the suite at the Welby as soon as Jonothan arrives."

Pepper padded to her side and nuzzled her hand before continuing over to be near Autumn and Allison. "Take good care of him, Mason," Brandi added. "He's the best."

"Who is the best?" Jonothan asked, striding into the kitchen.

"Oh, you are sweetheart," Brandi replied as she flew into his arms.

Alex Returns
Turtle Crossing

Jonothan led Brandi out of Granny's kitchen and to the swing on the far side of the recently screened-in porch. Pepper followed. A cool breeze rustled the leaves in the nearby lilac bush, and Brandi cuddled close to Jonothan. They hadn't had a moment to themselves all day. A dog barked in the distance. Pepper recognized it and disregarded it. The moon was full and cast tree shadows on the lawn.

Brandi laid her head on Jonothan's chest as he pulled her closer, running his free hand through her hair and brushing it away from her face. "Well, we're finally married," he said softly. "I never understood how my mom felt about my dad until today. She trusted him and loved him even after she found out about the double life he had been living all those years. But the look that passed between them at the hospital shortly before he died is something I'll never forget as long as I live. I felt that same connection with you when we faced each other and said our vows."

Brandi hugged him closer. "It certainly took us long enough, didn't it?"

He smiled and kissed her.

"How much time do we have before we fly out?" she asked breathlessly.

"We've got plenty of time, but not *that* much," he chuckled and hugged her tighter. "I want you all to myself for at least a week—with no interruptions."

But an interruption came almost at once as the voices in Granny's kitchen grew loud and heated.

"Dad!" Alex exclaimed. "Why haven't the business owners formed a coalition of their own?"

"Because we have been afraid the situation would escalate out of control as it has a few times in the past, and later we accepted it as a way of life—you know, like taxes."

"But it's already escalated hasn't it?" Alex questioned. "Look at what's been happening to Bea all this time. Don't you think the business owners will go along with us on this?"

"You've been away for a few years, Alex," her father replied. "Your mother and I were reminded of what happened to Bea's father all those years ago when the maps were recently found. They weren't really lost, just creatively hidden. Bea and her mom almost died in that fire."

The kitchen momentarily fell into a hushed silence. Then Granny huffed, "What maps are you referring to?"

"I didn't see them," Alex admitted, "but Bea and Jonothan were discussing them at Sadie's one evening."

When Jonothan heard his name mentioned he rose from the swing and stood outside the screen door questioning what else they had missed. Brandi joined him.

Spotting him, Alex asked, "Jonothan, may I have a word with you outside? In private?" When they were away from the house and had started walking down the lane that led towards the road, she began, "Did you know that I worked in Bea's father's office part-time while I was in high school and after I graduated?"

Jonothan stopped in his tracks and looked at her closer. "I was just in grade school, but I remember you now. You wore those glasses that were too big for you and you kept your hair braided."

"That's right. As you know, for several months, someone has been harassing Bea, but I'm starting to think she isn't the real target. I think their agenda is something else entirely. Did you ever hear Henry comment that Turtle Crossing was 'sittin' on a bloomin' gold mine?'"

"No, that's one I missed," Jonothan replied dryly. "Honestly, the less I hear about Henry, the better. At one time or another he has hurt every member of my family."

"As a child," Alex continued, "the tunnels were something we were forbidden to talk about. The old if-it-doesn't-affect-me-it-doesn't-exist syndrome."

"Your point?" Jonothan asked.

"A few of the townspeople got so deeply involved in

weekly poker games, they had to mortgage their homes or borrowed money at very steep interest rates. Others were intimidated by their own insecurities and fears. Remember how I did my best to keep local people from the Welby? You and Brandi wouldn't have even gotten as far as the registration desk if I had been there. I've been in hiding. I was doing what I felt I had to do—staying in my own little world and minding my own business.

"I'm just now realizing why Jamie tried to put me out of commission when he did. I had overheard him and Henry talking on more than one occasion, but I didn't know what their agenda was. Some of it is still blurry. And maybe they talked in riddles so I wouldn't understand."

"Ariel—I mean, Alex," Jonothan began, "are you saying either someone thinks you know more than you do, or they're not willing to take the chance you might remember something they don't want revealed."

"I suppose. I've had nightmares about both of those scenarios," Alex replied, pausing to look around—listening intently. She suddenly stopped when she heard rustling in the nearby field. When she saw headlights of an approaching vehicle on the road, she ducked behind Granny's favorite oak tree. After the truck passed by, she rejoined Jonothan. "Sorry. Habit," she explained.

"Alex, when you were a kid do you recall a man named Fast Foster?" Jonothan asked.

"Of course. Foster and Henry were running some form of gambling ring."

"And you know this how?" Jonothan asked.

"On the last Friday of each month, Bea's dad, Mr.

Longacre would hand me a business envelope to be deposited in a specific mail slot at 4:00pm. I worked in his office as his personal assistant twice a week after school and did all the filing in his hideaway file room. He swore me to secrecy. But I think he would forgive me now, since his daughter, my daughter and brand new granddaughter might still be at risk if anyone discovers that A. Lyndsey née Johnson didn't die but is alive and back in town."

"So, has anyone ever known your first name?"

"It wasn't public knowledge that I'm aware of. My mom and dad started calling me Lyndsey because a neighbor had just had a boy named Alex. Thus they just gave me the initial of A. Lyndsey on my school papers, but Alexandria is on my birth certificate."

"So Mr. Longacre was keeping secrets too," Jonothan remarked, bowled over by the information Alex had revealed. "We need to talk to Brandi and the Shadow Angels at once. Next to Judge Ogelthorpe, Mr. Longacre was the most honest and law abiding man I knew."

"I agree, but that's part of what I don't understand," Alex continued. "Bea was the third generation owner of the Longacre Building and her father trained her in the business, but apparently failed to warn her about this under-the-table graft that he had been paying for years—or did he? You've been working for her for awhile. Have you noticed anything unusual?"

"No. And I wouldn't know where to begin. I repeat; I need to talk this over with Brandi."

"No need," Brandi said softly, emerging from the field where Alex had heard rustling before. "Sorry Alex, but I wasn't about to let my husband take a walk with a woman who has a known past with Jamie Johnson."

"I should have known," Alex replied. "You've read his police file."

"I have. I've also done some research on you. You've either been very naïve or stupid, or very lucky."

"Just toss all of those together and you've got my profile on paper, except for the stupid part. In the beginning, yes, but later on I gathered information that I planned to use to get away from Jamie and Henry. But they knew my weak spot was my daughter. She was their ace in the hole." She sighed. "The first time I had any inkling that Autumn might be my lost daughter was at your wedding reception when I overhead her husband, Mason, call her by name. I still have trouble believing she's back in my life."

"Alex," Brandi began, "I apologize. You've apparently been a victim of circumstance; but I was just thinking about all your daughter has been through."

"I understand. You two go on your honeymoon. I know my way around the tunnels and back alleys of Turtle Crossing."

"And you know how to gain access to Bea's office without going in the front door," Brandi added.

"Well, everyone thinks we are leaving for our honeymoon tonight," Jonothan said. "Brandi, are you thinking what I am?"

"Yes. We made promises too, Alex. To each other."

"What about Jace?" Alex asked.

"What about him?"

"Isn't he standing in for you with Bea, Jonothan?"

"How did you know that was the backup plan?" Brandi asked.

"I overheard a conversation."

"It was the day that Brandi and I went exploring the tunnels with night vision and cameras, wasn't it?" Jonothan inquired, aggravated with himself for being so careless.

"You never saw me," Alex said.

"No. We felt a presence but didn't feel threatened," Jonothan replied.

"You're Miss Opal's son alright."

As they talked, they had been walking back to Granny's farm house. "We'll have to continue this conversation inside," Brandi stated. "The mosquitoes are coming out in force."

"I have protected my daughter all these years. I don't want her to know about any of this; especially not about her Dad," Alex demanded.

"She's not a baby anymore," Jonothan stated, "And it appears that she has managed just fine so far." He didn't need to add, *without your protection.*

When they re-entered Granny's kitchen, Alex realized they had no choice but to share with everyone what they had decided. Seeing her daughter so happy and surrounded by family and friends was not the result of anything she had done. *I need to change from being so independently selfish and earn my daughter's love.*

Granny handed each of them a tray with servings of potato salad, a chicken sandwich, a hot dog in a bun and a bowl of fresh fruit, plus their drinks and a couple of cookies. Brandi excused herself to call Bea—there were questions about her father's business that needed immediate answers—while everyone else took turns listening to and filling in details of Alex's story.

"While you were out," Granny began, "We have been looking through a box of photos that Wendy took. As you can see, being the little upcoming artist that she is, she is always looking for the unusual in her character shots."

"I've seen those men before!" Autumn pointed out. "They were regulars at the Fosters. Not ever for a meal, but definitely not just guests either. Do you have any other photos from Sadie's?"

Jonothan and Brandi started looking through the photos as well and were surprised how many photos Wendy had taken that didn't have anything to do with buildings and the history of Turtle Crossing.

Jonothan pointed out the man who had followed him his first day with the Shadow Angels, and asked Brandi, "Is this one of your men?"

Brandi shook her head no and Autumn cried, "That's my foster dad!"

"Brandi," Jonothan asked as she came back into the kitchen, "Were you able to reach Bea?"

"No. But the Sheriff put Jace on. I told him to get his shiny boots over to Bea's on the double. I told him we would fill him in tomorrow at around noon."

Granny's phone rang and she had barely said hello when she held out the phone to Jonothan. "Jace wants to talk to you."

"Jonothan?" Jace began. "I just spoke to Will. He said Bea is on the move. She told him, 'If anyone calls, tell them I'm going to see a man about a gavel.'"

Most of the people in Granny's kitchen understood that to mean Bea was at Judge Adam's home. "She'll be safe, Jace. Thanks. Wait a minute, Brandi wants to talk to you a moment."

"Jace? Ask the sheriff to help you find out when the Longacre Mercantile & Grocery burned and if the library has any newspaper accounts of the fire. Also, who was head of Children's Services between the years of 1950 and 1960? The Sheriff and my mom will have our private number."

"May I speak to Jonothan again," Jace requested.

"Sure," Brandi replied.

"Jonothan, when are the two of you leaving for your honeymoon?" Jace asked. "I owe the two of you so much. Another thing, I've been looking back into our dad's old books. The ones he had hidden? There are entries of him paying and receiving funds that I don't think had anything to do with Carpentier Trucking."

"Thanks, Jace. Be careful. And talk to no one but the Judge about this. Is that understood?"

"Jonothan."

"Is that understood?" Jonothan replied in a much sterner voice.

"Yes, Sir! Goodnight."

Jonothan hung up the phone and turned around. The entire room was silent, except for Allison's tiny burp. Even Pepper moved closer to Jonothan and rubbed against his leg. Then Brandi reached out and took his hand in hers. He knew he had to say something but his emotions were too raw. Anger and frustration of his father's past still had a way of sneaking into his heart when he least expected it.

How could he explain the memories that just hit him when Jace mentioned their shared dad's Carpentier Trucking Company's other set of books? Immediately, the memory of seeing a boy beside his father's truck flashed forward to his then and now look-a-like half-brother Jace, the adult. The difference? Today he felt like his dad's _other_ son.

"We'll be leaving," Brandi said softly. But, we'll be in touch." Jonothan and Brandi went back to the Welby for their honeymoon, in the guest bedroom in Alex's apartment. Their meals were to be delivered via a dumb-waiter, compliments of Alex.

"They should take a couple of days at least," Mason suggested. He knew how frustrated he and Autumn had been before they were married and even though they knew their timing hadn't been perfect, that hadn't stopped them from wanting each other. But their honeymoon would have to wait until Autumn had recovered from the delivery of their beautiful daughter.

"Haven't you ever wondered why the majority of the businesses seldom have money for renovations?" Alex asked. "They were afraid not to pay their growth percentages to Henry's Tunnel Rats after what happened to the Longacre."

"But that's been forty years ago. Do you have any proof?" Granny demanded because she recalled something her hubby had gotten trapped into that she failed to unravel until just before his death.

"Oh. You mean that he refused to invest in their scheme and their store became a tinderbox?" Alex replied. "Mom, don't you remember you used to tell me that Howard T used to brag about it in grade school?"

"That's right he did."

"Oh, I've got to talk to Bea," Granny said. "I can't say for certain, but Bea's flowers always had a note attached to them. Each was signed with a different letter of the alphabet. I saw a few of them, but put together they could have spelled Howard T. many times over."

"You don't really think he would hurt Bea or any of the other business owners in Turtle Crossing, do you?" Autumn asked, worried for her mom and grandparents and Sadie.

"We need to get the leaders of Turtle Crossing together," Mason suggested. Who will they listen to?"

"You and your partner, Richard Warren," Allen Ern suggested. "The two of you are investing a great deal of money in this community and neither of you has a history in Turtle Crossing."

"Alright then," Mason replied. "We need a list of names, telephone numbers and most important of all, a plan. Monday morning, the only business that will open its doors will be the pharmacy, the Sheriff's office and the hospital."

"Shouldn't they have a say in this?" Allen Ern asked.

"Mr. Ern," Mason said, "They've had how many years to do something and no one has stepped up. That's what this meeting is for. To make a pact and sign it; making all of them accountable—that they will stand together on whatever is decided. Alex? Are you with us?"

"I'm with you a hundred percent."

"Good. I'll call Richard. We've got two days to make the phone calls," Mason concluded.

"And those we cannot reach by telephone," Allen added, "I'll notify at their homes. It's our responsibility to make certain we clean out the tunnels for the public to enjoy and remove the mistrust that has been choking the entrepreneurship out of Turtle Crossing."

"Grandpa Ern?" Autumn asked. "Does what Alex said include you too?"

"It most certainly does, sweetheart. I believe the old-fashioned word for what we've accepted as normal all these years is called blackmail!"

On that note, thoughts were buzzing around the room, and one name came to mind: Henry. They knew he was in prison, but Henry always found someone willing to do just about anything if the money was right.

The next day Alex had finally had it—she read the deed which was titled in her name, Alexandria Lyndsey Welby, owner of The Welby. She had had her name legally changed before returning to Turtle Crossing. She knew her parents would understand that it was the only way she could stay.

The employees at The Welby adjusted quickly to the changes Alex was making. She felt free. She was having fun wearing her own hair loose, or piled up on top of her head, in a twist, however she pleased. When she walked into a room, it was with pride. Thus she appeared to be at least two inches taller thanks to wearing clothes that had style and elegance instead of the period clothes with petticoats galore.

The Welby Chapel had become an enigma. Visitors just needed to see for themselves whether the Chapel really was as beautiful as they had heard and didn't mind paying a token admission for that proof.

One of the visitors was Fast Foster's wife. She arrived with a group of church women. Of course she had no idea who Alex was or that she was Autumn's mother.

Alex breathed a sigh of relief on that note but Mrs. Foster was certainly envious of Alex having ownership of The Welby. "If we had known this place was for sale, all this would have been mine," she sneered. "The last time I was in this town was to pick up a kid. But you do what you gotta do, right?"

"Now Cora," one of the church women said. "That little red-haired girl was a real gem. We miss her. Didn't Howard T's mama help you with the paperwork, Cora? The way she despised children, it's no wonder they fired her."

"Your bus driver is ready to leave," Alex announced. "I hope you enjoyed your visit." She waved them on just as her secretary called her.

"Alex, I'm glad those women are the last visitors of the day. We had to keep our eyes peeled on that Cora woman. She kept trying to scratch a piece of stone with a pocket knife. No matter how often we told her it wasn't real gold.

She still didn't believe it. She tried to tell us she had just picked up a handful of the polished pyrite but one of the ladies said just weigh her purse because it's full."

"See," Alex began, "That's why we have to lock up the tunnels at night. But, you have to take the greedy with the honest."

Alex's stomach churned and guilt clutched at her heart. She wanted to shut herself away for a week and cry when she met the woman with whom Autumn had spent her adolescence. She would spend the rest of her life trying to make it up to her.

In the meantime, renovations were keeping her just as busy as her guests were. Local carpenters had built a temporary wall to show people the before and after part of the future renovation of the Tunnels with photos and design panels. Many of today's local visitors signed up to volunteer a certain number of hours to help with the restoration.

Couples were paying a deposit to reserve wedding dates for the chapel, plus the Bridal Suite and catered receptions. Part of this added revenue would be passed on to Alex's loyal employees, and a percentage to the restoration of the tunnels and the Welby.

All of the business owners in Turtle Crossing had anxiously signed the pact, despite the uneasy feeling that hung in the clouds. Nerves were singeing the phone lines.

Showdown

Turtle Crossing

Brandi woke with a start at 7:00am on day four of their honeymoon, and she woke Jonothan too. "We have to go." She dialed Granny and asked, "How is everyone?"

"Everyone here is fine. What is it, dear?" Granny asked.

"I don't know yet."

Brandi had just hung up when Jace called. "I want both of you in my office immediately!" he said in a harsh whisper. Without waiting for an answer, he slammed the receiver in her ear. The noise as effective as a cold shower.

"Something is very wrong, Jonothan. Jace has never spoken to me that way."

Next she dialed the sheriff, then Alex. "How fast can you get us to Bea's office?"

"Ten minutes," Alex said. "Meet you at the Jeepster in three."

Finally, Brandi called Tressie as per Shadow Angels protocol before rushing out the door with Jonothan on her heels. Outside, Alex had the Jeep running, and she headed for the tunnels the moment Brandi and Jonothan were aboard. She knew the combinations to all the business exits into the Tunnels, including Bea's.

Alex parked in an alcove and motioned they would go from there on foot. The patches of harsh light and absolute darkness in the tunnels were hard to acclimate to, but thanks to their previous visits to the tunnels, Brandi and Jonothan had come prepared. They donned their battery packs and "headlights."

Alex, who needed no such assistance, looked a little surprised, but suggested, "Hook these tandem clips to your belts and follow me."

Five minutes later, they arrived at the Longacre Building. Alex unlocked the door and they crowded onto the landing below the first set of stairs. Jonothan turned on his flashlight and they released their tandem clips before ascending the stairs.

Alex and Brandi raised the door of the second landing and Alex peered through the street level door of Donnelly's Vacations & Travel Service. When one of Will's men signaled they had that area covered, she closed the door but left it unlocked as they climbed the second flight of stairs.

When they entered Bea's daddy's private file room, it was apparent the Longacre files had been disturbed. Not by someone who was angry or frustrated by tearing-out and scattering files like confetti all over the floor, but stacked and marked according to the list that was posted on the framed corkboard on the wall. Jace had been busy.

"Jonothan, look at the photos propped up on top of the file cabinets," Brandi whispered excitedly. "Some of these photos were once very nicely framed. And here's one that has a stack of photos behind it."

"That's it! That's the one I've been seeing in my dreams," Jonothan said softly. "And I wouldn't be surprised if Bea hasn't been remembering it too."

"These are dated about the same time as those old postcard photos Wendy is using for the Turtle Crossing Insert," Brandi confirmed. "This eight-by-ten is a picture of the front of the Longacre Mercantile and Grocery just moments before it went up in a ball of fire."

"Wow!" Alex exclaimed, "Look whose reflection got caught on camera. It's old Homer, Howard T's dad, standing right in front of the Mercantile, holding a gasoline can and smiling—and one of the dolls in the display window is smiling back at him with black streaks running from her eyes like she was crying."

"So the flowers Howard T's been leaving at Bea's door weren't meant to frighten her at all. Just his way of acquiring her trust so he could find these photos," Jonothan added. "Boy, that man does not understand women, does he?"

"No time for that now," Alex remarked as she knelt on one knee.

Brandi and Jonothan watched her slide aside the black spine of a well-known book of Shakespeare's plays. She did not open the door, but motioned them to look and listen through the opening she had just created. Visible through the false bookcase, Jace was immobile, sitting in an awkward position in Jonothan's chair and glaring at a someone they could not see.

But Jace wasn't the only one in trouble. Tressie had told Brandi that Shannon and Bea had scheduled a self-defense training class this morning in her office. Brandi silently prayed that Shannon had reconsidered the location or they both might be in danger.

Jace was castigating himself for having been so careless. While Bea and Shannon worked on their practice moves, he had been at Jonothan's desk studying a 20-year-old Longacre file when he heard someone yelling Bea's name. No one he knew ever yelled at her in that tone of voice.

He immediately dialed Brandi's number and slid the file in the desk drawer seconds before Howard T frantically burst into Jonothan's office brandishing a gun. He strode directly up to the desk, a crazed expression on his blotchy face.

Behind Howard T's back, Jace saw a sliver of movement from the bookcase on one side of the office, and Bea's pale face peeking through the lavatory pocket door on the other. She had slid the silent pocket door partially open just when Howard T and one of his partners tied up Jace.

When the notch opened in the bookcase too, Jace breathed a sigh of relief.

It's time for the show to begin, he thought.

"Tell me, Howard T, how did you get mixed up in all this?"

"What do you care?"

"Well, I can't see that you're going to make any money now that the town council voted to open the Tunnels to the public. You'll have to find another place to do your dirty work."

"Yeah? Well, that Ariel is going to get her come-uppance real soon."

"How's that, Howard T? Don't you read the newspapers?"

"Why? You know something I don't?"

Jace almost told him that Ariel had already "got her come-uppance," as he called it, when she had driven off that cliff. But he held his tongue.

"Oh, I doubt it, Howard T. How could I know more than the guy who does most of Henry Carpenter's dirty work these days?"

"He takes good care of me."

"I'm sure he does. But you know that money he sends you? I'm afraid that well just went dry—as of today. The businesses in Turtle Crossing just closed their special accounts."

"We don't need their money. We're gonna get ransom money for lovely Bea, and you are going to make the calls."

"Really? Well, I want proof before I make any phone calls for you," Jace demanded.

"Bring her in here, Slim."

When he returned to Jonothan's office, it was apparent the captive was not Bea, but Shannon. Her range of movement was limited, but the rope was loose enough to allow her to walk. Apparently Slim had grabbed the wrong woman, and he still didn't know it.

When the phone rang in Bea's office, Howard T left Shannon with Slim. While he was in Bea's office, Slim turned his back on Shannon to check out the street below. Alex opened the revolving bookcase just far enough for Brandi to sneak through into the office. She quickly untied Jace and then had to crawl under the desk because there wasn't time to slip back out. Alex gently closed the bookcase door and Jace sat at the desk with his hands still behind him, but untied.

Shannon sent a partial hand signal across the room to Jace. Brandi, peeking under the desk partition, smiled and thought it was going to be fun to see Howard T eat his own words. Watching Shannon disappear right before his eyes would be her ultimate wedding present.

Howard T returned to Jonothan's office and bragged, "That was my contact. He says he has the owner of the Welby and the newlyweds tied up neat and tidy, so now we have quadruple the bargaining power. Thought you had me fooled didn't you?"

"Well, if that's true, then you won't mind helping me out here with a few questions. You know, I shouldn't have been surprised at how creative you and Henry have been with your accounting entries for Carpentier Trucking, but I was surprised that you took the time to include my dad in your maneuverings."

"Yeah. It took that sharp momma of yours to figure it out though, didn't it?"

"Oh, you're right about that. You know what they say. It takes one to know one—until she's the one being shafted."

"Yeah. That old lady of yours was madder than a wet hen and sure gave Henry an earful. That's why Henry set this in motion, you know."

"I'll just bet he did, but not without a bit of help."

Jace wanted to give whoever else was in the file room a bit of time to do whatever they planned, so he acted a bit miffed with his situation, and continued, "Foster was the sneaky one though, right?" Jace added.

Howard T spun around. "Never heard of the guy," he blustered. "Slim, go keep an eye on the entrance. I can handle things here, and we don't want any guests."

Slim nodded and vanished through the door.

In the meantime, with Howard T's focus on Jace, Shannon used her flexibility and limbered muscles to her advantage. She slipped out of the rope that Slim had tied around her wrists and waist. It dropped silently to the floor as she slipped behind Howard T, past the open connecting door to Bea's office, and behind the floor length drapes.

Brandi cautiously slid the front panel in the front of Jonothan's desk aside and even though she was expecting it, she was still amazed at how graceful Shannon disappeared from Howard T's vision.

Howard T, sensing that something had changed, spun again and stared down at the coil of rope that lay in the middle of the room like a lifeless snake. Shaking his head in disbelief, he called Bea's name several times.

Frenzied, Howard T darted back and forth, not knowing which way to turn. He spun back around and pulled out his gun. He just couldn't lose his bargaining chip. "Where'd you go Bea?" he yelled.

Jace figured his best bet was to sit and wait until someone told him what to do. With the way people were moving around in this office, he wouldn't have used his gun even if he had it.

Bea knew she couldn't bear it if anything happened to Shannon, and Brandi was too far away to be of any help, so she had to do something. Thus while Howard T's attention was focused on the bookcase—which had just emitted an odd scraping sound—Bea slipped out of the lavatory, sneaked up behind him and, like a kickboxer delivering a knockout blow, kicked the gun out of his hand.

"Bea?" Howard T questioned, wondering if she really was real.

Jonothan took the opportunity to squeeze through the bookcase door opening and crawled behind his desk to the drapes that covered the window behind Jace. Then Howard T's jaw dropped when Jace, a man he had tied to his chair, stood up, and Jonothan stepped out from behind the drapes to stand beside him.

How could one man he had tied up escape his bonds and become two men? He blinked, thinking his vision was failing him, but sure enough, there were two of them. They even had the same color shirt, pants and hair.

Shannon had remained hidden behind the other window drapes and pulled hard on the drapery cord. The drapes opened with a soft swish.

Howard T turned white as a sheet and his voice came out in a throaty whisper, "Ghosts!" and started towards the sun-washed window. "That you, Longacre?" he asked in disbelief.

Forgetting about the coiled rope as he dashed towards the window, slipped on the rope, fell forward, hit his head on Jonothan's desk and slithered to the floor, out cold.

"You say something, Howard T?" Slim asked as he stepped through the doorway. When he saw Howard T slumped on the floor and the room full of people who had not been there moments before, he turned and ran back out of Bea's office door—only to be handcuffed by Opal and Jewel, their faces shadowed in hooded black capes.

Bea was stunned. She had finally had the chance to disarm Howard T thanks to Shannon. But just as she was congratulating herself, a new voice echoed from the corridor. "Howard T?"

The room took on a surreal silence. Shannon was nowhere in sight. Jonothan and Jace remained standing, flanking the desk like matching bookends.

"Howard T? Answer me. I could hear you screaming all the way down the hall."

An instant later an old man in a gleaming wheelchair glided through the doorway. "Well, well, well, Miss Beatrice Longacre, you're as pretty as your mama," Homer announced.

The double-meaning in his gravely voice set her shivering, and she shook away the sensation. Anger raced through her like a raging fire. She turned towards him, stepped forward, clenching and unclenching her fists, and faced the shell of the man who had caused her family so much pain and heartache. She heard Shannon's voice echo in her mind, *Don't ever assume. Keep calm and alert for the unexpected.*

Homer's voice was strong, not nearly as frail and reedy as he appeared in his state of the art wheelchair. "You hurt my son," he accused, shaking his finger in her direction.

"No. Your son was clumsy, as usual, and knocked his fool self out on the desk," Bea replied. "What are *you* doing here?"

His attention had been directed at his son, still lying on the floor. It was apparent she had startled him by her aggressive tone of voice because he jerked his head up, his steely eyes filled with venom.

The morning cloud cover moved out and the sun once again brightened the room, the reflection diverting Homer's attention from Bea to Wendy's painting on the wall. The sunlight brought the reality of what he had done years ago to the forefront. He had listened to Henry's lies and, in a fit of jealous rage, had almost destroyed the woman he had, and to this day, still loved.

Homer's face turned pasty white as he gripped the arms of the wheelchair and stood. "I need that painting! It's mine!" he demanded.

"Oh? The painting on the wall, the photo of you stealing my gold heart from a jeweler's box on my wedding day? Or *this?*" she demanded as she dangled the gold heart in front of his face? You can't have *any* of them!"

He looked so confused; he plopped back into his chair and turned towards Bea. "Gotten kinda saucy, haven't you? But you and your ghostly accomplices can't stop me."

"But *we* can," Alex announced as she stepped out from behind the same drapes that Jonothan had previously occupied, followed by Shannon. Jonothan and Jace changed their stance, and Brandi scrambled out from beneath Jonothan's desk to handcuff Howard T. His face turned such a bleached white that Brandi took his pulse.

As Homer looked around the room, Bea grabbed up Howard T's rope; swung it like a jumprope over Homer's head and quickly knotted it in place, securely trapping his arms against his body and his wheelchair. The sound of his derringer landing harmlessly on the floor, was followed by cheers and the entrance of two of Will's men who had been posted at the Donnelly's Vacations & Travel Service, the Shadow Angels who had gathered in Bea's office, plus a couple of Deputy Sheriffs.

The following day, Brandi and Jonothan flew out on an extended honeymoon, the destination "classified," as Jonothan insisted whenever anyone asked. Also, personal letters were delivered to each business owner on the list, stamped *Paid in Full*. The arrest of Homer, his son, Howard T, Chub, Slim and Foster became top priority for the Sheriff's Department with a list of crimes almost as long as the tunnels—racketeering and kidnapping for starters. However front-page news featured a photo of Brandi and Jonothan's wedding at the Welby Chapel.

A souvenir insert headlined a miniature copy of future plans for the Welby, Warren, and Davies Expansion which included a sign up sheet for volunteers. They could help with the physical labor for the cleaning of the tunnels, offer to cook and serve meals for the cleaning crews or donate money. Clean up crews were to report Friday evening at Sadie's Diner. Checks for the money donations were to be written to the Turtle Crossing Tunnel of Safe Passage.

Epilogue

Three months after Brandi and Jonothan's "Wedding of the Century" in the Welby Chapel, the town celebrated the Grand Opening of the mile-long Turtle Crossing's Tunnel of Safe Passage, sponsored by the merchants of Turtle Crossing. Sadie's Diner had a new special they called the Bloomin Gold Mine that featured eggs, fried potatoes, and a great deal of butter.

A fleet of golf carts on loan for the Grand Opening were used for transporting children and adults who couldn't manage walking a mile. The tunnels were well lit and marked for underground access between Turtle Crossing and the Welby, plus the Pedestrians' Walkway.

The Merchants Council had banned all advertising on the breathtaking pastel sunset Tunnel Walls. Directions were marked in the pavement. Except for Jonothan and Brandi's wedding, people couldn't remember the last time Turtle Crossing had celebrated anything this exciting. Visitors arrived by passenger train, by bus, by car and others docked their boats on the Turtle Crossing River.

The restored Welby Chapel had gained wide acclaim because of the vaulted ceiling and the waterfall. A huge chandelier had been added and mirrors were used wherever possible to add to the spectacular golden sunset display. Exits had been redesigned so the tunnels could be locked between midnight and six a.m. to discourage vandalism and to save on the expense of hiring another full-time deputy. Plans were also on the drawing board to connect some of the businesses and the new Sycamore Shopping Mall with access to the Tunnels as well.

A few of the golf carts were enclosed for passenger safety. Of course none was as fancy as the Welby's. Alex had added fringe on the canopy and a banner across the back advertising the Welby's rooms and grounds. As for drivers, there was never any lack of enthusiastic volunteers to transport visitors through the tunnels while reciting the history of the tunnels in Turtle Crossing.

Tracks were to be installed the following year for an electric train, and Shannon's portrait of Daniel Welby, Richard Warren and Mason Davies would hang in the clubhouse of Golf at Welby Falls.

Alex hosted a special celebration at the Welby for the Shadow Angels, their spouses and children, plus anyone that claimed to be family. She said it was her way of thanking Bea for all she had done for her daughter, Autumn.

As they arrived, Marcie was kept busy taking group pictures. After everyone filled their plates of samples of the Welby menu and were seated, Jonothan stood to offer grace when Jace, Samantha, and Pearl entered the dining room. Jonothan had memory flashes of his Dad's empty chair in their living room or at the breakfast table, and his Mom sitting alone at school and sports events. All these memories did was make his stomach sour and crease his forehead in a frown.

But he also felt their indecision, questioning whether they had a right to be here, or where they fit in. Jonothan had lived this life.

"May I have your attention?" he began as he leaned down, hugged Brandi and kissed her on the cheek.

He approached the latecomers, led them to his table and announced, "Now that the rest of the family has arrived, I would like to say grace." He looked at his Mom, and with tears in her eyes, she nodded her approval.

"Dear Father in Heaven, we thank You for the opportunity for our fractured families to join in this celebration as a family. We can't change the rocky road of the past, but ask for your loving support and forgiveness. I know we can make it. Amen."

After he sat down and everyone started digging in to their meals, he leaned across the table and added, "Miss Bea, I need your opinion about a photo that was found recently. We think this is what Howard T was really looking for."

He handed her a reproduction of the newspaper accounting of the Longacre Mercantile & Grocery Fire. The photo caught Howard T's reflection in the Longacre display window. He was holding two gasoline cans high in the air. His eyes were jet black and wild, his smile one of satisfaction.

Bea stared at it in silence. It was her worst nightmare, come to life. "I saw him that night," she said softly. "My favorite beautiful doll was crying in the window."

"We know," Autumn said softly. "Bea," she pleaded, as she took Bea's hands in hers. "When my mom saw the photo of that doll in the window, she recognized it. This must have been one of Mrs. Welby's favorites too because this little red-headed doll named Victoria Anne was stored in the attic in a special glass display case. Now she is yours."

"The good news doesn't stop there," Granny said, standing. "May I have everyone's attention please?"

The voices quieted.

"Bea," Granny began, "Jonothan found sketches for a privately financed Longacre Museum and Veteran's Chapel to be built where the Longacre Mercantile and Grocery once stood. This plaque—" She held up a handsome golden plaque with Bea's name embossed under those of her parents. "—will be embedded in the cornerstone."

Applause filled the room as Granny laid the plaque on the table in front of Bea.

"Bea," Jonothan began as he pulled up a chair beside her. "I also found two plat maps of Turtle Crossing dated 1829 in your Dad's desk. These are copies of the original and a forgery. You might be interested in the name on the forgery where your Mom and Dad's Mercantile was located—Homer T Ragamuffin I."

"And you think this is what they've really been looking for?"

Jonothan just shrugged his shoulders, smiled, and added, "They would have been disappointed. The forgery was never recorded."

"Thank you, Jonothan," Bea said with tears in her eyes. "I'm so happy, I could dance!"

In addition to eating, taking photos, and general fellowship, everyone also took turns passing around the new babies. Mason and Autumn had little Allison Ellen; Sheldon and Marcie had Amber Beth-Eden, who was already nine months old; and the youngest of the bunch by a single day was Will and Wendy's infant, Storm Tomas. The babies, for their part, tolerated the delighted squeezing, cooing, and rocking with bemused stoicism.

Awaiting her turn to hold Allison for the third time, Brandi couldn't wait to tell Mason the good news. He was going to be an uncle/cousin. Next year at this time she and Autumn and Marcie and Shannon and Wendy could bring their children to ride the train and go shopping together. Shannon and David Donnelly's twins, Lily Anneé and Lauri Rose, were already making plans to be the next generation Shadow Angels when they grew up, and they didn't really mind that Allison Ellen was named after her grandma rather than with the name they had suggested. The name Storm fit Will's feisty little boy better anyhow.

Acknowledgments

Stories, characters, and possibilities swirled through me after a visit to the Marblehead Light House and Keeper's House on the shore of Lake Erie, Ohio. It has also inspired numerous artists, including my favorite, James A. Andrews.

I would like to thank the members of the Bluffton Creative Writers for their support and encouragement. Special thanks to Amy Joseph, Elaine Rich, and André Swartley for their editing skills.

Genealogies

Donnelly

Robard J. Donnelly m. Rose L. Fields

Charles Donnelly	Kristopher Donnelly	David J. Donnelly	Marcie M. Donnelly
SaraElizabeth Carpenter	Nancy A. Jordan	Shannon Warren	Sheldon Warren
David J. Donnelly	Jacob Donnelly	Lily Anneé Donnelly	Amber Beth Eden Warren
Marcie M. Donnelly	Jordan Donnelly	Lauri Rose Donnelly	

Warren

Winthrop Warren (WW) 1st. m.
E. Tessa Montgomery {m. annulled}

Winthrop Warren (WW) 2nd. m.
Constance Stephanie Strange
|
Richard C. Warren 1st. m.
Summer Eden Fox
|
Sheldon Warren
Shannon Warren

Cecil Warren (CW) m.
E. Tessa Montgomery 3rd. m.

E. Tessa Montgomery 2nd.m.
Tom Sands
|
Wendy Warren Sands m.
William {Will} Fox
|
Storm Thomas Fox

Carpenter

Henry Carpenter	Tressie Carpenter	Jacob Joseph Carpenter	aka	Joseph {Joe}Jacob Carpentier
Jewel Hendrix	Fletcher Brown	Opal Fields		Pearl E. Peltiers 2nd.m
SaraElizabeth Carpenter		Jonothan Arden Carpenter		Jace Carpentier
Charles J. Donnelly		Brandi Elaine Davies		Samantha Carpentier
Marcie M. Donnelly				
David J. Donnelly				

Welby / Erne

Daniel Welby
Ellen Winters

Allen B. Ern
SueLynn Winters
|
Ariel Ern
Alexandria Lyndsay Ern {Alex}
Jamie Johnson
|
Autumn Winters Johnson

Mason Davies {cousin of Brandi}
Autumn Winters Johnson
|
Allison Ellen Davies

About the Author

Marilyn R. Stark writes daily, and in various capacities: letters to family and friends, recording family memories, updating the family genealogy for an annual newsletter, and interviewing people as a former feature writer for a local newspaper, *The Senior's Beacon* (now out of print).

Her previous novels in the Children's Home Mystery Series include *The Flutist and The Dancer, The Pianist and the Locksmith, Broken Arrows/Broken Promises,* and *Trails End Isle and Wings.*

She is also the author of *A Pictorial History of Lima/Allen County, Ohio* and *The History and Purposes of Allen County Institutions, Buildings and Government.*

CPSIA information can be obtained
at www.ICGtesting.com
Printed in the USA
FFOW03n0604211014
8182FF